A Rose from
the Dead

**Center Point
Large Print**

**This Large Print Book carries the
Seal of Approval of N.A.V.H.**

A Rose from the Dead

A Flower Shop Mystery

Kate Collins

CENTER POINT PUBLISHING
THORNDIKE, MAINE

This Center Point Large Print edition
is published in the year 2008 by arrangement with
NAL Signet, a member of Penguin Group (USA) Inc.

The text of this Large Print edition is unabridged. In other
aspects, this book may vary from the original edition.
Printed in the United States of America.
Set in 16-point Times New Roman type.

ISBN: 978-1-60285-148-1

Library of Congress Cataloging-in-Publication Data

Collins, Kate, 1951-
     A Rose from the dead : a flower shop mystery / Kate Collins.--Center Point large print ed.
     p. cm.
     ISBN 978-1-60285-148-1 (lib. bdg. : alk. paper)
     1. Knight, Abby (Fictitious character)--Fiction. 2. Florists--Fiction.
3. Women detectives--Fiction. 4. Large type books. I. Title.

PS3603.O4543R67 2008
813'.6--dc22

2007043087

This book is dedicated to those genuinely caring men and women of the funeral industry who provide gentle guidance and understanding to grieving families, performing a service that most of us could not do.

ACKNOWLEDGMENTS

A list of thank-yous can be entertaining or boring depending on how creative the author feels after laboring for months over dialogue, plots, characters, words, sentences, scenes, and chapters, not to mention the whole comma-versus-semicolon dilemma. With that said, I confess I had intended to write a clever limerick, weaving in the names of everyone who'd lent expertise, advice, wisdom, support, chocolate, et cetera. But after searching my remaining brain cells and coming up with some seriously horrendous duds (to wit: I have so many people to thank, but first I need a great big drank), I'm taking the easy route.

Thank you to Martin and Janice Moeller for their expertise on the funeral industry.

A big thanks to my sis, Nancy, for her excellent critiquing skills and for keeping my story on track.

Another big one to my hubby, Jim, for his legal proficiency, support, ability to make emergency runs for office supplies on a moment's notice, and, of course, male viewpoint.

Yet another to my son, Jason, for designing Abby Knight's very own MySpace site (www.myspace.com/abbyknightflorist) and lending his musical talents to it.

Thank you, David Cergizan, for creating a virtual Bloomers that is exactly what I'd imagined. (You can see the photo on Abby's site, above.)

Thank you, Sandi Kuntzmann, for helping with the Brit bits.

Thanks to my Spark* team: Karla, Kiersten, Annie, Val, and Britta, and their adviser, Dr. Bonita Dostal Neff, associate professor, Valparaiso University, for their creative input and hard work, even with finals looming.

As always, thank you to Barb for being my unofficial PR lady; to my daughters, Julia and Natasha, for their enthusiastic support and twentysomething vantage point, and to Bonnie, the dearest stepmom anyone could ask for.

Now, off to get that great big drank.

*Spark Public Relations is a student-run agency at Valparaiso University sponsored by the Public Relations Student Society of America (PRSSA). Students who are actively studying public relations offer their communication expertise in publicity and promotion, research, event planning, strategic thinking, and media relations to individuals and organizations needing public relations support.

Chapter One

Okay, guys, great joke. Phone booth in a coffin. Ha-ha. Now, let me out. The door is stuck."

I waited a moment, then pressed my ear against the smooth pine finish, listening for snickers coming from the other side, but all I heard was silence. I pushed against the wood, but it didn't budge. "Ross? Jess? Are you leaning against the door? Come on. It isn't funny anymore. I'm claustrophobic."

When the booth still didn't open, I pounded on it. "Let me out of here!"

More silence. I pictured them pinching their lips shut so they wouldn't guffaw.

And the reason you trusted a pair of twenty-three-year-old males in the first place was . . . ?

I ignored that smug little voice of rationality. Right now, my only concern was breathing, because the air in the two feet of space I occupied had suddenly become unbearably stuffy.

Sweat beads gathered at my temples, plastering my hair to my skin. Why wasn't this phone booth air-conditioned? Was a little vent in the ceiling too much to ask for? I gave the door one last smack with the heel of my hand, then rested my forehead against it. "You guys are in major trouble now because I'm phoning the police."

The silence roared in my ears. Or was that my shallow breathing?

I ignored the ebony receiver behind me, a replica of the old coin-operated phone of my mother's generation. I didn't have any money with me, anyway.

Luckily, I never went anywhere without my cell phone. I pulled out the sleek stainless-steel case, flipped it open, and thumbed in 911. "Hello, yes, I'd like to report being locked in a coffin. Wait. Don't hang up. This isn't a joke. My name is Abby Knight. I own Bloomers Flower Shop, and I'm at the morticians' convention in—yes, my father is Sgt. Jeffrey Knight, formerly of the New Chapel PD. Anyway, could you send someone over to—yes, he *is* doing well, considering his injury. Sure, I'd be happy to pass along your best wishes—if you'd send someone over to get me *out of here!*"

At once the door to my jail opened, flooding the space with bright light. I blinked several times, holding up a hand to shade my eyes until the blurry male shape before me came into focus. To my relief, it wasn't either of the two pranksters who had imprisoned me. It was Marco Salvare, the Hunk of the Midwest, the man who could make me breathe shallowly—and *like* it— just by sauntering into a room.

"Never mind," I said to the dispatcher. I slipped my mobile phone back into my pocket. "Marco, thank God you came. I was starting to hyperventilate."

"What were you doing in there?" he asked as I emerged fanning my face.

What, indeed?

There I was, a bright young florist of some note—

10

okay, maybe half a note (I had owned Bloomers for a mere six months), and maybe only bright because of my red hair. But there I was, nevertheless, in the middle of a morticians' convention, trying to drum up business, only to find myself wedged in a phone booth as if I were some ditzy female who couldn't find her way out of a—well, phone booth.

That it resembled an antique coffin straight out of a vampire movie only made my humiliation worse. What person of even *average* intelligence would be gullible enough to walk into an upended coffin? Talk about the height of embarrassment.

On the plus side, Marco had proven once again to be my go-to guy. He was not only an ex-cop and new bar owner but also a former Army Ranger, a tough, savvy, modern-day warrior whose group motto said it all: "Rangers lead the way." And if anyone had found a way into my heart, it was Marco.

He was all man—hard jawed, firm mouthed, straight backed, and taut bellied—with nut brown eyes that knew how to cut through pretense and a strong, masculine nose that was slightly askew. His wavy dark mop drooped casually onto the left side of his forehead and ruffled onto the nape of his neck but never reached farther than his collar. He was sexy, sincere, and thoughtful, the kind of guy girls like me dream of snagging. Yet he remained something of a mystery.

At this moment, however, there was nothing mystifying about what he was thinking. His most captivating feature, aside from his penetrating gaze and that hint of

11

five o'clock shadow, was his expressive mouth—straight, firm lips that curved up at the corners when he was amused and slanted down when he was bemused. Judging by what I saw now, he was perplexed.

"How did you get locked in?"

"That's what I'd like to know. Just wait till I get my hands on those two idiots." Huffing angrily, I started to charge past him, but he caught my arm.

"What two idiots?"

"Ross and Jess Urban—or, as I now prefer to think of them, Thing One and Thing Two. We met them early this morning while we were setting up our display, remember? Dark blond hair with light blond tips, large teeth, big dimples in their chins, very tan? One of them looked like a model for *GQ*—he had on Ferragamo loafers and a Tag Heuer watch—and the other one looked like a homeless skateboarder. They manage a chain of funeral parlors for their father."

"You still haven't told me how you got locked in."

"After you left earlier, they came to our exhibit and said I had a phone call and brought me here. So I stepped inside, and the door—lid, whatever—latched behind me."

Marco examined the latch in question. "Abby, this slide bolt isn't automatic. They locked you in."

"I had a feeling they might be trouble, but I ignored it because they're *funeral* directors. What if I had passed out from a lack of oxygen—or even worse, died in this coffin? I don't even want to think about the irony."

"Take a look back here," Marco called. "This isn't even a working phone."

I went around to the back of the tall booth. There on the ground lay a disconnected phone cord—and not a phone jack in sight. Obviously the coffin–phone booth was just for display, but how was I to know? I'd never been to a funeral directors' convention before.

Displaying my floral wares at the Midwestern Funeral Directors' Association's regional convention was actually the brainchild of my friends Max and Delilah Dove, owners of the Happy Dreams Funeral Home, located around the corner from Bloomers and just off the town square in New Chapel, Indiana. Max and Delilah had suggested I rent a booth alongside the other businesses that supplied products and services to morticians, as a way to generate more income for my shop, a small business struggling to hold its own against the giant chain competitors. The convention was being held at the Woodland Hotel and Conference Center, on Lake Michigan, about twenty-five miles north of New Chapel.

Since the $1,500 rental fee was a little too steep for my budget, Max and Delilah had generously offered to split the cost and share booth space. Even at the bargain rate of $750 I'd still hesitated to commit the money, until I learned that I'd get to attend the Saturday night banquet with a guest of my choice. The banquet, Delilah had promised, was an event not to be missed, with food provided by an excellent caterer and entertainment afterward.

I'd signed up immediately. I was all about free food. But I was not about looking like an ignoramus.

"Boy, are those two Urban jokers in trouble. How dare they lock me in a phone booth and put my life in jeopardy. And for what? A laugh? Well, I'm going to have the last laugh because . . . Marco, are you listening?"

He was staring up the long, brightly lit corridor toward the exhibition hall at the end, his jaw hard and his eyes narrowed to slits of steel-edged fury.

Uh-oh. I knew that look. My twin tormentors were toast.

Chapter Two

Marco, wait," I said, and dashed after him, catching up just as he stepped into the big warehouselike room where hundreds of people were browsing the wide, carpeted aisles of display booths. "Ross and Jess did this to *me*. If anyone is going to teach them a lesson, it should be me."

Both corners of Marco's mouth curved down, a clear sign that he strongly disagreed, but since that had never deterred me before, I paid no attention. I pulled the convention brochure from my purse and turned to the index. "Where would two young guys hang out? The extreme-marketing seminar?"

That snapped him out of his funk. "Whoa. Hold it. Before you put on your brass knuckles, Sunshine, you'd better think this through."

"You're right. They're probably at the computer software booth."

"That's not what I mean. You're here on business. You don't want to cause a scene that might jeopardize your chances of picking up new clients for Bloomers."

I blinked as his words sank in. *Rats.* He was right again. How professional would I look if I walked around punching out morticians, even young ones who thought they were crafty stud muffins?

"Fine. I'll let them go for now, but if they pull anything else, they're going to find out Abby Knight is a force to be reckoned with. I may be small, but I'm mighty." I flexed a bicep, which, I might add, was looking pretty hot. Chalk that up to toting heavy bags of potting soil from the depths of Bloomers's basement to the first-floor workroom.

Ignoring my demonstration, Marco made a visual sweep of my five-foot-two body, as if to remind me that I wouldn't be much of a threat to two full-grown, testosterone-charged young males. "Don't worry about the Urbans. I'll take care of them."

It was my turn to grab his arm. "Not so fast, Rambo. Legally, you're here as my agent. What you do affects my liability. So, touché. You can't do anything, either."

"Agent? Is that a new term for pack mule?"

"Pack mule. Ha. All you did is carry in three floral arrangements and help Max and Delilah put together the portable walls of our booth. Stop complaining."

He finally relaxed, put an arm around my shoulders,

and bent his head close to my ear to murmur in his husky low voice, "You're foxy when you're stubborn."

All it took was the brush of his lips against my earlobe to send flutters of excitement all the way to my toes. "Want to come to my den this evening?" I murmured back.

"You have a banquet this evening."

Double rats. In the heat of the moment, I'd forgotten. "Actually, *we* have a banquet. You're my date, don't forget. And don't roll your eyes. I know you hate to put on a jacket and tie, but Delilah said the food is fantastic. It'll be over by eight o'clock anyway."

"Have you ever known a banquet to be over in an hour?"

"No. But honestly, Marco, take a look at the people around us. What do you see? Morticians. Is there any group deadly duller than a bunch of morticians?"

"Deadly duller? Were you trying to make a pun?"

"I was trying to say that I can't imagine there being any fun and games with this crowd. Think about it. They work with dead people. On the whole, they're a serious bunch—except for Thing One and Thing Two, who are aberrations."

Marco turned me around to see a man wearing a big sandwich board that read, CASKET RACES, SUNDAY, 2:00 P.M. EAST PARKING LOT. Beneath the print was a picture of a long pine box on wheels, with racing stripes down the sides. A morticians' soapbox derby?

The man turned to display the back of his board:

POST-BANQUET VAMPIRE VIP PARTY TONIGHT. DRACULA
DRESS REQUIRED. BLOODY MARYS AT MIDNIGHT.

"What were you saying about a serious bunch?"
Marco drawled.

"I take it all back. But you'll still come with me to
the banquet, won't you?"

He scratched behind his ear. "There's a hitch."

I groaned.

"Gina wants me to have dinner with her and Mom
tonight to decide on her baby shower plans."

"Why didn't you tell me a month ago, when I
accepted Max and Delilah's invitation?"

"She called me this morning."

"I asked before she did."

"You can eat with Max and Delilah."

"And Gina can eat with your mom, her husband, and
your nephew. That's three to two in her favor."

"It's a tie. Gina's husband is away on business."

"I don't get it. Your mother has already decided on
the menu for the shower. I'm providing the flowers,
my mother made the favors, and you donated the use
of your bar. There's nothing left to plan."

"She needs me to run interference. You remember
how it is with those two."

Fat chance. I'd been with the two Salvare women
exactly once, when Marco's mom invited me for her
lasagna dinner and kept refilling my wineglass until I
couldn't remember my own telephone number. Marco
had later explained that she'd been testing my alcohol
tolerance. The higher the tolerance, the less she'd like

me. It had been one of the few examinations I'd passed with flying colors. I was blotto after two and a half glasses.

So it was a standoff: Gina or me. Considering what a close-knit family the Salvares were, and that Marco's younger sister had him on a short leash, I was bound to lose this contest. After all, Marco and I weren't engaged, pre-engaged, or thinking about considering being pre-engaged. We'd known each other for five months, had dated for four, and were nowhere near being ready for the picket fence–diaper routine. So what chance did I have against his sister? Unless . . .

"Okay. I understand. Family comes first."

He studied me apprehensively. "You're fine with me not going tonight?"

"Hey, it's no big deal."

"So, you're not angry?"

"No, but if you keep asking me if I'm angry, *that* will make me angry. Forget about it, okay? I don't mind if you miss the banquet. Have a great time with your family."

"All right, Sunshine. What's going on?"

"Marco, what don't you understand about the phrase *I don't mind?*"

He let out an exasperated sigh. "Fine. I'll go to the banquet. What time should I pick you up?"

"Six o'clock."

It was an old strategy, but it had always worked with my father. "I saw a Starbucks at the food court. Let's get some coffee."

He checked his watch. "I really need to get back to Down the Hatch."

"*Pfft*. It's early yet. Besides, we've got one more load of flowers coming, and we need a pack mule." My attention was drawn to a glassblower creating beautiful vases at a nearby booth. The sign above the booth read: FROM ASHES TO ART—THE ULTIMATE BURIAL EXPERIENCE.

"Is she using what I think she's using to make those vases?" I asked Marco as he escorted me around a group of curious people who had gathered to watch her shape the glass.

"I need to get out of here," he muttered. "This convention gives me the creeps."

"It's just business, Marco."

He pointed out two mannequins on display—a male in a gray pinstripe suit and a female in a navy blue dress. On a folding screen behind them were enlarged photos of the outfits in different colors. "See? That's what I mean. Who would buy their clothes here?"

"That's burial clothing. Funeral homes sometimes offer a selection in case the deceased has nothing appropriate to wear."

"Nothing appropriate? So did the person walk around in a bath towel? And then there's the angel music. Is that really necessary?"

"Angel music?" I paused to listen. "Oh, that's harp music. Remember the girl setting up the harp at the booth across from ours—that new age-y–type place?"

"The chalk-faced chick in a black lace nightgown?"

"It was a black dress, but yes, that's the one. I think her business is called Music of the Soul."

"She gave me the creeps, too. And what the hell is this booth about? A souvenir shop? You've got to be kidding me."

We stopped to inspect a glass jewelry case where hearse-shaped tie clasps, coffin cuff links, and tombstone paperweights were on display. Okay, that *was* creepy. I saw a rack filled with T-shirts and picked one up, laughing. It read GOT FORMALDEHYDE?

"Look, Marco. Like the advertisement 'Got Milk?'!"

He didn't seem to find it as amusing as I did, so I tried another one. "Okay, this one will definitely make you laugh." I showed him a shirt that read YOUR HEARSE OR MINE?

But Marco had found something more to his liking: a whoopee cushion. "This would ratchet up a funeral service a few notches."

I took it out of his hands and put it back. Some things were just not funny.

"Now, that's more my style," Marco said happily, and veered toward another booth where a big-screen TV was playing a video that had lots of loud engines revving. Then he realized the video was about hearses and limousines, not Jeeps and motorcycles, and he veered back, scowling. "How long until that load of flowers gets here?"

I was about to answer when I spotted something that

alarmed me. "Marco, isn't my booth at the end of this aisle?"

"Why?"

"Because something's happening down there, and it doesn't look good."

Chapter Three

"A crowd isn't necessarily a bad thing, right?" I said, dodging poky walkers. "I mean, it could be that my floral arrangements are a big draw, couldn't it?"

Then I heard a loud, harsh female voice say, "We have rules at this convention, Mrs. Dove. You were given a copy of those rules before you set up your booth. Now, you'll have to dismantle your display at once and move everything in by a foot on each side."

Dismantle it? After we spent two hours setting it up? Okay, *that* was bad.

We wove through a dozen onlookers to find the source of that grating voice—a startlingly attractive, fortysomething woman in a tight, zebra-print, sleeveless wrap dress. The woman was obviously a fitness buff, as was evidenced by her well-toned arms, firm bust (with a major display of cleavage), tiny waist, long, shapely legs, and curvaceous rear end—which every male seemed to be checking out. To her outfit she had added a bloodred rose tucked above one ear into her long sweep of platinum hair. She held a clipboard in one hand and a red marker in the other, and was fixing Delilah with a glare that would make ice shiver.

It wasn't fazing Delilah, however, who calmly regarded her from beneath the wide, translucent brim of her pale pink hat. "Sybil," she said with her easy Southern drawl, "we've been coming here long enough to know how to set up a booth. We are well within the limits."

Max Dove pushed through the crowd to step up beside his wife, but anyone who knew Delilah knew his support was unnecessary. She might have been a genteel lady with a soft voice, big hairdo, and impeccable manners, but beneath that deceptively innocent heart-shaped face, Delilah was the proverbial steel magnolia.

Not only was she strong willed, but she was also physically strong, a quality that enabled her to do the heavy lifting often required in her line of work. Yet Delilah was able to hold her own without flexing a muscle, uttering a single swear word, or even raising her voice. It was all in her attitude.

"If you have any doubts, Sybil," Delilah continued, reaching into a box of supplies hidden beneath the table skirt, "perhaps you'd be kind enough to see for yourself?" She smiled angelically as she offered Sybil a tape measure.

The sudden strum of harp strings across the aisle made the crowd chuckle. The young woman I'd noticed earlier was seated at a tall golden harp, running her delicate fingertips up and down the strings, the wide sleeves of her long, flowing black dress falling back to reveal thin, pale arms. Her eyes were closed and her pale face gazed upward as though she were somewhere far away. I doubted she even knew what was happening in front of our booth.

Sybil maintained her frosty glare for another ten seconds, then swung around to cut a swath through the onlookers, calling over her shoulder, "I'll be back to measure later, *Mrs. Dove.*"

"We'll be here," Delilah sang out.

Sybil marched past, giving me a glimpse of what could have been a model's face, except that it was coated with makeup that gave her skin an other-worldly, almost plastic appearance. Her full lips, painted with an iridescent rose red lipstick, were now twisted in annoyance, and her big amber eyes glared from inside a shimmery, smoky circle of eyeshadow. Her long platinum mane slapped her back like a treacherous wave beating against the shoreline, telling the world that Sybil Blount was not a woman to be messed with.

Then she saw Marco and stopped in midstride, her march becoming a hip-swinging sashay, her hostile expression dissolving into a flirtatious smile. "Well, *hello.* I haven't seen you around here before." She reached for his hand, which he reluctantly let her shake. "I'm Sybil Blount, chairperson of the convention."

"Marco Salvare," he said, watching her with slightly narrowed eyes.

"Marco, is it?" she said in a sultry voice, behaving as if they were the only two in the room. "What mortuary are you with, Marco?"

"I own a bar."

"A bar? Well, aren't *you* a hottie." Sybil still had his hand, and now her gaze was stripping away his clothes. "What's the name of your bar, Marco?"

"Down the Hatch." He politely withdrew his hand but didn't step back, even though she was edging closer. Hadn't he figured out yet that she was hitting on him? Wasn't he aware of the people around us straining to hear their conversation?

Sybil leaned into him, murmuring, "Maybe you can drop down *my* hatch one of these days, Marco. What do you think about that?"

Okay, that did it.

"Hi, I'm Abby Knight from New Chapel," I said, inserting myself between them, although I had to step on Marco's foot to get him to move back. I grabbed her hand and shook it like a dusty throw rug at the back door, raising a cloud of the sharp, tart scent she wore. "I own Bloomers Flower Shop. Marco came with me to help me set up my flower display." I pointed from him to me so she'd be absolutely clear about our connection.

"How nice for you." Her unmerciful gaze swept over my face. "Stop by my booth after lunch. I'll help you hide those horrid freckles." She turned to Marco and, with a wink, said in a husky whisper, "See *you* later, cutie."

"I don't think so, Sybil," I muttered as she turned to talk to someone else.

"Behave," Marco growled.

"Me? I'm not the one who let Sybil paw me. And she's old enough to be your mother, by the way."

"No way."

Delilah took us by the arms and ushered us back to the booth. "Don't let Sybil get under your skin, Abby. She's just a big ol' clucking hen who likes to strut around reminding everyone that she's the chairperson. And she's forty, by the way."

"See?" Marco said to me.

"Darlin', gloating is ungentlemanly," Delilah chided. "And just so you know, Sybil *was* pawing you. See all those males watching her strut up the aisle? Purely half of them have felt her pawing and the other half are waitin' their turns." Delilah gave a gleeful laugh.

"Listen to Delilah," Max said. "She knows Sybil's ways. At every convention we've ever been to, Sybil has always tried to get a rise out of Del." He cupped a hand around his mouth, pretending his wife couldn't hear. "That's because Sybil is jealous of Del's natural beauty. Nothing artificial about her looks."

Delilah blushed prettily. "Darlin' man, she's not jealous of *me*. She's jealous of my hats." She patted the one on her head.

Delilah adored hats and had a closet dedicated to them. She never suffered from hat head because her blond hair was back combed, then sprayed to a helmetlike stiffness with her favorite hair spray, which she carried in her purse at all times, along with her powder compact and a tube of pink lipstick. Her clothing style was classic, mostly pastels, and her ever-present pearls were always the genuine article. She was a true Southern lady.

Hearing laughter, I turned to see Sybil halfway down the aisle, slapping the chest of a young male sales rep as if he'd just told the funniest story she'd ever heard. He put his arm around her waist and whispered something in her ear, and when she turned to whisper something back that had him nodding excitedly, I noticed a piece of paper stuck to the seat of her skirt that read: STAND BACK! I BITE.

Everyone around us saw it, too, which caused a lot of snorts and titters as people drifted off, leaving me with a perfect view of Ross and Jess giving each other high fives. The sign writers, obviously. I would have found the joke funny if they hadn't already gotten me.

Hmm. Maybe it was time to settle that matter.

"So, we don't need to worry about the booth being the wrong size?" I asked the Doves.

"We measured everything carefully," Delilah assured me. "Besides, Sybil will be onto something else in a minute anyway, won't she, Max?"

"Or onto some*one* else," I said, giving Marco a pointed glance. He responded by rolling his eyes.

As if on cue, we heard a furious screech. "There she goes," Delilah said. "She must have discovered that sign on her derriere."

At the end of the aisle, Ross and Jess were laughing so hard they had to hold each other up.

"Would you excuse me for a few minutes?" I asked my friends. "I have to take care of something."

"Abby," Marco called, "where are you going?"

He'd figure it out.

"Hey, guys," I said, striding right up to them. "I need to talk to you."

I would have expected them to appear at least slightly embarrassed when they saw me, but not those two. They had the nerve to look quite pleased with themselves. Thing One, dressed in designer loafers, khakis, and a green golf shirt, stepped forward. His blond-tipped hair was styled so that one lock curled perfectly above his right eye, unlike Thing Two, whose hair had a bed-head look. He wore brand-new Nikes and ripped-at-the-knees blue jeans with a white T-shirt that said DROP DEAD. Real professional.

"What's up, Red?" Thing One asked, flashing his pretty-boy smile.

"I'm not a crayon, okay? It's Abby. Remind me again—which one are you, Dumb or Dumber?"

"It's Jess, and what's *your* problem?"

"Hey! *I'm* Jess," Thing Two said, giving his brother a not-so-playful punch in the arm. Jess the Mess. He'd be easy to remember.

"Hey, man, lay off me," Ross said, knocking his hand away.

"*You* lay off."

I let out a bored sigh as the brothers argued and shoved. *This* was why I never dated younger men. Go below the age of twenty-four and you're asking for a babysitting gig. "Hello-o-o. I just wanted to thank you for locking me in the phone booth this morning. It was a great way to start the day."

"It was a joke," Ross said with a shrug of one shoulder. "Lighten up."

"Jokes have punch lines," I reminded him. "Here's one for you. What do you call two individuals who confine another individual in a phone booth—coffin?"

"I give," Jess said dryly.

"Felons—which is what you'll be if you ever pull a stunt like that on me again, because I will press charges so fast your skulls will spin. Got it?"

Ross patted his mouth, as though yawning. "I'm sorry. What was that again?"

Jess took a more serious stance. "Cool down, little dudette. We thought you were, you know, looking for some fun. Not like the old farts around here."

"The old farts, as you call them, deal with death and loss," I said. "That tends to diminish the fun aspect."

"Give me a break," Ross said. "These booths, this convention—it's all about commerce. So there's no reason why these dudes have to take things so seriously. I mean, okay, so you're a mortician. Get over yourself. Everyone gets bagged eventually. Have some fun with it."

"Bagged?"

"Toe tagged, gone sour, whatever." Jess flicked his

tongue at me, which had a silver stud embedded in the tip. It explained the clicking noise when he talked. Charming.

"That's not an attitude you see much in funeral directors," I said. "How do your clients feel about that, considering their state of grief?"

"We don't deal with clients. We're management." Ross nudged his brother. "Hey, look, Jess. Here comes the Diva of Death again. Is our sign still there?"

I glanced around and saw Sybil with her clipboard.

"It's gone," Jess replied with a snicker, clicking his tongue stud. "You should have seen her, Red. She was strutting around like, 'Oh, look at me, I'm so hot.' She didn't have a clue that there was a freakin' sign on her ass." They both laughed.

"Why do you want to embarrass her?" I asked them. "What has she done to you?"

"Nothing," Jess the Mess said, "and that's the way we want to keep it. We're too cool to fool. Hey, Ross. Let's get her again."

"Dude, what should we do?"

"You're asking me? Come on, Mr. Cool, you're the one with the ideas."

"If she finds out who's behind these pranks, I wouldn't want to be you," I told them.

"It won't be a problem." Ross cast a sly glance at his twin. "She'd think it was an invitation."

"An invitation to what?"

"Well, *hello,* boys," I heard Sybil say from behind me, her voice dripping with sweetness. She practically elbowed me out of her way in her eagerness to get close to them.

Have at 'em, Sybil. I turned and headed toward my booth, but just a few yards short of my target, I stopped when a fragile figure in black suddenly appeared in front of me, her incense enveloping me in a dry, dusty fog of aroma.

I pulled back in surprise as the harpist said in a sad, whisper-thin voice, "No one understands her."

"Understands who?"

"Sybil." The harpist closed her eyes, swaying to some inner tune as her gossamer dress billowed around her. She had a very large forehead, short, dyed-black hair parted in the middle, silver glitter eye-shadow, white makeup, and black lipstick. Up close, she was also much older than I'd thought, appearing to be in her midthirties.

"I've heard Sybil's soul," she said, as if this were a serious matter. "So *dissonante.* So *bellicoso con fuoco.* I've never met anyone like her. You can see why she must be recorded."

"Sorry. I don't understand Italian."

The harpist pinned me with a look that bordered on repulsion. "I'm speaking in musical terms."

"Oh, right." I moved around her. I mean, it wasn't like I'd said I ate worms. Besides, Italian, music— they were pretty much the same to me. One year of piano lessons had proved that, besides having short fingers (which actually went well with my short body), I had no comprehension of music.

Before I could escape, she held out a small, slender hand with black-polished fingernails and silver rings stacked on her thumb. "Angelique DeScuro."

I took her hand, which was a lot like squeezing a damp rag. "I'm Ab—"

"Sh-h-h!" She put her other palm on top, making my extremity feel like the meat between two pieces of soggy white bread. She closed her eyes for a few seconds, then looked at me with contempt as she practically spit out, *"Staccato,"* before stepping away from me as if I were fungus on a garden plant. She drifted back to her harp, took a seat on her stool, closed her eyes, and began to play.

Okay, then.

I saw Marco, Delilah, and Max watching from our booth, looking amused.

"That was bizarre," I said, joining them behind the long display table, which Delilah had decorated in my absence. It was now covered with an array of Happy Dreams Funeral Home brochures; Bloomers business cards; mints in a shallow glass bowl; an album of photos of funeral flowers, wreaths, and blankets; and three fresh flower arrangements that I'd made the day before.

We'd hung several of my funeral wreaths from hooks on the portable pastel green walls, one of which was my new square design made with purple anemones, white carnations, dusty pink hellebores, the interesting saw-toothed banksia foliage, wispy wild grass, and Green Goddess callas, whose graceful stems crossed through the open center of the wreath. We placed more arrangements on floral stands, along with a big vase of mums on the table to give away.

"Angelique is a different sort of person," Delilah said tactfully. "I met her at last year's convention. She claims to be able to record a soul's melody at the very moment it leaves the body and passes on to the next life. She's trying to get all of us morticians to hand out her brochures to our customers who come in to make prearrangements, so that when they're at death's door, so to speak, she'll be at their bedside with her recorder."

"That's where the term *soul music* comes from," Max said, then waited for a laugh.

Delilah patted his cheek. "Pumpkin, you're simply not cut out for comedy."

She was so right. Max was a very ordinary-looking, mild-mannered guy with kind eyes, a gentle voice, a receding hairline, and the air of assurance that people needed when they were overwhelmed with grief. A comedian he was not.

"Don't feel bad, Max," I said. "Apparently, I'm *staccato*."

Marco's mouth twitched in amusement. "Short and disconnected? Yeah, I can see that."

I gave him a glance that said, *You are so not funny.* Lucky for him, he was hunky enough to get away with it. "How do you know what staccato means?"

"I took guitar lessons in high school. So, did you straighten out the Urban legends?"

"Urban legends," Delilah said with a laugh. "I like that. See, Max? *He's* funny."

"As a matter of fact, I did straighten them out," I said, "and trust me, they won't pull any more pranks on me. But I can't say the same for Sybil. When I left, they were plotting something. That reminds me. Is it just me, or does her face look plastic? And what's with that rose in her hair?"

"What you witnessed is a walking advertisement for her line of cosmetics—Sybil's Select," Delilah said. "The red rose is her trademark. Her business hasn't been successful, and I'm sure you can see why, but that makeup sure doesn't discourage the men from coming around."

"They're not looking at her face," I noted.

"You lost me," Marco said. "Why would Sybil push cosmetics here?"

"It's for those loved ones who pass on, dumplin'," Delilah explained. "It makes their viewing more tolerable for their families. Some people are jaundiced when they leave us, you know. They need purple to normalize their skin tone. Then others are more of a green tone—"

"Too much information," I said, preparing to stick my fingers in my ears.

"If you want to see the full line of her products, her booth is number four," Max said, "right next to Chet Sunday's make-it-yourself booth."

"*The* Chet Sunday?" I asked. "From television? Marco, you know who he is—the star of *Make It Easy,*

33

the Saturday afternoon cable TV show on the handyman channel."

"I work Saturday afternoons," Marco reminded me.

"No offense, Max, but what is Chet Sunday doing at a morticians' convention?" I asked.

"It was Sybil's idea," Max said. "She said his name would be a big draw. Apparently he came as a personal favor to her."

"I can't imagine why," Delilah said with a wink.

"Chet is even going to tape two shows from here," Max finished.

"That is so cool," I said. "We have to see his shows, Marco."

Marco looked less than thrilled.

Delilah pulled out her convention schedule. "Today's show starts at eleven o'clock, so why don't you two use the rest of the morning to see his show and the booths, then take over for us after lunch?"

"Sounds like a plan." I glanced at Marco, knowing he wanted to get away. "Don't worry. You'll be off the hook by noon."

Suddenly, we heard a deep voice behind us boom out in fury, "Young men, you have just pulled your last prank."

I turned around to see Ross and Jess dart between two booths as a tall, dark-suited man with ruddy cheeks, a red-veined, bulbous nose, and a bad comb-over strode after them, shaking his fist.

"Now those boys have done it," Delilah said. "They've got the colonel riled."

Chapter Four

Marco, who had never quite gotten the army out of his blood, perked up. "A full-bird colonel? What outfit was he with?"

"I don't believe he's ever said, has he, Max?"

"No, come to think of it. His full name is Walker T. Billingsworth. He and Sybil Blount's husband did a tour of duty together in Vietnam, then came back and opened a mortuary and crematorium. They made quite a name for themselves by offering free cremations for veterans. Billingsworth and Blount. They were highly respected in the industry."

"My uncle was cremated there," Marco said. "He was a Korean War veteran. I remember seeing the Billingsworth and Blount names etched in the urn that sat on my aunt's coffee table."

I wrinkled my nose. "She kept the urn on her coffee table?"

"She said he rested his feet there, so why not all of him?"

"You're making that up," I said. Marco winked, so I didn't know whether it was true.

"It was a brilliant marketing strategy," Max said. "It helped them become the biggest name in northeastern Indiana. The colonel is retired now—he left the business when Sybil's husband passed away last February—but he stayed on as president of the Midwestern Funeral Directors' Association."

"You'll have to ask him to show you his Purple Heart," Delilah said to Marco. "He got it for an injury he suffered in 'Nam. He always wears it on his suit coat. He's so proud of it. He even has one of those customized license plates that says, 'PRPL HRT.' "

"He's so patriotic," Max said, "that his cell phone plays 'America the Beautiful.' "

Marco seemed impressed, and it took a lot to impress him.

"When it comes to the funeral business, the colonel is strictly old-school," Max said. "Suits and ties are required attire, and rules must be followed. He has no tolerance for the Urban twins' practical jokes. His three sons are models of professionalism, basically younger versions of himself, all running their own funeral homes. If he could find a legitimate way to ban the Urban boys from these conventions, he'd do it in a minute."

"One of these days those two young men will pull something on the wrong person," Delilah cautioned, "and then they'll get their comeuppance."

Marco glanced at me, and I knew he was waiting for me to tell them my phone-booth story. Right. Like I wanted to revisit *that* embarrassment.

My cell phone rang, and I heard my assistant Lottie's big, cheerful voice on the other end. "Hey, sweetie, I'm in the parking lot with the flowers. Can you lend a hand?"

"We'll be right there." I slipped the phone in my

pocket and said to Marco, "The flowers are here. You want to saddle up, Mr. Mule?"

"Bring your flowers through the service entrance," Max said. "It's faster." He pointed us in the right direction.

I grabbed my jean jacket and slipped it on as we skirted the outside of the cavernous exhibition hall to reach the back hallway, passing a kitchen, the men's and ladies' restrooms, and a storage room, where I came to a sudden stop. I backed up to peer through the doorway. At least two dozen decorated caskets filled the room, leaving only a few feet of space around the perimeter, where metal shelving stacked with boxes, tools, and equipment lined the walls.

"Come take a look, Marco. This is where they're storing the entries for the themed casket contest."

"The what?"

"Casket contest. Didn't you see the flyer on the table? Let's see if we can guess which one is Delilah's."

"I'll pass."

Intrigued, I stepped inside to see more. "Here's one that looks like a race car, and there's one that looks just like an iPod. How clever. And there's one that looks like a piano keyboard. Someone even decked out this interior to look like a day at the beach, with real sand in the bottom. How crazy is that?"

"See you later," Marco called.

"Spoilsport." I hurried after him, exiting the building through a pair of heavy steel doors that opened onto the parking lot. About fifty yards west of us was the glass-fronted public entrance, which also faced the parking lot. Connected to the convention center was the Woodland Hotel, a five-story L-shaped structure that attempted by color and design to blend into the woods behind it.

As we left the building I was surprised to see two police cars pull up—one from the county sheriff's department and one from the New Chapel PD. On the sidewalk near the public entrance stood a group of sign-carrying protesters, along with a photographer and a camera crew from the local media. The seven protesters were dressed in brown burlap robes that tied at the waist with lengths of ropes. Around their necks hung strings of garlic bulbs, and their signs read, GO NATURAL and GREEN BURIALS SAVE THE PLANET.

Sign in hand, their leader, a reedy, hollow-cheeked man with thick, iron gray curls covering his head like a fright wig, was urging them on through his bullhorn as they chanted, "Ashes to ashes, dust to dust."

As the cops exited the squad cars, Sybil came marching out of the main entry shouting, "Officers!" She made sure the cameras had swung in her direction before pointing to the group and calling, "I want those people arrested immediately."

"She's the one you should arrest," the leader shouted at the cops through his bullhorn. He used his sign to point directly at her. "She and all the other phonies that run the funeral directors' association. They're the reason we're out here and not in there. They denied us the right to rent a booth."

"I can't imagine why," Marco said under his breath as the protesters booed and hissed at Sybil. "Abby, where are you going?"

"Reilly's here," I called over my shoulder. "Didn't you notice him get out of the car?"

"I was hoping you hadn't," he said with a sigh, and started after me.

After my father, who was now retired, Sgt. Sean Reilly was my favorite police officer in the entire world, partly because he had come to my assistance at least five times in the past year, and partly because he was highly tolerant of my natural curiosity. As a young rookie, Reilly had worked with my dad and still greatly admired him, and had also become fast friends with Marco during Marco's stint on the police force.

Reilly was a big, gruff forty-year-old with intelligent-looking hazel eyes and brown hair starting to show a bit of gray on the sides. He was an honest, no-frills kind of cop who preferred to play by the rules but didn't feel he had to push anyone around to prove he was in charge.

At that moment, Reilly was standing in front of his squad car sizing up the protesters. He saw me come up and said out of the side of his mouth, "Imagine finding you here."

"I knew you'd be thrilled to see me, Sarge. I'm attending a convention. What's your excuse? This isn't New Chapel PD territory."

"Sheriff's department is running shorthanded

39

because of a toxic-waste spill on Highway 20. They asked for backup, and lucky me, here I am." He saw Marco come up beside me and managed a quick nod of greeting before his attention was drawn back to the leader of the small band of protesters, who was attempting to argue his position with Sybil. She was too busy posing for the cameras to notice.

"These people are lunatics," Sybil said into a microphone thrust beneath her face. "Look at them. They're wearing burlap, for God's sake."

"We're not the lunatics," the leader shouted through his bullhorn, his hollow cheeks puffing out in indignation. "You're the lunatic! You and your self-serving committee of asses!"

"Sir, you're going to have to leave," Reilly said, stepping between the two combatants. "You're trespassing on private property."

"I'm not here to cause trouble, Officer. I'm an upstanding citizen who just wants to be able to promote my natural burial bags." As the cameras focused on him, he said, "Allow me to introduce myself. My name is Eli Cotton." He offered a hand to Reilly, who was having none of that.

"Do you know anything about natural burials?" Eli asked him, undeterred. "Here, I'll show you." He thrust his hand into his robe pocket, sending a strong wave of garlic-scented air our way.

"Keep your hand where I can see it, sir," Reilly barked as the other cops moved to surround him.

Eli carefully withdrew a pamphlet, which Sybil

promptly snatched from him and ripped into pieces. "Here's what I think of your natural burials." She threw the pieces into the air, then brushed her hands together. "Now, Officers, as the convention chairperson of the Midwestern Funeral Directors' Association, I order you to arrest this lunatic and his motley crew at once."

"You can't have us arrested," Eli shot back at her. "We have the right to free assemblage."

I started to raise my fist to show my solidarity, but Marco put a hand on my arm. "Stay out of it," he said quietly, "or you'll be on the six o'clock news."

"Sir, do you have a permit to assemble?" Reilly asked Eli.

Before Eli could answer, Sybil screeched, "I don't care if he has three permits. Arrest that crackpot right now."

With a roar of rage, Eli grabbed his sign and swung it at Sybil, narrowly missing her but causing several rose petals to fall off the blossom above her ear. She stamped her foot in outrage while one cop seized the sign, two more pulled Eli's arms back, and Reilly snapped the cuffs over his wrists and began to recite his Miranda rights.

Once Eli had been subdued, Sybil gave a nod of satisfaction. "Thank you, officers," she said, making sure to display as much cleavage as possible. After ensuring that her rose was securely in place, she sashayed back to the center.

"Too bad Eli's aim wasn't better," I muttered to Marco.

Poor Eli looked so dejected as they stuffed him into the backseat of the cruiser that I couldn't resist stepping up to the car window to say through the glass, "When you bond out, picket across the street. It's public property. They can't arrest you there."

At Reilly's furious scowl, I said, "What? I thought he could use some free legal advice."

"You want free legal advice? Here it is. Go back to law school and get your degree."

Ouch. That smarted.

"What did you expect?" Marco asked as we hurried across the parking lot. "You were interfering with police business."

"I got caught up in the moment. Besides, Sybil looked so self-satisfied that I couldn't resist trying to help Eli. Why shouldn't he be allowed to rent booth space if he can pay the fee?"

"How do you know whether he can pay it? And don't give me that look. You don't have to get involved. Eli isn't your concern, so just erase this whole incident from your mind, and let's get back to what you came here to do, okay?"

"Fine. It's erased."

"Good."

Men are so gullible.

As we hurried toward the white minivan we rented for large deliveries, I could see Lottie sitting inside fanning her face with a folded newspaper, even though it was a chilly October day. She gave off so much heat that she wouldn't need a coat until the snow fell in December. She was dressed in a pair of black Keds, black jeans, and a short-sleeve T-shirt with scenes from Paris on the front and back, and had her usual pink barrettes clipped into her brassy curls to keep them out of her face.

"Sorry," I said. "I got sidetracked."

"Don't ask her how," Marco said.

"Fair enough," she answered as we loaded our arms with boxes.

Hailing from the lovely bluegrass state of Kentucky, Lottie Dombowski was a raw-boned, big-hearted, full-bodied, forty-five-year-old dynamo who had given birth to quadruplet sons seventeen years ago and was now trying to survive their teenage years. Originally, she had owned Bloomers and I had worked there as her summer help.

Half a year ago, while I was busy flunking law exams, being dumped by my fiancé *and* my insurance company, and crossing off my dream to become the success my brothers were, Lottie's husband developed serious heart problems, starting a cascade of financial difficulties that threatened to sink her ship—er, shop. Since we were both looking for a life raft, Lottie suggested what seemed like a crazy idea at the time. And now, one gi*normous* mortgage later, I owned a flower shop and she worked for possibly the best employer in the whole country.

We'd trudged back to the center with our boxes and, as we set out the flowers, Delilah and I filled Lottie in on the events of the morning, including Chet Sunday's upcoming show and the pranks pulled by the Urban twins. Prudently, I waited until Marco was out of earshot before telling the others about Eli's clash with Sybil.

"Isn't that just like Sybil," Delilah said. "I do wish I could have seen Eli swing his sign at her, though."

"Sybil Blount," Lottie mused. "Seems like I read something in a gossip column linking her with a TV star not too long ago."

"Doesn't surprise me," Delilah said. "After her husband passed, she went hog wild with the menfolk."

Suddenly, the beginning strains of a familiar song blared over the PA system—"Make It Easy on Yourself," sung by Jerry Butler, which also happened to be the theme song of Chet Sunday's show.

"It's showtime," I announced. "Who's coming with me?"

"I'm heading back to Bloomers," Lottie said, slinging her purse over a hefty shoulder. "I'll be back at two o'clock."

"Del and I will stay here," Max said to me. "You and Marco go."

"I'm going only because you asked me to," Marco grumbled.

Did he need another reason?

The *Make It Easy* set had a wooden stage, the familiar backdrop of the inside of a workshop, lights, cameras, electronic equipment, grips, a director wearing headphones, and a man in a suit (possibly a representative of the show's sponsor, Habitation Station). The only thing missing was Chet.

The six long rows of folding chairs in front of the stage were already filled, so we had to stand in back with other latecomers as the director gave instructions to the audience, spoke with his cameramen, then signaled to his soundman. The theme music swelled, the director started the crowd clapping, and Chet Sunday strode onto the stage.

At six feet tall and in his midthirties, Chet had shiny, honey brown hair, a neatly trimmed goatee, a muscular body, a strong, aquiline nose, and the squarest jaw I'd ever seen. As usual, he had on his trademark blue plaid cotton shirt, dark blue jeans, and yellow work boots, with a fully-loaded leather tool belt around his waist.

The audience members instantly got to their feet, whistling, clapping, and *woo-woo*-ing, until the director finally got them to quiet down. The *Make It Easy* show had been on the air for two years and had garnered a huge following of men and women alike. Habitation Station loved Chet for his wholesome image and all-American good looks, even if he had immigrated to America from Eastern Europe ten years earlier. It hadn't hurt his image, either, that he had recently been nominated for a Humanitarian of the Year award and often made appearances on behalf of his favorite charities.

Each of Chet's shows had a theme, and the one they

had selected for today was called "Build It Easy," in which Chet demonstrated how to put together a simple pine box casket, line it with foam padding, and cover the padding with satin—all material available in a kit sold at Habitation Station. It wasn't until halfway through the taping that the irony occurred to me.

I leaned over to whisper to Marco, "If Chet Sunday is allowed to promote do-it-yourself caskets, why shouldn't Eli be allowed to do the same with his burial bags?"

"Forget about Eli," Marco whispered back. "The man is off balance."

"He's a concerned environmentalist."

"You've got the *mental* part right."

"Shhh!" someone behind me whispered.

At the end of the show, Chet took off his tool belt and hung it on a peg, his standard routine. "Be sure to tune in for our next episode, 'Transfer It Easy,' when I'll show you how to build a space-saving CD/DVD stand you'll be proud to display anywhere. As a bonus I'll even demonstrate how to transfer those old video-tapes and reel-to-reel movies onto DVDs. Until then, remember, make it easy on yourself."

The music swelled, his director said, "It's a wrap," and the cameras shut off. As the crew packed up, Chet had a brief conversation with the director, then walked down the two steps to sign autographs. Quickly, I fished in my purse for my notepad, something I never left home without.

Marco glanced askance at me. "Tell me you're not going up for his autograph."

"It's not for me; it's for Nikki. She's a huge fan." Nikki, my best friend since third grade and also my roommate, watched Chet's show every Saturday with me, except for the weekends she had to work an extra shift at the hospital, when I taped it for her.

"Put away your notepad, Sunshine. Looks like Sybil has other plans for Chet."

I looked up to see Sybil whisper something in Chet's ear that didn't seem to please him, judging by his slight frown. He frowned even harder after she plucked her rose from her hair and tickled him under the chin with it. But he put on his star smile to turn back to his fans and say with just a hint of Slavic accent, "Go get a cup of coffee and a bagel and I'll be back to sign autographs at one o'clock."

The murmurs of disappointment didn't bother Sybil. She seemed almost effervescent as she and Chet headed out of the convention hall and up the main hallway past the phone booth–coffin toward a glass-ceilinged atrium at the far end. From the atrium one could either exit the building through the wide glass doors of the public entrance or head up a corridor that connected the convention center to the hotel. It was the latter route that the pair took.

"Why would Sybil drag Chet away from his fans now?" I asked. "Do you think she just wants to show how much power and influence she has, or do you think the two of them have something going on?"

"I don't really care," Marco said. "It's noon. Let's go grab some lunch."

"It's always about your stomach, isn't it?"

He put an arm around my shoulders and drew me close. "Not always."

We found a café in the food court at the back of the convention hall and were seated right away. I ordered my usual turkey and Swiss cheese, and Marco got a burger with the works. He ordered a side of fries, which we shared, and we each had a Bud Light.

We had finished our sandwiches and were working on his fries when I heard a cell phone behind me begin to play "America the Beautiful." I glanced over my shoulder and saw Colonel Billingsworth holding a cell phone to his ear. Then he snapped it shut and said to his companion, "That's it. Something's got to be done about those Urbans. Their behavior borders on the criminal. Did you hear about their latest stunt?"

The man sitting across from him said something I couldn't catch, even after I'd shushed Marco. "Listen," I whispered, discreetly hitching my thumb over my shoulder as their conversation continued.

"Did you know they're the ones who pushed this vampire drinking party and casket race through?" the colonel asked. "A casket race! Do you know what will happen if the media gets wind of it? Do you have any idea what that will do to our image? The public has their expectations of us, you know, and the behavior of those young men makes a mockery of everything we stand for."

Marco stole a fry from my plate. "Are you going to talk to me or listen to them?"

I pointed with my thumb again. "Them."

"Then I'm taking back my fries."

I pushed the plate toward him and tipped my head back to hear more.

"Have you tried speaking to their father?" the other man asked.

"Of course I have," the colonel replied. "Not that it's done any good. The truth is, Conrad Urban is too busy jetting around the country buying out funeral homes to discipline them. I'll just have to find a way to ban the boys from future conventions. I'm considering taking away their association memberships."

"Conrad would never stand for that," his companion said. "He has enough money to put on his own convention, and you know we couldn't compete with that. Have you discussed the problem with Sybil?"

"What's the use? You know what a pushover she is with young men."

"Pushover? Is that what they're calling it these days? So the Urbans will continue until something happens, and then their father will pay money to make the problem go away." The colonel sighed. "Short of banning them, all we can do is hope they cause Conrad a great deal of disgrace. Maybe then he'll take action."

"Did you hear about the young woman they locked

in that phony phone booth this morning? Perhaps, if we can locate her, we can persuade her to press charges."

I leaned toward Marco to whisper excitedly, "They're talking about *me*."

He trapped my hands under his. "Don't even think about turning around."

Chapter Five

Don't turn around, when the two men clearly needed to talk to me? That was like handing me a Ghirardelli bar and telling me not to eat it. "Why shouldn't I let them know what happened to me?" I asked Marco.

"Do you really want to testify in court against the sons of a mortuary mogul, a man who could crush you like a bug? Do you think that will be good for your business?"

"But it's not right that they get away with their stupid pranks because their father is rich. I could have suffocated in that booth."

Marco traced a fingertip along the back of my right hand, sending shivers of delight up my arm. "But you didn't suffocate, Sunshine, so no harm, no foul. Besides, the booth wasn't airtight, and people are in that hallway all the time. If I hadn't come along, someone else would have heard you calling to get out."

I took in his sensual eyes, the dark hair waving onto

his forehead, and that rough shadow of a beard, and said in a sexy purr, "Lucky for me, it *was* you."

His mouth curved up at both corners. "How lucky?"

"Talk to me after the banquet."

The afternoon passed slowly, as more of the convention's guests attended the workshops than browsed the displays. Even Max and Delilah had gone to a seminar, and Marco had escaped back to his bar in New Chapel, so I stood behind the table waving mums at anyone who passed, hoping they'd stop to chat. This was not only to gain customers but also to discourage Angelique from drifting over to share tales of her bedside death watches. I couldn't seem to get her to understand that her stories did not thrill me and that her eerie music made my skin crawl.

Thankfully, Lottie returned at two o'clock carrying a cup of coffee for her and a mocha latte for me. She opened a folding chair and sat down while I took careful sips from the cardboard cup in case it was still at tongue-blistering temperature.

"How's it going, sweetie?"

"We've had slow but steady traffic." I leaned closer to whisper, "And that traffic includes our neighbor across the way."

"You should have been here when she tried to get Delilah to sign up for a recording. 'Beggin' your pardon, sugarplum,' Delilah told her, 'but recordin' me wouldn't do any good. I'm tone deaf.'" Lottie slapped her knee and howled with laughter, which made Angelique stop strumming her harp strings and glance our way.

"Great. Here she comes again," I muttered.

Lottie bent down to hunt for something in her mountain of a purse on the floor beside her, then straightened and nearly jumped out of the chair. Angelique had planted her elbows on the table and was leaning across, her face inches from Lottie's, studying her with unblinking, emotionless eyes.

"Good golly, woman," Lottie cried, a hand against her heart. "You scared five years off my life."

Angelique continued to stare into her eyes. *"Pesante,"* she said at last, dismissing Lottie with a wave of a pale hand. She drifted back to her booth, put on a CD, and began a slow pirouette to the strange, unharmonious sounds.

"Pesante?" Lottie repeated. "What's that supposed to mean?"

"I don't know, but I'm *staccato,* which Marco says means short and disconnected."

"Then *pesante* must mean built like a plow horse. Uh-oh. Trouble is on the way."

Coming up the aisle was Sybil, clipboard in hand, stopping at each booth to impart information. At the Music of the Soul booth, she paused to listen to a selection from a CD that Angelique had obviously persuaded her to hear; then she put an arm around the harpist's shoulders and gave her a hug before heading our way. The intimate gesture made me think they

52

were friends, but the next words out of her mouth disabused me of that notion.

"Angelique wants to record my *soul* music," Sybil said, rolling her eyes. "What a freak show. And if her face isn't screaming for a makeover, I don't know whose is."

Lottie stared at Sybil in disbelief, while I tugged at a hangnail to keep from suggesting that Sybil might want to grab a hand mirror and have a gander at her own plasticine complexion.

"Now then," Sybil said to Lottie, having dispensed with her snarky comments, "have you signed up for the casket contest?"

"Yes, ma'am," Lottie said.

I couldn't help but give Lottie a look of surprise as Sybil put a check mark beside the first item on her list. Then she asked, "Have you registered your group for the banquet tonight?"

"Yes, ma'am."

I gave Lottie another surprised glance while Sybil checked off the next box.

"Be in your seats promptly at six fifty," Sybil ordered. "At seven o'clock I'll open with a welcome; a chaplain will deliver a short prayer; then dinner will be served."

"Yes, ma'am," Lottie said again.

As soon as Sybil moved to the next booth, I said, "We don't have an entry in the contest, and you're not coming to the banquet tonight."

"Sweetie, life's a whole lot simpler when you plow around the stump."

I wasn't exactly sure how the stump applied to our situation, but at that moment Angelique caught my eye. She was standing in the middle of the aisle with her hands clasped to her bosom, staring longingly after Sybil.

"Bellicoso," she cried in her ethereal voice. *"Tremendo."* She pirouetted over to our table and leaned toward us, arms over her head. "If Sybil doesn't let me record her *omaggio,* I'll wither like a vine in winter. *Feroce al fine."* To emphasize her statement, she crumpled gracefully to the floor.

"You want to translate for us simple folk?" Lottie asked, looking very grumpy. She had a low tolerance for people with attitude.

The harpist rose, gave us a haughty glance, and toe-danced back to her harp to strum her strings.

"That woman is getting on my nerves," Lottie said, then saw me jotting in my notebook. "What are you doing?"

"Writing down what Angelique said. The next time she tries to impress us with her knowledge, I'm going to be prepared." I opened my cell phone and called Bloomers. "Hey, Grace, can you translate some musical terminology for me?"

"Did you mean to say, '*Will* I'?" was Grace's reply. Because of course she *could.*

Grace Bingham was my other assistant at Bloomers, an intelligent, energetic, stylish, often picky six-tysomething Brit whom I'd met when I clerked for Attorney Dave Hammond. Grace had been Dave's legal secretary at the time. Besides running the coffee and tea parlor at Bloomers, she also served as my resource person. If she didn't know the answer, she knew how to find it.

A minute later I hung up and said to Lottie, "Grace is on it."

At five o'clock all the booths were to close in preparation for the evening gala, so Delilah and Max returned to help Lottie and me pack up the fresh flowers for storage in an empty cooler in the industrial-size kitchen located just off the back hallway. On our way back from the kitchen, Delilah had us detour to the storage room to see the Happy Dreams entry for the casket contest.

The Happy Dreams casket was covered in a tapestry material and embellished with a trimming of small beads and lace. Delilah opened the lid for us to see a pair of giant, wire-rimmed eyeglasses inside.

"An eyeglass case!" I announced. "Very cool, Delilah."

"You don't think this contest is a little far-out?" Lottie asked, keeping her distance.

"Morticians like to have fun, too," Delilah said, then let out a little gasp of dismay. "The lace is coming off this side, Max. I'll have to come back with the glue gun."

He glanced at his watch. "We promised Mark and Jane we'd have a drink with them before dinner, so why don't I take care of it while you get ready?"

"Sugar pie, I love you to pieces, but you're down-right dangerous with a glue gun. Besides, this is my creation. It won't take me any time at all to fix this. If it makes you feel better, I'll get all gussied up before I come down here. I'll just have to remember to put on my smock so I don't drip glue on my dress. I'm sorry you'll miss all the fun, Lottie."

"My philosophy is, if you've been to one banquet, you've been to them all," Lottie said.

"I'll see you and Max at the banquet hall at six thirty," I said to Delilah. With the convention center located only half an hour's drive from New Chapel, I was able to go home each night, saving the expense of a hotel room.

"Don't be late," Max called. "You don't want to incur the wrath of Sybil."

At six o'clock Marco arrived at my apartment, looking—according to Nikki, who'd answered the door—super-hunky in a soft gray jacket, white shirt, hand-painted silk tie with a swirl of colors, and slim-fitting black pants.

"That man is a *treasure,*" she whispered.

As best friends went, so was Nikki. She was a tall, slender blonde with a peaches-and-cream complexion and an easygoing nature. We'd met the summer between third and fourth grade, and our friendship had been rock solid ever since. Back then, we were the same height and weight and even wore matching ponytails, but by seventh grade she had left me in the dust as far as height was concerned. I was still hoping to catch up, but at the ripe old age of twenty-six, I knew the odds weren't in my favor.

Nikki had offered to share her apartment with me after my wedding and law school plans fell through, and I had quickly leapt at the offer. Since she usually worked afternoons as an X-ray technician at the county hospital and didn't get home until almost midnight, we saw each other only briefly during the week, which was why our arrangement worked so well.

Now, standing in front of the full-length mirror hanging on the back of my bedroom door, I held a pair of silver hoop earrings against my ears. "How do these look with my dress?"

"Ugh. Not with that color green. Try your crystal dangling ones." She dug through the little blue jewelry box on my dresser. "Oh, wait. I borrowed those last week. I'll be right back."

While Nikki dashed to her room across the hallway, I took two steps backward and squinted at my reflection (a trick that made me appear slimmer.) Just as I'd feared, the earrings weren't the problem. It was my sleeveless wrap dress, a designer knockoff I'd found at Marshalls. With my extra-curvy body and my upswept red hair, I looked like two scoops of key lime ice cream with a cherry on top. Oh, well. It was too late to change now.

"Here you go," Nikki said.

I shoved the posts through my earlobes, grabbed my leather clutch purse, slipped into my black sling-back heels, and hurried up the hallway, around the corner, through our tiny living room, and up another short hallway past the kitchen, where I found Marco leaning against the door, arms folded, looking like he'd just stepped away from a *GQ* photo session. As always, I had to stop to catch my breath. How could anyone be that scrumpti-hunkalicious?

He looked me over and one corner of his mouth curved up in approval. "Nice."

"You're not looking at me and thinking, 'Hmm, I could really go for an ice cream sundae'?"

"Not the direction of my thoughts at all." He lifted an eyebrow suggestively.

Good enough for me.

As we wove through clusters of men in dark suits and women in cocktail dresses, hunting for table seventeen in the banquet hall, I found Max seated at our table with the Doves' friends Mark and Jane Vale, and another couple, Alicia and Walt Tyler. Max explained that Delilah would be arriving momentarily. She'd had problems with her glue gun.

At another front-row table I saw an older, more sophisticated version of Ross Urban, right down to his highlights. The only difference was that his hair was curly, where Ross's was wavy. He had to be Conrad Urban. With him was a contingent of assistants watching his every twitch, eager to do his bidding. Surprisingly, the twins hadn't yet arrived, and Conrad seemed edgy because of it, glancing from his watch to the wide, double doors in the back. There was also no sign of Chet Sunday.

At seven o'clock everyone began to drift to their seats. Delilah, however, had yet to make an appearance, and by the frown on Max's face I knew he was starting to fret. Delilah prided herself on punctuality. It would be unthinkable for her to arrive late.

"Where's the happy harpist?" Marco leaned close to whisper, his husky voice sending scintillating tingles to locations I could only describe as strategic.

"She's in the back at a table all by herself, draped over her chair like a black fog. I think her vampire costume is scaring people off." My stomach rumbled, so I reached for the poppy-seed roll on my bread plate. "I hope Sybil starts this soon so we can eat. I'm hungry."

At that moment Ross and Jess came scooting through the crowd and plopped down across from their father, drinks in hand. At first I couldn't tell them apart, as one had on a navy suit and the other wore a black suit, and both had neatly combed hair. However, one of the twins was sporting a tie that appeared to have been hastily knotted, with an unbuttoned collar to boot. I was guessing he was Jess the Mess. He got a fierce glare from Conrad, which prompted him to quickly adjust his tie.

"It's after seven o'clock," Marco muttered, twisting in his chair to glance around the room. "Still think we'll be out of here at eight?"

At that moment Delilah swept up to our table. "I do

beg your pardon," she said breathlessly as Max jumped up to seat her. "I had a slight difficulty, but everything is under control now."

"Are you sure?" Max asked, which was exactly what I was wondering. Delilah's pastel pink hat was askew, and several wisps of her blond hair had managed to break free of the hair spray and were flying about her face as though she'd been in a wind tunnel.

"Of course I'm sure," she said, tucking her hair in place. "I had a little delay, is all. I ran out of glue and had to go out to our van for more."

"You should have beeped me," Max said. "I would have gone for the glue."

"Darlin', I was in the storage room, just yards from the back door. It didn't take long to get to our van from there. Now, don't fret."

"Did you happen to see Sybil on your way in?" Mark asked her.

Delilah leaned forward to say quietly, "Sybil was in the storage room when I went to fix the lace. She kept insistin' that I leave because of some silly rule that says no one is allowed in after six, but I could tell by her jittery behavior it wasn't about a rule. She was waitin' for someone. So I told her, 'Honey, I have one little-bitty thing to glue on, and I'm not leavin' until you let me in to do it.'" Delilah smiled. "She let me fix it, although she was as nervous as a cat the whole time."

"But even if she'd been waiting for someone," Jane said, "Sybil would never allow herself to be late to the banquet, not when she's in charge."

Everyone at the table agreed with her.

Over the PA system I heard, "Sybil Blount, please come to the banquet hall."

I turned to glance around the room, but even the announcement failed to produce Sybil. I saw Chet Sunday seated near the back with a group of men in tuxes, no doubt his sponsors from Habitation Station. The far table where Angelique had sat was now empty.

By seven fifteen, we were not only hungry but also annoyed. The servers were poised outside the kitchen doors, their carts loaded with salad plates; the bowls of bread and rolls on the tables had been emptied and filled again; and all around me exasperated guests buzzed with speculation.

"She probably found herself a bellboy toy," I heard one man say.

At seven twenty the colonel strode up to the podium. "We seem to be missing our chairperson, so I'd like to ask Reverend Schmidt to come up and give a blessing. Then we'll get started."

Applause greeted his announcement, and the dinner took off at last. We ate field greens topped with goat cheese, blueberries, and walnuts in a light balsamic vinaigrette; pecan-crusted chicken breasts stuffed with spinach and Gorgonzola cheese on a bed of couscous; and white asparagus spears in a lemon beurre-blanc sauce. Delilah hadn't misled me. It truly was a spectacular meal.

But a rushed one. At seven forty-five, as dessert was being served—a chocolate torte with raspberry sauce—Colonel Billingsworth again went to the podium. "I'd like to ask for four volunteers to judge our casket contest. If you're interested in judging, please raise your hand. I'll announce the winner in half an hour, after our judges have had a chance to review the entries. In the meantime, could I ask the ladies who have prepared a skit for tonight's entertainment to please come forward?"

"Sybil must have taken ill," Jane said. "She'd never let anyone take the contest judging away from her."

"Marco," I said quietly, "I have a funny feeling about Sybil's absence."

He grabbed a bottle of white wine from the table and splashed some into my glass. "This will make it go away."

"I'm serious." I picked up my clutch purse and whispered to him, "I'm going to look for her. Want to help?"

He gazed at me for a moment, probably trying to decide whether he could get away with saying no. Then, muttering "I know I'll regret this," he followed me out of the banquet hall.

Chapter Six

We explained the situation to the hotel manager, who tried to ring Sybil's room. When he didn't get a response, he sent a woman from housekeeping up to the fourth floor with us to knock, and when that didn't work either, the woman used her master key card to unlock the door and call inside, "House-keeping, Mrs. Blount. Hello?"

"Why do I keep picturing that shower scene from *Psycho*?" I whispered to Marco, gripping his hand.

The housekeeper scowled at me but proceeded inside anyway, making us wait in the hallway. A few moments later she returned and said, "I'm sorry, but no one is in the room."

Then where was Sybil?

We headed for the exhibition hall to check her cosmetics booth. The vast hall was deserted because of the banquet, and the huge lights overhead had been dimmed, making the rows of booths feel like a ghost town. At booth four we found a big silver makeup case; several oval mirrors on stainless-steel stands; a stack of brochures; jars holding her blushes, foundations, and powders; and a dummy's head wearing a wig and the shiny makeup that was Sybil's trademark look, but there was no sign of Sybil.

As we paused at the top of aisle two, trying to decide where to search next, I happened to glance over at the mannequins on display at the funeral outfitters' booth. To my surprise I saw a black fishnet stocking dangling from the female dummy's fingers. And that wasn't all. Someone had removed the mannequin's navy dress and shoes and replaced them with a zebra-striped wrap dress and black patent spike heels.

"Marco, look at that mannequin. Isn't that the outfit Sybil had on today?"

"Sunshine, I don't even know what *you* had on today."

"Gee, I feel so flattered." Walking over to bat the dangling stocking, I said, "Looks like Ross and Jess got Sybil again."

Marco gave me a skeptical glance. "How did they get hold of her clothes?"

"Are you kidding?"

Over his shoulder I suddenly noticed the pulsing red and blue lights of police cars shining through the windows near the back hallway. "Marco, look."

He started jogging toward the back exit. "I'll check it out. You wait here."

Right. I was going to stand *here* while he was over *there* where all the excitement was.

Um, no.

I slipped off my high heels and hurried after him, not an easy feat in a skirt that's tight at the knees. As I hobbled down the hallway I could hear men's voices coming from the storage room, and when I peered inside I saw two young cops from the county sheriff's department talking to Marco. They were standing on the left side of the room by the last row of caskets, directly in front of one on a low stand, its lid open to reveal a silk lining that had been plumped up and painted to look like big, fluffy clouds. I remembered the entry: It was supposed to be a beach scene, and the casket itself had been filled with several inches of sand. Had someone vandalized it?

Pausing to put on my shoes, I slipped up behind

Marco and ventured a glance around him, then instantly pressed my fingers against my mouth to stifle a horrified gasp. Inside the casket lay Sybil, her glassy, bulging eyes staring up at the ceiling with a terrified expression, her mouth gaping like a fish, and her body nude except for a sexy black lace teddy, with garter straps dangling, stocking free.

My stomach churned as I gazed down at the ghastly sight. Her shiny funeral makeup was in place but her lipstick had worn off, revealing blue-tinged lips. Her arms were bent at the elbow, with her hands near her shoulders, palms up, as though she were pushing something away from her face. I glanced around for a likely object, like a loose pillow, but all I saw was a big gray tool chest lying on its side behind the casket stand.

Marco noticed me and instantly drew me away. "Why didn't you stay in the hallway?"

I signaled for him to wait as I took a slow, deep breath, hoping the shock would wear off. Unfortunately, it wasn't happening. "Marco, did you get a look at her face?"

"I saw it."

"Sybil didn't just crawl into that casket and die."

"I know. Come on, Sunshine. Let's get out of here."

I was trembling all over as he led me out of the room. I lurched to the wall and let my back flatten against it, my hands against the hard surface, trying to ground myself. It wasn't the first time I'd seen a dead body, but it was still a terrible shock.

"There's a kitchen next door," Marco said. "I'll get you some water."

I clasped his wrist. "Was she suffocated? Strangled? Shot?"

"I don't know."

"The cops didn't offer an opinion?"

"No."

"*You* don't have an opinion?"

"I got here two seconds before you did."

"Her mouth was open and her lips were blue, Marco. Make a guess."

"Why are you snapping at me?"

Why *was* I snapping? "I'm sorry. I'm just rattled. I wasn't prepared to see her . . . like that." I took another breath. "Poor Sybil. And what an ironic place to die."

He took my hand and rubbed it between his own. "Think of it this way. At least it was convenient."

I pulled my hand back. "That is *so* not funny."

"Come on. I'm just trying to lighten the mood."

"How do you lighten death?"

"Isn't that what everyone at the convention has been doing all day? Now, stay here and rest while I get that water—or would you rather have coffee?"

I couldn't have swallowed anything if my life depended on it. "Nothing right now, thanks."

I glanced toward the doorway, where I could see the cops cordoning off the crime scene with bright yellow tape. "Marco, do you think it's significant that she's wearing only her undies and is lying in a casket that looks like the seashore? Is someone sending a message?"

"Nah." Standing at my shoulder, Marco said, "I'm guessing there was some kinky sex going on."

"In a casket? That goes way beyond kinky. But you know, it *is* a possibility. Remember what Delilah said about Sybil waiting for someone down here? Maybe she and her lover climbed inside for a little romp in the sand, and right in the middle of—well, whatever— she had a heart attack and tried to push off whoever was with her. And then when the guy saw she was dead, he panicked and ran."

"That would be a pretty callous thing to do. There would also be sand on the floor where he climbed out, and I didn't hear anything crunch under my shoes."

"You're right. Plus, her clothes didn't walk themselves out to that mannequin. You know what I'm thinking?" I heard the back door open and glanced around to see Sgt. Reilly coming up the hallway toward us. With an exasperated shake of his head, he said, "Look who's right in the thick of things as usual. Abby Knight."

He had apparently missed the Italian American hunk standing beside me.

"You're still on duty?" Marco asked.

Reilly hooked his thumbs in his thick leather belt. "Like I said earlier, today's my lucky day."

"Your luck is about to get worse," I said. "The chairperson of the morticians' convention was found dead in a casket. Sybil Blount. You met her this morning."

67

"In a casket." Reilly nodded slowly, as if he heard that sort of thing all the time. "Fitting."

"Convenient, too," Marco added.

"You guys are sick," I said, turning away. "I am *not* listening to this."

Reilly stepped to the doorway to take a look. "Those are caskets? They look more like circus props."

"Contest entries," Marco explained.

"A casket contest?" Reilly blew out a big breath. "And this was supposed to be my day off."

When he strode into the storage room, I couldn't help but follow. Although I was still a little nauseated from the shock, my curiosity was too strong to keep me away. I motioned for Marco to come with me, but he grabbed my hand. "Where are you going?"

"You don't really need an answer to that, do you?"

"Abby, you know how Reilly feels about you nosing around."

"I'm just going to stand inside the doorway. I'll be quiet." I pretended to lock my lips, then turned to watch as Reilly made his way over to the other cops, staying outside the boundaries of the yellow police tape.

"Okay, what do we have?" he asked the county cops, taking out his notepad and pencil. Reilly wasn't in the sheriff's department, but because of his rank and experience, the younger cops had no problem letting him take charge.

"Victim's name is Sybil Blount," one of them said, reading his notes. "No ID on the body. Salvare gave us the name. The vic was in charge of—get this—a funeral directors' convention." He started to chuckle, but since no one else looked amused, he dropped it.

"Who called it in?" Reilly asked, craning his neck for a view of the body.

When the cop pointed toward the opposite side of the room, I peered around the doorjamb for a look. Someone else was there? Why hadn't I noticed earlier?

I had to stand on tiptoe to see over a row of caskets, and much to my surprise, there sat Angelique against a black metal shelving unit on the black-and-white linoleum floor. She was hugging her knees to her chest and rocking to and fro, totally lost in her own world. Her eyes were closed, her white face was wet from crying, and her bare ankles and black ballet slippers peeked out from beneath the hem of her long black dress. No wonder I hadn't spotted her. She blended right in.

I whispered to Marco, "Did you know she was there?"

He shook his head.

"Anyone get her name?" Reilly asked, studying her.

"Angelique DeScuro," I offered, earning a scowl from Reilly and a nudge from Marco. Angelique didn't even bat an eye.

The young cop told Reilly, "When we got here she was sitting cross-legged in front of the casket stand. There was a black fishnet stocking wrapped around her hand and she was stroking it against her cheek."

"Fishnets, huh?" Reilly said. "You came up with that awfully quick, didn't you?" At the cop's embarrassed shrug, Reilly said, "Did you bag the stockings, Romeo?"

"There was only one, Sergeant, but the lady still has it. We bagged the tape recorder that was in her lap."

Reilly's eyebrows drew together. "A tape recorder?"

"One of those little portable numbers."

There was no way I could keep quiet. "Angelique uses that tape recorder for her soul music," I whispered to Marco. "Maybe she was trying to record Sybil's soul before she died."

That spurred another thought, so I turned again to add, "But if Sybil was alive when Angelique got here, why are Sybil's hands in that palms-up position?"

Marco shrugged. He wasn't in a talkative mood.

Reilly gave Angelique another appraising glance. She still had her arms wrapped around her knees, and tears continued to course down her cheeks, making flesh-colored valleys in her white makeup, but now her head was tilted back and her mouth moved, forming silent words, as though she were praying. "Has she given you a statement?" Reilly asked the cops.

"The only thing she would tell us was that she found that tool chest on top of the casket when she came into the room"—the young cop pointed to the big, gray metal container behind the casket stand—"and had to shove it off before she could open the lid."

My mouth fell open. Now the position of her hands

70

made sense: Sybil had been pushing against the lid. Poor Angelique must have arrived too late to save her. No wonder she was so distraught.

A chill ran through me as I tried to imagine the terror Sybil felt when she couldn't get the lid open, reminding me of my own frightening experience in the phone booth. There were only two people I knew of who would be cruel enough to shut another person in a casket. The Urbans.

I turned to tell Marco, but he held a finger to his lips and pointed toward Reilly, who was crouched in front of the metal container. "Where was the tool chest when you got here?"

"Where it is now, and the coffin lid was up. We tried to question the witness further, but she got up and moved back there and hasn't said a word since."

Reilly rose to look around the crowded room. "The tool chest must have come from those shelves beside the door."

I peered around the doorjamb again to see where he was pointing. On the bottom shelf a few feet away from me was a metal box identical to the one on the floor.

Marco whispered in my ear, "I'll be right back," then pointed down the hall toward the men's room.

"Wait, Marco." I stepped away from the doorway so I wouldn't be overheard. "Am I the only one who sees a coincidence here?"

"What do you mean?"

"Sybil locked in a casket, and me locked in that

71

phone booth? I think we were both tricked by the Urban twins."

"A prank gone wrong?" His lips pressed into a line as he pondered it. "How would they have convinced her to take off her clothes?"

"How would two good-looking young guys convince Sybil to get naked? Gee, let me think. This is *Sybil* we're talking about, Marco."

He didn't look convinced. "Let me think about it."

While he strode off to the men's room, I hurried back to the doorway in time to hear Reilly ask the cops, "Any other witnesses?"

"Not that we noticed, but we got here only about fifteen minutes ago. The outside hallway was empty when we came in. We did a brief check of the restrooms and the kitchen right away. No one was around, but the back door isn't locked, so anyone could have entered or exited through it. The techies will be here soon to process everything, the coroner is on his way, and the hotel staff has been advised of the situation."

"Good. Anything else?" Reilly asked.

"That's all we have."

Maybe that was all they had, but I had more. I raised my hand like a schoolkid trying to get the teacher's attention.

Reilly beckoned me over. "Do you have anything helpful to add? And please note the word *helpful*."

"Yes, I do," I said eagerly.

"Of course you do."

He was being snide, but I ignored him. "I know how she died."

"I can't wait to hear it."

And I couldn't wait to share it with him. So, as Marco rejoined us, I laid out my theory, starting with my own experience with the Urbans up to our finding Sybil's clothes on the dummy, watching Reilly's expression turn from snide to skeptical to interested. "That's *U-R-B-A-N*," I spelled out for him. "Ross and Jess."

Reilly wrote it in his notepad, then sent one of the cops to secure the booth with the mannequins.

"And one more thing that supports my theory on the Urbans," I said to Reilly. "Delilah Dove told me that when she was down here around six o'clock this evening, Sybil appeared to be waiting for someone. So, guess who that someone—or someones—must have been."

Reilly was still taking down the information. "Dove?" he asked. "As in the bird?"

"As in the Happy Dreams Funeral Home Doves," Marco clarified.

"Oh, right. What was she doing in the storage room?"

I turned to point out Delilah's decorated casket. "That's her contest entry. She had to glue something on before the judging started. So, anyway, back to my theory—"

At that moment, Angelique rose and stretched her body like a graceful swan awakening from a nap.

Gliding effortlessly around the caskets on the right side of the room, she approached Reilly, her expression registering no emotion. The only indications of her grief were the deep tear tracks down her cheeks. "I'd like to leave now. May I have my recorder, please?"

"The recorder is evidence, ma'am," Reilly said.

"But I need it. I have work to do."

"You can have it when the investigation is over." Reilly motioned to another cop. "Take her to the kitchen and get a statement. And make sure she gets fingerprinted."

The cop tried to escort her to the door, but Angelique drew away from him with a sharp, *"Scherzo!"*

Reilly and the cop exchanged puzzled glances.

"It's a musical term," I whispered to Reilly. "Pretend you're not impressed."

"Ma'am, you'll need to go with this officer," he said. "We have to clear this room so the investigators can get in to work."

"Not with *him*," she said of the young cop. Using her index finger to point, Angelique swung her arm around, stopping at Marco. "Him."

I nearly laughed at Marco's stunned look, but Reilly wasn't seeing the humor in the situation. "He's not an officer, ma'am."

She crossed her arms over her chest and turned her head away. "Then I won't go."

Reilly frowned at her, but she wasn't paying any attention to him.

"You have to accompany the officer, ma'am. Now."

Angelique did a pirouette, then sank to the floor beside a casket decorated like a TV remote control and wrapped her arms and legs around the stand, casting Reilly a glance that said, *Make me.*

"Is she nuts?" Reilly whispered to me.

"Oh, yeah."

"Sean," Marco said, and motioned for Reilly to step out of Angelique's earshot, as I tagged along. "Look, if it will help move things along, I'll sit in on the interview."

Reilly lifted his hat to scratch his head. "I know you've got the experience, Marco, but it's not something we normally allow. And if brass gets wind of it . . ."

"Sean, it won't be a problem. I'll be there for support, and that's the extent of my involvement. You know I can keep my mouth shut. But if you don't want to chance it, that's fine with me. I'm ready to go home. How about you, Sunshine?"

Before I could reply, Reilly said, "Hold on a second," and signaled for the other cop to join the huddle.

While the three guys conferred, I took the opportunity to get another look at the body. Since the whole back row was now officially off limits, the best I could do was to stand between the harmonica casket and the miniature jet plane and lean over the yellow tape. Fortunately, the casket holding Sybil's corpse sat on a low enough stand to give me a good view from that distance.

Don't look at her eyes. I focused on Sybil's long mane of hair instead, then her ears, nose, and mouth, down her neck, over her body, and up again. I couldn't see any signs of blood, wounds, or purplish marks on her throat that might have indicated strangulation, but by the way her mouth was positioned, it was obvious that she had been gasping for air when she died. She was lying on a good three inches of sand, and the silk lining inside the casket lid had been stuffed so full that, when shut, it would probably have pressed against her face, further terrifying her.

A hard shudder rippled through me as I imagined her struggling to get out, crying for help even as she fought to draw a breath. Meanwhile, in the exhibition hall, the Urban twins had been dressing the dummy and having a good laugh. I couldn't fathom why they had put a heavy object on the lid. Leaving her naked in the storage room, her clothing on the mannequin in the hall for everyone to see, would have been embarrassing enough. Didn't they realize she would run out of air?

My fists tightened in outrage. This was one prank the Urbans would *not* get away with.

"All right, ma'am," Reilly said to Angelique as I rejoined them. "Mr. Salvare will accompany you, but he's not allowed to advise you in any way. Do you understand?"

At her nod, Marco and one of the cops helped her up, each one taking an arm. But before they could usher her into the hallway, she broke free and twisted around for another look at the casket where Sybil's body lay.

"Let's go, ma'am," the young cop said to her.

She had something soft balled in her palm and quickly tossed it high into the air. As the ball fell to the ground, it unfurled into Sybil's black fishnet stocking. "Roses are red and violets are blue," she called, as Marco and the cop took a firmer hold of her arms. "Find the petals and a killer, too."

Reilly watched the three of them go, then said to me, "What was that about?"

"Sounds like a new twist on an old poem." A thought suddenly occurred to me. I hurried to the back row to lean between the two caskets for another look at the corpse. "Sybil had a red rose in her hair today, Reilly, but now it's gone. That's what Angelique meant. She must think that whomever Sybil met here took it."

"Couldn't she have just said, 'The rose is missing'?"

"You're lucky she didn't say it in musical terms. I wonder if she has an inkling as to whom Sybil met."

As Reilly jotted more info in his notepad, I glanced toward the empty doorway. "May I go sit in on the interview?"

"Not on your life. I'm already bending the rules for Marco. Besides, I've got something better for you to do." He pointed to the doorway. "Go home."

"But I have questions for Angelique."

"I think we can handle the questions, Abby."

"Can I at least stick around long enough to see the Urban twins taken away?"

"No. Now, go home. That's an order."

At that moment, a contingent of crime scene investigators and the coroner descended on the storage room. Startled, I backed straight into the pointed nose of the jet plane. Luckily, every male eye in the room was focused on Sybil's body, so my windmilling arms went unnoticed—or so I thought. But no, there was Reilly standing by the door, an amused look on his face. I straightened my skirt and made my way up the row of caskets, pretending nothing had happened.

Suddenly a booming voice from the hallway called, "Where is she? What happened to Sybil?" and in the next moment Colonel Billingsworth appeared, leading his troop of new judges. He tried to get into the room, but Reilly's arm shot out to bar his way.

"Sir, please step back."

The colonel turned left, then right, trying to see what was going on, but there were too many men blocking his view. "Has Sybil been found? Is she here?"

"Are you a relative, sir?" Reilly asked.

"Her late husband's business partner. Did something happen to her?"

"Your name?" Reilly asked, flipping open his notebook.

"Walker T. Billingsworth, president of the Midwestern Funeral Directors' Association. Why are the medics here? Did she have a heart attack?"

"I'm sorry, Mr. Billingsworth, but she's dead."

The colonel blinked several times, mouth agape, as though the words wouldn't register. "Dead?"

"Yes, sir."

He let out a huge sigh. "Thank God."

Chapter Seven

Reilly stopped writing and the new judges looked startled. "Excuse me?" Reilly said.

The colonel looked flustered. "I didn't mean that the way it sounded. I'm not relieved she's dead. I'm relieved she's been found. She didn't show up for the banquet or answer her page, and we—by that I mean the convention committee—were growing concerned. With good reason, as it turns out. Would you tell me the cause of her death, Sergeant?"

Reilly scratched his ear. "It's unknown at this time. Do you know if the deceased has family in the area, Mr. Billingsworth?"

"We prefer to use the term *loved one,* rather than *deceased,* Sergeant, and to answer your question, Sybil has no family in the area. I believe there's a distant cousin in Honolulu."

"How did you know to come down here to look for her?"

"She was supposed to be here earlier to judge the entries for our casket contest, so this seemed a logical place to look."

"Did you search anywhere else?"

"Her room and her booth."

"When was the last time you saw her?"

"Just after two o'clock, when she was making the rounds of the exhibit booths."

Reilly finished jotting the information in his notepad, then pointed up the hallway. "Do you see that officer? Would you give him your name and a number where you can be reached?"

"Certainly, sir. I'll help in whatever way I can." He pointed to the Purple Heart medal on his lapel. "I served in 'Nam, Sergeant. I know how to get things done." He saluted, did an about-face, and strode away, followed by his small group, who fell into a single line behind him.

Reilly glanced at me and sighed wearily. "It's going to be a long night."

It was almost ten o'clock when I left the storage room and went to see whether Marco was finished. But the only person in the kitchen was the young cop.

"Check for Salvare outside the building," the cop told me. "He said he had to take a phone call."

A phone call at ten o'clock on a Saturday night? That couldn't be good news, especially since ninety-nine percent of Marco's calls came from either a bartender at Down the Hatch complaining about a problem at the bar or a member of his family complaining about another member of his family. I started for the back exit only to have *my* cell phone ring. I checked the screen. Strange. My dad never phoned this late.

"Hi, Dad. What's up?"

"Sorry to bother you, honey. Are you busy right now?"

I pushed open the heavy back door and saw my hunk-a-hunk-of-burning-love standing outside near the curb, his phone pressed to his ear. He glanced at me and shook his head to signal that things weren't going well with his conversation.

"Marco and I are just leaving the convention center. Is there a problem?"

"Your mother is throwing clay, Abby. I don't know what to do."

There was nothing odd about her throwing clay. That's what my mom called it when she sat at her potter's wheel producing her weird sculptures. It was a hobby she'd started a year ago, although she'd since moved on to other media to produce her works of art, such as mirrored tiles and feathers. What *was* odd was how tense my dad sounded.

"Whatever she's making can't be worse than her Naked Monkeys Table," I joked. Marco glanced at me with raised eyebrows.

"You don't understand, Abby. She's actually *throwing* clay—at the walls, on the floor . . . I don't know how to help her. Listen. Can you hear that?"

In the background I could hear my mom shrieking, "I *hate* this clay. Hate it, hate it, hate it!"

"Let me talk to her."

"I don't know if I want to get that close."

"Come on, Dad. This is your wife of thirty-five years."

"No, this is an alien life form *disguised* as my wife. Hold on. I'll give it a try."

I waited while he maneuvered his wheelchair toward the spare room at the back of the house, where Mom had set up her art studio. My father had been wounded in the leg while chasing down a drug dealer, and while on the operating table had suffered a stroke that had left one side of his body paralyzed. Although he'd retired from the force, that hadn't stopped him from living a full life.

"Maureen," I heard him say, "your daughter is on the line."

"Did you phone her?" the alien life-form snarled as she took the phone; then in a sweet voice, my mom said, "Hello, Abigail."

"Mom, is everything okay?"

She let out a tinkling laugh. "Of course. Why? What did your father tell you?"

"That you, well, aren't yourself."

"How silly. Who else would I be?"

I didn't dare mention my dad's theory on the subject. "Then you're feeling all right?"

"I'm perfectly fine."

She certainly didn't sound like the same woman I'd heard screeching moments before, but my dad wouldn't have called unless he was truly concerned. "Are you working on a new sculpture?"

"I'm trying to finish a gift for Marco's sister's baby shower, but the clay isn't cooperating"—she took a tense breath and let it out—"and naturally it has to be finished by next weekend, not to mention that I have to find a dress, and a pair of shoes, and my hair needs cutting and highlighting, and of course my stylist couldn't get me in until Friday, and you know how I hate my hair the day after it's been cut, so when am I going to do all that, huh? *When?*"

She was making a sculpture for Marco's sister's *baby shower?* Oh, no! How would I ever live down the embarrassment? Trying not to betray the lump of anxiety in my throat, I asked pleasantly, "So, you're making something for Gina's shower?"

"Isn't that what I just told you?" she said churlishly.

I was determined not to let her irk me. "What are you making?"

"A lamp."

I knew my mom's creative tendencies. It might be an octopus-armed lamp with a snake scale–covered shade and an elephant-footed base, but it would never be *just* a lamp. With more than a little trepidation, I asked, "Do you want me to come over to see it?"

"Abigail, I said everything was fine. And the next time your father complains about me, you can tell him that he's going to have to be a little more under-standing of my artistic temperament. Now, go back to whatever you were doing before he interrupted you."

Okay, then. Time to step back and let them duke it out. As I hung up, I noticed that Marco had shut his phone and was listening to my conversation. "Every-thing all right?" he asked.

"Depends on whether you ask my mom or my dad. How about on your end?"

"There's a gas leak at the bar, and they've had to evacuate the building. I need to get over there."

So much for salvaging the evening. I leaned into Marco, letting him wrap an arm around my shoulders. "I guess we'll have to put our evening on hold."

He kissed my forehead. "I'm sorry. This has been one hell of a day, hasn't it?"

"And more fun to come tomorrow. I have to be back here at ten in the morning, assuming the convention hasn't been canceled. I'll have to call Delilah before I head out, just to be sure."

"You still want me to help you pack up at five o'clock tomorrow evening?"

At my eager nod, he lifted my chin and gazed down into my eyes, a sexy little grin tugging at one corner of his mouth. "And afterward we can pick up where we left off tonight?"

"Which is?"

The little grin turned to a big smile as he pulled me close. "Here's a sneak preview." He kissed me then, hot and heavy, an intense meeting of our mouths, a melding of our lips. I twisted my fingers into his glossy hair and felt the rough stubble of his chin like sandpaper against mine and his firm chest pressing against my breasts. As his kiss deepened, my insides became all soft and gooey and my blood pulsed like molten fudge through every part of me.

I was just about to wrap myself around his body

when someone cleared his throat behind us. Loudly. Twice. We broke our kiss and glanced around to see Colonel Billingsworth holding the door open. Inside, two cops flanked someone in handcuffs. Looked like I was going to get my wish to see at least one of the Urbans hauled off to the police station after all.

Unfortunately, it wasn't Thing One or Thing Two who came through the doors. It was a limping, burlap-robed, wild-haired Eli Cotton.

"So much for your advice to Eli to picket across the street," Marco said.

"What happened?" Marco asked the colonel as the cops hustled Eli toward a waiting squad car.

"Apparently, Mr. Cotton gave the police the slip and came back here. An officer found him crouched under a table at one of the booths. He claims he was only handing out pamphlets, but that's hard to do from under a table, don't you think? Makes one wonder what he was really doing here tonight." The colonel paused to watch a cop pat Eli down. "In light of his clash with Sybil earlier, I told the officers to treat him as a suspect."

As Eli was being tucked into the car, he twisted around to call, "I know you're afraid I'll steal your customers, Colonel, but you can't stop free enterprise. I'll talk to the press. I'll call the media. I may be one little independent against the entire funeral industry machine, but who do you think the public will rally behind? You and your pompous committee can't keep me out forever."

Whether Eli was a suspect or not, I couldn't help but feel sorry for him, because I knew exactly where he was coming from. Bloomers was one little flower shop against the big chains of the floral industry, with their endless inventory and enormous advertising budgets. It wasn't fair at all, but I doubted that Eli would commit murder because of it. His ranting about taking his cause to the media didn't sound like something a man who'd just suffocated someone in a casket would say. My gut told me he was innocent.

"Why wasn't he allowed to rent booth space?" I asked the colonel. "If Chet Sunday can hawk Habitation Station's Make-It-Yourself Casket kits, then Eli should be able to exhibit his burlap bags."

"Abby," Marco said quietly, "it's none of our business."

"I don't mind answering," the colonel said. "I agree with you, young lady. Neither one of them should be allowed to exhibit at our convention. Bringing Chet and his sponsors in here was all Sybil's doing. I told her those kits were completely incompatible with the other companies who exhibit here, but when Sybil makes up—er, *made* up—her mind, there was no changing it. As for Mr. Cotton, Sybil and I and the other committee members agreed that his presence here would be completely disruptive. Take a look at the man. He is wholly unsuitable for this staid convocation. Now, if you'll excuse me, I have things to do, so I'll bid you both good evening." Giving us a polite nod, he turned on his heel and marched inside.

"I think Eli was right," I said. "The funeral industry is afraid of him. Do you know how much money people would save if they used biodegradable body bags instead of caskets and burial vaults? Thousands of dollars. It would kill the casket industry."

"All I know is that *my* ashes are going into a pickle jar," Marco said.

"A *pickle* jar?"

"Dill, I think, or maybe sweet. I haven't decided. We go through a lot of them at the bar."

"You are *so* making that up."

We headed for the parking lot, pausing to watch the squad car pull away, Eli's long, sad face pressed against the side window. "They can't seriously consider Eli a suspect," I said. "Can you imagine him convincing Sybil to undress and climb into a casket?"

"How do you know he didn't force her?"

"They patted him down, Marco. No weapon found . . . unless he held a garlic bulb to Sybil's head." I pretended to be Eli. "Get into that casket or I'll stink you up good, lady."

Marco hit the remote control to unlock his car doors. "Eli could have ditched the weapon. And remember, he was hiding when the cops found him. That makes him look a little suspicious, don't you think?"

"Well, of course he hid when the cops arrived. He wasn't supposed to be in the building. He probably got scared, ducked under a table, and waited, hoping he could sneak out later."

"We'll see if his fingerprints show up on the casket."

"You get it that Sybil had her own reason for allowing Chet and his sponsors to promote their casket kits, but not Eli, right?"

"You mean, besides Eli being a wack job?"

"He's not a wack job. He believes in his cause."

"He's wearing a potato sack and has a string of garlic bulbs around his neck. You tell me that's not a wack job."

"It has nothing to do with Eli's mental state. Chet is a hot TV star. We saw Sybil putting the moves on him after his show, and guess where her booth is located? Right next to Chet's. Gee, I wonder who was in charge of the booths? Let's see. How about Sybil? What surprises me is that Chet has this reputation as a wholesome family man. Why would he jeopardize it?"

Marco put his hands on the car on either side of me and leaned in. "First of all, you're jumping to conclusions. We don't know where Sybil and Chet went after his show. Don't assume the worst. Second, so you think Chet is hot, huh?"

I walked my fingers up the front of his shirt. "I'm just saying that *Sybil* would have thought so. Me, I go for the kind of man who aspires to pickle jars."

"Good save," he murmured against my lips, causing all kinds of wicked thoughts to race through my brain, including a strong desire to wring the head bartender's neck for not being able to handle the gas leak himself.

We kissed for a moment; then Marco stepped back. "Stop distracting me. I have to get to the bar. I don't want anyone turning blue from the gas leak."

The word *blue* immediately brought Angelique's cryptic rhyme to mind. As we buckled ourselves into his Prius, I said, "When you sat in on the interview, did Angelique mention anything about Sybil's rose, or did she recite her poem again?"

Marco thought back a moment, then shook his head. "Neither."

"Did the cop even ask her about it?"

"Nope."

"I knew I should have been there. Do you remember the red rose Sybil had in her hair this morning? There was no flower in her hair when I saw her body tonight, which I made sure to point out to Reilly. Angelique noticed the missing flower, and that's what her poem was about."

"Do you really think the person who shut that lid on Sybil would take the rose out of her hair first?"

I tried to imagine the Urbans plucking the blossom from behind her ear, then closing the casket, but, unfortunately, it wasn't working for me. Young guys simply wouldn't be concerned with minor fashion details. "I concede that you have a point."

"Isn't it possible that Sybil left the flower in her room?"

"Another point for your side. Then what *did* Angelique talk about in her interview?"

"If I tell you, you have to promise to drop the whole topic afterward."

"Deal."

We shook on it; then Marco started the engine, put

the car in gear, and took off. "Yesterday afternoon, Angelique overheard Sybil on her cell phone arranging to meet someone in the storage room before the banquet. When Sybil failed to show at the start of the dinner, Angelique went straight to the storage room to look for her. She saw the tool chest on top of one of the caskets right away, but it wasn't until she saw a fishnet stocking that she became suspicious and checked inside. She said it was apparent at once that Sybil was dead."

"Did the cop ask her why she had her tape recorder with her?"

"It didn't come up."

I smacked my palm on my knee. "Another reason why I should have been there. Think about it. If Sybil was already dead when Angelique found her, why did she have her tape recorder out? Does that make sense to you?"

"Remember our deal?"

"You have to admit it raises questions."

"Which is why there will be an experienced detective working on the case. Now, how about some music?" Marco reached for the radio button. "What are you in the mood for? Jazz? Rock?"

"How about the blues?"

Minutes before my alarm went off at seven thirty the next morning, something furry settled on my head, covering my forehead and eyes, which played right into my dream about being shut in a coffin. I awoke with a gasp and pushed the warm object off my face, only to hear a loud meow of protest. The alarm buzzed just then, sending Simon scrambling off the bed, down the hallway, and into the kitchen, where he would lie in wait so he could ambush my ankles on my way to the refrigerator for orange juice.

Simon was Nikki's white cat. This was the same Nikki who swore to me in sixth grade that she would never, *ever* have a cat; that, in fact, she hated cats and couldn't stand the gray and white feline that ruled as Supreme Overlord of the Knight household. Now she claimed it was tropical fish she hated, so I fully expected to come home one day to a fifty-gallon aquarium in the living room.

As I stumbled out of bed and made my way to the kitchen, I heard Nikki talking to Simon in the hateful baby voice she always used with him. "What does him want to eat today?"

"What him always eats." I grabbed the orange juice carton from the counter. "Kidneys in gravy, and you can skip the kidneys because all he does is lick the gravy anyway."

"He does not. He's a good boy, aren't you, Simmy-Simey?" Nikki plopped a large spoonful of the canned food in Simon's dish and we watched as he licked off the sauce. I felt so vindicated.

Nikki pretended not to see it. "How's the convention going?"

"I can tell you, but you may be sorry you asked."

"Not on your life. You never say that unless you

have a juicy story." She patted one of the kitchen stools. "Have a seat. I'll put on the coffee."

Perched on a stool, I related Saturday's events to her, starting with my close call in the phone booth and continuing all the way up to when Marco dropped me off at the apartment the evening before, leaving Nikki with eyes as large as Frisbees. "Omigod, Abby, you could have died the same way Sybil did!"

"Tell me about it."

She poured the brewed coffee into two purple mugs and gave me the one with the chip in it. As if I wouldn't notice. "So you think Sybil was the victim of a prank played by the two jerky Urban guys?"

"I'm not saying there aren't a few others I'd want to check out if I were investigating, but the Urbans are so obvious it's scary. I mean, who but the Urbans would think it was funny to shut someone in a dummy phone booth? So it makes sense that they'd also shut Sybil in a coffin and dress a dummy in her clothes. Maybe there'll be more information in today's newspaper." I hopped off the stool and went to get the paper in the hallway outside our door.

Taking it back to the counter, I unrolled it, and the banner headline leapt out at me: DEATH AT FUNERAL CONVENTION.

"Isn't that like an oxymoron, or something?" Nikki asked, peering over my shoulder.

"Irony."

"I said *or something.*"

While Nikki made toast with peanut butter and

92

honey for each of us, I read the article out loud. Surprisingly, there was no mention of any arrests being made. In fact, there was nothing at all about the Urbans even being questioned. "How could that be possible, Nikki? Their fingerprints had to be all over that casket, not to mention Sybil's shoes and the tool chest."

"Well, duh, Abby. You just got done telling me their father is loaded. He probably used his money to get them off the hook. Don't look so shocked. You know people pay bribe money all the time."

"In our county? The prosecutor gets lazy with his investigations sometimes, but he's never been accused of being crooked."

"So you believe Melvin Darnell wouldn't even be tempted to take a bribe of, let's say, fifty thousand dollars to go after someone else and leave the Urban twins alone? What does a chief prosecuting attorney make in one year? Seventy, eighty thousand? Do you really know the man that well? Don't forget about Marco's little run-in with him."

"Darnell was all set to prosecute me, too, and no one was paying him to do that."

"There you go," Nikki said through a mouthful of toast.

"So you think the Urban twins will skate?"

"Oh, yeah."

I sipped my coffee, getting angrier by the second. If there is anything I can't tolerate, it is injustice. "It's unfair, Nikki. The wealthy should have to play by the same rules the rest of us do."

"You know what you're going to have to do, right? Go after the Urbans yourself."

My anger fizzled. "I can't. I promised Marco I'd stay out of it."

"I know you too well, Abby. You won't be able to stop yourself."

"I don't have any reason to get involved, Nik. Let the detectives deal with Sybil's death. The only thing I'm going to do today is try to drum up more business for Bloomers—if the convention is still on. And I might even be able to get Chet Sunday's autograph for you."

Her eyes lit up. "Really? Abs, I would *so* owe you. Oh, crap. It's eight o'clock. I'm taking an extra shift at the hospital today, so I'd better shower." She stopped to hug me before she dashed off. "That's for Chet's autograph."

I wolfed down my toast and was just finishing my coffee when the phone rang.

"Hi, Abby, this is Max."

"Hey, Max, I was just about to call you. Is the convention still on?"

"It is, but we're not going to be able to make it. We've been at the police station all night."

"Why?"

"The detectives are questioning Delilah about Sybil's death."

"What do you mean questioning her? As a witness?"

Max sighed heavily. "The prosecutor is calling Delilah a person of interest, Abby."

My stomach dropped about two floors. "A person of interest? That's absurd. How could Darnell possibly think Delilah had anything to do with Sybil's death?"

"You remember that silly scene Sybil made yesterday morning at our booth? Well, that is now being called an altercation. Del tried to explain that it was just Sybil throwing her weight around, but she might as well have been talking to a cement wall. The prosecutor was told that there was a longstanding rivalry between the two women, so he's considering that a motive."

"You've got to be kidding me. There have to be a dozen people who saw what happened. I know they'll testify on Delilah's behalf."

"Then there was Delilah showing up late for the banquet."

"Big deal. I saw any number of people arrive late."

"We told him that, Abby."

"So basically all they have are Delilah's late arrival, an altercation that never happened, and a rivalry that can be disproved. That's so flimsy, Max. How could that possibly make Delilah a person of interest?"

"Because of that little run-in Delilah had with Sybil in the storage room before the banquet. That was at six o'clock, and they're estimating the time of Sybil's death to be between six and seven. According to them, that makes Del the last person known to have seen Sybil alive. Darnell called those her means and opportunity, and *that* makes her a person of interest."

My throat was really, really dry, but I had to ask

anyway. "How did they learn about Delilah's little meeting with Sybil in the storage room?"

"Someone apparently told one of the cops on the scene."

Oh, no. That someone was me.

Chapter Eight

This is a nightmare, Abby," Max continued. "I'm still in shock, and poor Del is exhausted from their all-night grilling. They actually tried to badger her into confessing. Do you believe that? As if Delilah could ever hurt anyone. When she wouldn't give them a confession, the detective tried to get her to imagine how she would have killed Sybil *if* she had wanted to. They called it a vision statement. Thank goodness Delilah didn't cave in to their pressure. That steel in her spine really came through."

But for how long? She'd surely be called back again if they couldn't find another likely suspect. I was so overcome by guilt, I blurted, "I'll help in any way I can, Max. Just name it and it will be done—call an attorney, whatever you need. I'm here for you."

"Thanks for the offer, Abby. We hired Dave Hammond, and with any luck he'll get it straightened out soon."

"Of course he will. Delilah is in good hands with Dave. Besides, the allegations the cops are making will be awfully hard to prove."

"Those were my feelings, too. I hate to say this

because I voted for Melvin Darnell in the last two elections, but it sure seems that he's railroading her."

I didn't want to alarm Max, but people were railroaded all the time by prosecutors eager to get a case off their desks and score points with the voting public. Chief Prosecuting Attorney Melvin Darnell was no exception. With elections coming up, Darnell was eager to maintain his reputation as Protector of the Realm by removing bad people from the streets and putting them behind bars, which was all well and good, except that his definition of bad people sometimes included unlucky people who happened to be caught in circumstances that made them look bad. At that point, it fell to Darnell to make his targets look even worse in front of a jury so he could win his case and come out the hero. Never mind if those unlucky people were innocent.

I had been one of his targets not too long ago because I'd delivered a flower to a professor at the law school during a noon lunch break when another professor with whom I'd had previous run-ins was found murdered. Being in the wrong place at the wrong time had nearly cost me my freedom. Fortunately, I'd found the real killer before Darnell could indict me.

With that horrible memory in mind, I knew I had to make sure Delilah didn't suffer a similar fate. It would devastate her, Max, *and* their business. And it would be my fault for opening my big mouth to Reilly.

"So no one wanted to cancel the convention because of Sybil's death?" I asked him.

"Nope. Colonel Billingsworth is prepared to proceed as planned, although I'm certain it will be very subdued. I'm sorry we won't be there to help you, but you probably won't have much traffic anyway, especially with Sybil's memorial service for the convention attendees already planned for this afternoon."

"Don't worry about a thing. I'll take care of the booth, and I'm sure Grace and Lottie will pitch in, too." And Marco, I really hoped.

"Keep me posted, okay, Abby?"

"Will do, Max. You do the same for me. And give Delilah a big hug and tell her everything is going to be fine."

Because somehow I had to make it fine.

First thing I had to do was to line up some help, so I called my assistants, who were horrified by the news and more than happy to lend a hand. We arranged to meet inside the exhibition hall at ten o'clock, giving them time to make it to church first. Grace even promised to bring a plate of her homemade scones.

Second, I needed to find out where Delilah stood on the suspect list. I couldn't call the prosecutor's office until the next morning, so I phoned Reilly. I figured he owed me information for passing along my innocent comment about Delilah's meeting with Sybil.

"Hey, Super Sarge, it's me, your favorite florist. Are you working today?"

"No and no."

"What's the second no for?"

"Whatever you're going to ask me to do."

So much for the sweet talk. "Delilah Dove is being questioned in Sybil Blount's murder, Reilly, and now you have to help me get her out of it because it's your fault she's in it."

"Whoa. Wait a minute. *My* fault? What the hell are you talking about?"

"Remember me telling you that Delilah met Sybil in the storage room at six o'clock?"

"So?"

"So you told someone who blabbed it to the DA, and now Darnell has his sights set on Delilah as a person of interest. I need to know who else they're talking to so I can—"

"Stop right there. You know I can't discuss an ongoing case."

"Come on, Reilly, we've had this conversation before, and you've always managed to give me a little assistance in the end, so let's skip the part where I nag and nag and you finally give in, and go straight to the part where you drop a big hint. So how about coughing once if the Urban twins are being questioned?"

"Look, Abby, I'm not unsympathetic to Delilah's plight, but my superiors aren't stupid. They've seen us talking enough times that they're going to figure out how you're able to come by your information. I've got a kid to support, a teenager who'll be off to college soon, and an ex-wife who gets testy if I miss a support payment. I can't afford to be suspended. So I'll help in whatever way I can, but official police business is strictly off limits. Understand?"

"I understand, Reilly. I know you have to be careful, and I wouldn't ask you to do anything unethical. But we both know Delilah could very easily be railroaded by the DA, so all I'm asking you to do is cough. Just cough. You don't have to say a word. Okay?"

He sighed, but he didn't cough.

"Okay, have Ross and Jess Urban been questioned? Remember, once for yes."

This time he did cough.

"So they *have* questioned them. That's good. Are there plans to bring them back for more questioning?"

Silence. Was that a no? "So the Urbans *have* been questioned but they aren't being considered persons of interest?"

Dead air. Good thing I could hear him breathing or I'd think he'd passed out.

"Did you tell the detectives about the prank those two pulled on me? Do they know about Sybil's clothes on the mannequin? Did you tell them the twins actually told me they were going to get her again? Because if you did, then how could those two idiots have been cleared? I mean, it's so obvious what they did. Weren't there any fingerprints left at either scene?"

Silence.

"Are you saying everything was wiped clean?"

"I'm not saying anything, Abby. That's as far as I go. I'm hanging up now."

"Just give me one more minute, Reilly. Please? Are they talking to *anyone* other than Delilah?"

"Abby."

"Just tap out the first name. Once for *A,* twice for *B*—"

"If you want more information, talk to Darnell." *Click.*

I hung up with a groan of frustration just as Nikki appeared, wanting to know who had called. I gave her a quick rundown on my conversations with Max and Reilly, then put my head in my hands. "This can't be happening."

"Call Marco," she said, rinsing her cup in the sink. "He'll know what to do."

My finger was already pressing the speed-dial button. It didn't occur to me until I heard his sleepy voice that he might have been up late because of the gas leak.

"Got to bed at three in the morning," he said with a yawn.

"I'm sorry. I wouldn't have bothered you this early, but Delilah is in serious trouble. Darnell is calling her a person of interest, and you know what that means—she's a suspect. And it's all my fault for opening my mouth to Reilly in the first place. I have to get her out of this mess, Marco, before it goes any further."

"Whoa, Sunshine. Slow down. You're talking way too fast for my tired brain." In the background I heard sheets rustle, as if he were climbing out of bed. "Tell me what happened."

"Darnell questioned Delilah all night, and needless

to say, Max is a basket case. He retained Dave Hammond and I'm sure Dave will do a good job for them, but you know that if Darnell decides to indict Delilah, even if she's proven not guilty, her life will be ruined, not to mention their funeral-home business. The best defense attorney in the world wouldn't be able to prevent that from happening. I've got to make sure it doesn't get that far."

"Okay, steady now. You realize what you're saying, don't you?"

"Yes. That I have to prove Delilah's innocence."

"No, that you have to find a killer."

"I like my way better."

"Do you have a plan?"

"Not yet. I talked to Max only a few minutes ago. All I know is that the convention starts at ten o'clock and ends at five, which gives me seven hours."

"That gives *us* seven hours. There's no way you're doing this alone."

I could have smothered him with kisses. "Thanks, Marco. Your help means a lot. I know Max and Delilah will be grateful, too."

"What time do you want to go?"

It was eight fifteen. I still had to shower, dress, and dash down to my flower shop to catch up on orders before heading up north to the convention center.

"Pick me up at Bloomers at nine thirty," I told him.

As I hung up, Nikki paused at the door to wish me good luck. "And by the way," she said, "I knew you wouldn't stay out of it."

• • •

Bloomers is the second shop from the corner on Franklin Street, one of the four streets that border the courthouse square. The store occupies the first floor and basement of the old three-story building and has two bay windows with a yellow-framed door in between. The left side of the shop is the sales area, incorporating one of the bay windows, a glass-fronted refrigerated display case, an armoire, a bookcase and several antique tables that hold a variety of floral arrangements, and a small counter with our cash register. A purple velvet curtain separates the shop from the workroom in back.

On the right side of the shop is our Victorian-themed coffee and tea parlor, where customers sit at white wrought-iron tables in front of the other bay window, drinking out of china cups and saucers, eating Grace's scones or biscuits, and watching the happenings on the square. It's a cozy, comfortable place to hang out, and it draws customers into the flower shop.

Around the square is the typical assortment of family-owned shops, banks, law offices, and restaurants, including Marco's Down the Hatch Bar and Grill, located two doors north of Bloomers. In the middle of the square is the stately courthouse, built in 1896 from Indiana limestone, that houses the county and circuit courts, plus all the government offices. Five blocks east of the square marks the western edge of the campus of New Chapel University, a small private college where I would have graduated from law school if I hadn't flunked out.

On that unhappy thought, I unlocked Bloomers' bright yellow door and walked into the sweet fragrances of roses, lavender, and eucalyptus as I felt again the thrill of being in my very own oasis. I headed through the curtain to where my floral creations came to life. It was a paradise filled with colors, shapes, textures, and scents, with dried and silk flowers in vases on the floor, ribbon-festooned wreaths hanging from hooks on the wall, and all manner of flowerpots and containers on the shelves.

Two stainless-steel walk-in coolers lined the right wall, and a desk holding my computer, telephone, and the normal assortment of items was on the left. In the middle was the big worktable with wooden stools tucked beneath, where Lottie and I sat for hours doing what we loved best, arranging flowers. That's what I needed now—a few blissful moments before the race to clear Delilah's name began. When I was creating, my mind was fully engaged and my thoughts were at their keenest.

I checked the orders that had come in over the wire during the night, printed out one I knew I could put together quickly, and went to work. The order was for an anniversary arrangement in autumn colors. I stepped into the big cooler and glanced around for inspiration. The Red Rover mums would be a good start. Foxtail fern? Perfect. Definitely the Konfetti roses, along with several stems of hypericum, some

Spanish moss, and oh, yes, thin twigs of curly willow for accent. Maybe I'd add some purple carnations for a surprising jolt of color.

I pulled the flowers, took out the tools I'd need from the drawers built into the worktable, then stepped back to survey my supply of containers. Aha! A small ceramic pumpkin. Just right. As I affixed a base of wet foam inside the pumpkin and began to put physical shape to the arrangement I had worked out in my mind, I also began a mental list of whom I wanted to question at the convention. Appropriately, numbers one and two on my list were Thing One and Thing Two. If my hunch was right, I wouldn't need to go any farther.

I finished my design, wrapped it in clear cellophane, marked it for delivery, and put it in the cooler. I checked the time and saw that it was almost nine thirty, so I threw on some peach-colored lip gloss, pulled my hair back with a tortoiseshell barrette, grabbed my purse, and left.

Marco's car was parked in front of Down the Hatch, so I headed toward it just as he strode out of the bar. Seeing him gave me the same heady rush of pleasure that I'd had when I first laid eyes on him. Then, as now, he had on a black leather motorcycle jacket, slim, faded blue denims, and black boots. With his olive complexion, dark eyes, and cocky swagger, he was not merely sexy but *dangerously* so. It was one of the things that gave him an edge over every other guy I'd ever met.

"Morning, Sunshine," he said, flashing that devilish grin that had my heart singing. He appraised my outfit—a fitted beige jacket and bronze-colored shirt over tan jeans, finished off with knee-high brown boots—and gave me a thumbs-up. "Hot look for an amateur Sherlock."

Had to love those compliments. Had to love the guy who gave them, too.

"Are you ready to track down a murderer?" he asked.

"I think you mean *murderers*," I corrected. "Ross and Jess."

"It *could* be them, Sunshine, but we know Sybil wasn't the most popular person at that convention, so keep yourself open to all possibilities."

"Okay, but we don't have any other possibilities yet."

"That's our first order of business."

Chapter Nine

For once Marco was wrong. Our first order of business was to get the refrigerated flower arrangements from the kitchen to booth twenty-nine before the convention officially opened for the day. Lottie and Grace, who had arrived earlier, had already made two trips, so Marco, being our pack mule, volunteered to get the rest.

Grace had donned a traditional navy shirtdress and sensible navy pumps, the dark blue setting off her fair

English complexion and short silver hair. She had a watch on a fob pinned to the bodice of her dress, and simple pearl studs in her ears. The surprise was her shiny orange belt, but Grace always did have a certain flair. She had brought a basket of scones as promised, along with jam and clotted cream, a supply of napkins, and a thermos of coffee. Being a proper Brit, she'd also brought a china pot for serving, and cups and saucers.

Lottie's outfit hadn't changed appreciably from yesterday's, except that her cotton knit shirt now depicted Rome, Italy. It was part of her world tour collection. She might not have the money to travel the globe, but she had the T-shirts.

I stowed my purse under the table. Then, as we arranged the display, I explained in greater detail the events that had led to the discovery of Sybil's body and my suspicions as to who had killed her.

"The Urbans do seem to have the burden of proof on their shoulders," Grace said after a moment's consideration, "especially in light of what Walker told me."

"Walker?" I asked. "Do you mean Colonel Billingsworth?"

"Yes, dear. He stopped by the booth to introduce himself, so I poured him a cup of coffee and offered him a scone, and we had a pleasant chat."

"You're already on a first-name basis with him?"

"Am I not allowed to make a new friend now and then?" Grace asked.

There was a definite twinkle of mischief in her eye,

making me think she had something up her sleeve. "A friend, huh?"

"You should have seen Gracie in action," Lottie said with a chuckle. "She was just a-flirtin' away, and the poor guy was blushing so hard his scalp turned pink. I could see it through those twelve strands of hair he combs over to the opposite ear."

"I was *not* flirting," Grace said, lifting her chin. "I was merely taking an interest in Walker's stories. It's amazing what one can learn when one asks the right questions."

"So basically you were snooping," I teased.

"Certainly not! I was gathering information. And frankly, Abby dear, not to sound cheeky, but your investigation could use a bit of a boost. After all, Delilah is our friend, too, and we're quite concerned about her. As Benjamin Franklin once said, 'You may delay, but time will not.'"

Grace was a walking library of quotations. I could always count on her to have one at the ready.

"I'm staying out of it," Lottie said. "The last thing I want to do is screw things up for Delilah by poking my nose where it isn't wanted."

"Okay, Grace." I folded my arms across my chest and leaned against the table. "What information did you gather from *Walker?*"

"Among other things," Grace said, straightening the brochures on the table, "he said that Sybil was quite infamous for having affairs with younger men."

I cast Marco a pointed glance as he returned with

a box of flower arrangements. "I'm not surprised."

"There's a first," he quipped as Lottie and I helped him unload. "Alert the media."

"Good one," Lottie said with a laugh, and gave him a high five.

I laughed with her only to show my strength of character, because I certainly hadn't found it as amusing as she had.

"Seriously, don't you think Sybil exuded a raw sexuality when she was near a younger man? Look how she came on to you the instant she met you, Marco."

"I get that a lot," he said, giving me a flicker of a grin. "You did it, too, the first time we met."

"You came on to *me!*"

"And you loved every minute of it." He arched an eyebrow, giving me a very hot look, which he also did that first time.

I ran my hand up his arm. "I'm not saying I didn't love it."

"Hey, you two," Lottie said, "Grace was telling us what she learned from Colonel Billingsworth, remember? Go ahead, Gracie."

"Very well, then. Walker also said that Sybil has been stalking Ross and Jess Urban since they turned twenty-one, and the colonel is of the opinion that one of the boys finally succumbed to her, shall we say, *attentions* this year."

"That would explain why Ross wasn't worried about what would happen to him if they pulled a prank on Sybil," I told the group. "When I warned him that she'd be furious, his exact words were, 'It won't be a problem. She'd think it was an invitation.' It's clear now what he meant. Can't you see how easy it would have been for him to coax her into that casket?"

"I don't like to speak ill of the dead," Lottie said, "but from everything I've heard about her, I doubt Sybil had to be coaxed. More like a wink and a pat on the butt."

Marco, who was listening with a frown of concentration, said to Grace with mild skepticism, "How did the colonel know about this alleged affair?"

"He was merely giving an opinion," Grace said. "But since Walker and Sybil's husband had been long-time business partners, it seems logical to think he'd know a little something about Sybil's activities."

"Could be that the colonel picked up on some of the rumors going around about Sybil," Lottie said. "When I was standing in line for coffee yesterday, I heard a few choice bits of gossip myself, some I wouldn't care to repeat."

Juicy gossip? "We'll talk later," I whispered to her.

Grace said, "Walker also mentioned that he had spoken to Conrad Urban yesterday morning about his sons' behavior here at the convention. Apparently, Conrad was astounded to hear of it. It seems that he had become so fed up with the boys' irresponsibility that, in an attempt to get them to mend their ways and govern themselves as adults, he had told Ross and Jess that their conduct over the next six months would determine which one of them would succeed him as

CEO of his company. The one who exhibits the most maturity and business acumen is to be his successor. He thought they had taken his ultimatum to heart, thus the reason for his astonishment."

"That's a little extreme of Conrad, isn't it?" I asked.

"Personally," Grace said, "I think it's a dreadful way to pick an heir. It will pit his sons against each other. Why would a parent want to foster such rivalry?"

"Maybe Conrad is just that desperate," Lottie said. "Maybe he's tried everything else, and this is his last resort."

"He could cut them off and let them fend for themselves," Marco said. "They'd grow up fast then."

"Tough love," Lottie said, nodding in agreement. "That's always been my motto. I wouldn't have survived raising my quadruplets if I'd been soft on them."

"Since we know little about their family, it would be hard to say what's best for those young men," Grace remarked. "One shouldn't judge until one has walked a mile in another's shoes."

"I'll tell you one thing we can say for sure," Lottie put in. "If the Urban twins are responsible for Sybil's death, Daddy Big Bucks had better have another successor waiting in the wings, because his boys will be cooling their heels behind bars."

"Unless only one of them is involved," Marco mused. "Then his choice would be easy."

"You're right," Lottie said. "The innocent twin would be an automatic shoo-in."

It was my turn to weigh in on the subject. "I can't imagine only one of the Urbans showing up at the storage room to pull a prank on Sybil. They were both eager to get her. I still say they were in on it together."

As we pondered the idea, the first shoppers of the day strolled up to look at our display, causing us to table our conversation.

"I've got one more box to bring out," Marco told us, "and then this mule is off duty."

"Your carrot will be waiting," I replied, giving him a flirtatious smile.

He winked at me, then strode away.

I poured myself a cup of coffee, still thinking about our discussion on the Urbans.

"Have you considered the young lady across the aisle as a suspect?" Grace asked.

Lottie and I turned to gaze at Angelique, who sat at her harp with her eyes shut and an intense look of concentration on her face as she plucked strings in what seemed to be random order. Today she was dressed in an all-white gauze dress with white ballet flats, and she appeared to be listening to a tape recorder through earbuds. This machine was larger than the one she'd had with her the evening before. It must have been her backup.

"After all," Grace remarked quietly as she went about hanging a wreath on one wall, "she is the angel of death."

Lottie nearly dropped the arrangement she'd been fixing. "Excuse me?"

"Angelique is another form of Angel, and DeScuro translates as *of darkness*; hence, Angel of Death," Grace explained. "I would be quite suspicious of her."

Lottie rolled her eyes. "Because of her name? You can't help what your parents name you."

"She might be using a stage name," I said.

"We must also consider the musical terms Angelique used to describe Sybil." Grace removed a piece of stationery from her pocket and carefully unfolded it. "I researched these yesterday."

She cleared her throat and began to read in a soft voice: "*Bellicoso con fuoco*—aggressive, warlike, with fire. *Tremendo*—frightening. *Feroce al fine*—fiercely to the end. *Dissonante*—just what it sounds like, dissonant."

"Whee, doggies," Lottie said, unfolding a metal chair to have a seat. "Makes that *pesante* she called me seem pretty tame, doesn't it?"

"At least she didn't call you short and disconnected," I said. "I feel like a dropped phone call."

"It's obvious that Angelique was attracted by Sybil's aggressive nature," Grace said, slipping the paper into her pocket. "It speaks volumes about Angelique's personality, doesn't it?"

"So does her all-white outfit," I joked. "She must have checked her wings at the door."

"And what's up with that white stage makeup?" Lottie asked. "I can't tell where her throat ends and her dress begins."

"You should have seen her black garb yesterday,

Grace," I said. "The only way I can describe it is goth."

"Make that goth-awful," Lottie said, and we had to clap our hands over our mouths so we didn't laugh out loud.

"Another reason to consider Angelique," Grace said, ignoring our silliness, "is that she had her tape recorder with her when the police arrived. Has anyone asked why she happened to bring her recording equipment to a dressy banquet?"

"The cop who conducted the interview didn't think to ask," I told Grace. "Of course, if Reilly had allowed me to sit in, we wouldn't be having this discussion."

"Men," Lottie said, shaking her head. "They do their best thinking below the belt. Everything between their ears is an afterthought."

"Bonus equipment," I said, and we both giggled.

"It could be that Angelique carries a tape recorder like others do their mobile phones," Grace suggested, pronouncing the word *mow-bile*. She had such class.

Lottie tried to look thoughtful. "Sure. I can see it. In that line of work you never know when you'll be called upon to do some serious soul searching."

We laughed again until Grace said with a sniff, "When you're finished being catty, you must admit it's possible Angelique was in the right place at the right time to do Sybil in."

"I'll add her to the suspect list, but I still like the Urbans best," I said. "They had the motive, the opportunity, and certainly the means to get Sybil inside the

114

casket. Angelique thought too highly of Sybil to want to do her harm."

"Perhaps she doesn't view death as harmful," Grace said. "As Bertolt Brecht once noted, 'Do not fear death so much, but rather the inadequate life.' "

Across the aisle, Angelique's music grew louder and more cacophonous.

"Someone ought to give Jolly Roger over there some music lessons," Lottie muttered, rubbing her temples. "I'm getting a headache."

Grace eyed Angelique thoughtfully, her finger tapping her chin, leading me to believe that another quotation was forthcoming. But a moment later she picked up her dessert plate and held it out to me. "Have a scone, Abby."

Only too happy to oblige. But no quote? I glanced at Lottie, who shrugged.

I was just about to bite into the buttery treat when an announcement came over the public address system: "A memorial service for Sybil Blount will be held today at one o'clock in the Redenbacher Room on the mezzanine level of the hotel. Please join us there for a brief service to honor the woman who made this convention possible."

I glanced at Angelique, who had gone as still as a statue. Lottie and Grace were watching her, too. "I wonder what she's thinking," Lottie said.

As though she was aware of our scrutiny, Angelique turned her head slowly toward us, glared for a long moment, then went back to her string plucking.

"She certainly is an odd duck," Grace commented quietly.

"Make up your mind, Gracie," Lottie said. "Is she an angel or a duck?"

"If it walks like a duck and quacks like a duck," I said, repeating one of Grace's sayings, "you can be reasonably sure it's a duck."

"Either way, she'd have wings," Lottie said, sending us both into gales of laughter.

Grace put her hands on the table and leaned forward to scowl at us. "You two," she said sternly, "are really—quacking me up."

At that, all three of us dissolved into giggles, drawing curious looks from the people passing by. We immediately donned sober expressions, and Lottie jumped up to talk to a couple who were admiring the floral arrangements.

"Are you ever going to try that scone in your hand?" Grace asked me.

"Yes. Right now." I took a big bite just as, at that same moment, I spotted Ross and Jess walking past the end of our aisle, arguing and shoving each other. In my eagerness to point them out to Grace, who had never met them, I swallowed the bite too hastily. "Urban"—*cough*—"twins," I said, jabbing an index finger in their direction.

She glanced around at the very moment that messy-haired Jess delivered a hard punch straight into Ross's gut and stalked off, leaving his brother doubled over in pain.

"Good gracious," Grace remarked. "I wonder what brought that on."

There was one sure way to find out. Ask.

I put down the scone and wiped my fingers on a napkin. "I'll be right back."

Chapter Ten

Bastard," Ross swore under his breath, tucking his polo shirt into his pants where it had come loose from the impact of his brother's punch. He was neatly dressed in a gray UMS shirt, black slacks, and tasseled black loafers, his hair carefully styled.

"You took quite a hit," I said, laying on the concern. "I hope you're all right."

Ross winced as he touched his stomach. "Not a problem."

"Brothers," I said, shaking my head in sympathy. "What a nuisance. So, what provoked Jess?"

"It was nothing."

"*Nothing* doesn't get you sucker punched."

"I've been a sucker all right," Ross muttered, glaring after his brother.

A sucker? That was an interesting comment, and much too juicy to let slide. "You want to talk about it?"

He made a scoffing noise. "What are you, my shrink?"

"Fine. It's your loss. Too bad, though, because I'm a good listener and I know what it's like to have annoying brothers."

Ross's eyes narrowed. "Why are you being so friendly all of a sudden?"

"I'm always friendly, Ross, except when idiots pull dangerous stunts on me. Then, not so much."

"It's old news, Red. Get over it."

I was going to take exception to Ross's use of the *Red* moniker but decided I'd better grab his attention quickly and ignore the irritating nickname. "There sure is a lot of gossip going around about your buddy Sybil's odd demise."

"My *buddy?* What are you talking about?"

"What do you guess it would have taken to convince Sybil to strip down and climb into a casket right before her appearance at a banquet?"

"What is this, a quiz?"

"More like a news bulletin. Flash! Abby Knight locked in coffin. Flash! Sybil Blount locked in casket. See what I mean? The similarities are almost too coincidental, wouldn't you say?"

"Are you hinting at something, Red?"

"Well, gee, Ross, let me think. I didn't lock myself in that phone booth, and I'm betting Sybil didn't shut herself in that coffin, either. How's that for a hint?"

He thrust his face close to mine, giving me a strong whiff of musky men's cologne and a close-up view of the large pores on his nose, which was not at all flattering. "I don't like hints, Red, so why don't you say what you mean? You think we locked Sybil in that casket?"

I gave him a shrug. "If the fishnet stocking fits . . ."

Ross smirked, being his usual smart-ass self. "Here's a hint for you, Red. Prove it."

"I'll let the detectives take care of that." But if they didn't—and I wasn't holding out much hope—I was going to take great pleasure in nailing him.

Ross gave me a smug smile. "Hate to disappoint you, Red, but the cops are done with me. I'm in the clear. Mr. Cool's no fool."

"Did your daddy hire a really smart lawyer for you, Mr. Cool?"

Ross's smile dissolved. "Get bent," he said, and turned to walk away.

"Is your brother in the clear, too?"

"Couldn't tell ya. I'm not my brother's keeper." He snickered, apparently amused by his witticism. His cell phone began to play "SexyBack," so he pulled out a razor-thin phone and answered it as he sauntered off toward the Starbucks counter.

Laugh now, Loafer Boy. Ross might think he was in the clear, but he had no idea how tenacious I could be. When I was on a mission, nothing could stop me. I was the Little Red Engine Who *Did.*

I waited until Ross was in line for his order; then I hurried to the next aisle and darted up it, hoping to find Jess at his family's booth. I hadn't yet seen the UMS exhibit, because, frankly, I hadn't cared to, and now it brought me to a stunned stop. Their elaborate display occupied half of the right side of the aisle and was undoubtedly the largest and splashiest booth at the convention.

Designed to resemble the inside of a cozy country chapel, complete with stained-glass windows and an old-fashioned pipe organ, the booth had ornately crafted caskets lined up like rows of pews and a marble-topped altar topped with an array of expensive crystal urns. Burial clothing hung on antique hall trees at the back, a collection of pearl and diamond jewelry glittered in long, glass-fronted cabinets along the side, and enormous flower arrangements on gilded risers were scattered throughout. Presiding over all were a bevy of eager salesmen wearing cleric's collars. But no Jess.

I bypassed the salesmen and headed for a genial-looking woman in a gold choir robe. She was standing at the front end of the mock chapel handing out samples of something from a basket over her arm.

"Would you like to try our new fragrance, hon?" she asked pleasantly, spraying a strip of white paper with essence from a glass bottle shaped like a coffin.

I waved away a cloud of pungent mist. "UMS sells perfume, too?"

"No, hon. Funeral fragrances." She leaned close to add, "You know how unpleasant some of those funeral odors can be." She offered me the scented paper. "This is Mortu-Airy, a lovely blend of gladioli, rose hips, and disinfectant. It's part of our Urban's Decay line."

Urban's Decay? *Ew!* "I don't think so. Thanks, anyway."

She fished another bottle out of her robe and

sprayed a sample onto a fresh piece of paper. "Try some of our original scent—Crema-florium. It has just a hint of ash touched with a smoky pine scent and a splash of lily of the valley."

"No, really, that's okay. I'm looking for Jess Urban. Have you seen him?"

"He came by a few minutes ago." She glanced around. "You might try the Internet café. It's right next to Outer-Space Burials in aisle four."

"Thanks." I started to walk away, but when her words registered, I stopped and turned back. "Did you say *outer-space* burials?"

"Exciting concept, isn't it? They offer two choices—Shoot for the Moon, which is their budget line, and A Space Odyssey, their deluxe design. I believe UMS is looking into offering them next year."

"Okay, just so I understand the concept, when a person dies, the body is jettisoned into outer space?"

She laughed as though I had cracked a joke. "They don't send bodies, hon. They send the ashes in a memorial capsule."

"Right. Okay, then, thanks for your help." An outer-space burial—death's final frontier.

I found Jess the Mess in his usual wrinkled shirt, paired with khakis today, hair sticking up at odd angles, playing a computer video game at the Cyberary Café. The seat next to him was unoccupied, so I sat down. "Hello, Jess."

"Hey," he said absently, his gaze glued to a screen where race cars were screeching around a track, crashing into barriers and each other and exploding into fireballs.

"How's it going? Punched anyone lately?"

He glanced my way, then did a double take. "Yo, little dudette. What are you doing here?"

"Looking for someone."

Jess must have sensed something was up, because his expression quickly grew wary. "Good luck with that." He returned to the game, and I could hear his silver tongue stud tapping absently against his teeth as he worked the controller.

"Maybe you've seen him. Young, nice looking, able to lure women into coffins, sometimes with their clothes off."

"Don't know anyone like that. Sorry." *Click, click, click.*

"What a shame. I'd really like to chat with him about how Sybil ended up in a casket."

When he ignored me, I leaned closer to say, "I'm staying right here until you talk to me, Jess. Don't think I'll be the only one to see the coincidence between what you and Ross did to me yesterday morning and what happened to Sybil. It's just a matter of time until the police catch on."

Jess tightened his jaw, and his stud clicking grew faster, but he made no comment. He probably thought if he stayed silent long enough, I'd go away. Too bad he didn't know that only made me more determined. I'd have to see whether I could push some guilt buttons to get him to confess.

I paused while a man in a blue suit took a seat at a computer station on the opposite end of the long counter; then I said quietly, "I know Sybil had been after you, Jess. I know what kind of woman she was, always preying on younger men. And I heard that she propositioned you this weekend, so I wouldn't blame you for wanting to embarrass her so she'd leave you alone. But if you played a prank on her and it went wrong, you'd better speak up, because by keeping quiet you make yourself look guilty of murder."

He smacked his hands on the keyboard and swiveled his chair to face me. "Why do you keep saying *you?* I have a brother, you know. Did you ever think of that?"

Jess had latched onto that *you* pronoun awfully fast. That was worth poking with a stick. "I just talked to your brother, as a matter of fact. We had an interesting little conversation." The *little* part was true, anyway. "Seems Ross was cleared by the cops. The puzzling thing is that he wouldn't say the same for you."

"What are you telling me? That Ross said I had something to do with Sybil's death?"

I shrugged. Jess could take that to mean whatever he wanted.

"He wouldn't do that to me," Jess said defiantly.

"Are you sure? He was pretty smug about it."

"Ross knows I have a solid alibi."

"Gee, I wonder why he wanted me to think otherwise."

Jess pondered my question a moment, then shrugged it off. "It doesn't matter. The cops have a videotape made by the hotel's security camera that proves I was at the bar yesterday evening, right up until it was time to go to the banquet." He pulled out his cell phone and tried to hand it to me. "Here. Call the cops. They'll tell you."

A security camera caught him? *Damn.* It was a solid alibi, all right, not to mention that it threw a major wrench into my case against the Urbans. What was odd was that Ross hadn't offered up *his* alibi.

"That's okay. I have a phone. So, was Ross with you at the bar?"

Jess studied me guardedly as he put his phone in his pocket, probably realizing he'd done more talking than he should have. "Didn't he tell you where he was?"

Oops. Bad move, Abby. "Well, sure, but I'd like to hear your side of it."

"Yeah, right." He gave me a look of disgust, then swiveled back toward the screen.

Okay, so Jess the Mess was shrewder than I'd thought. Still, I wasn't about to give up, especially because his cautious reply made me more suspicious. Maybe I could appeal to his ego to get more answers.

I leaned closer so that the man at the other station wouldn't overhear. "If you were at the bar, Jess, then Ross must have met Sybil in the storage room alone. As far as pranks go, he pulled a good one—coaxing her into the casket and making off with her clothes. I'm surprised you weren't in on it, though. You were the one who suggested getting her again."

"Go away," he muttered, his thumbs vigorously working the game controller.

"Really, Jess, I'm truly amazed that Ross managed to pull it off without your help. I hadn't figured him to be that resourceful, but I guess I was wrong, because it would take quite a salesman to convince a vain woman like Sybil to ditch her clothes and lie down in a sand-filled casket right before she had to be at a banquet."

Jess glanced at me slyly, and I caught a spark of interest. Hoping I was making headway at last, I kept up the chatter. "Naturally I don't condone Ross's prank—the woman died, after all—but I can appreciate the ingenuity behind it. I've played a few tricks on people myself. So, tell me how Ross did it. How did he convince her?"

Jess played with his tongue stud, twisting it with his fingers, watching me. Then he wiggled his index finger, beckoning me nearer, until I was close enough to hear him whisper, "You seriously think I'd rat out my brother?"

If Conrad Urban was fostering a rivalry between his sons, pinning the prank on Ross would be exactly what Jess should want to do. But maybe he couldn't bring himself to admit it. So how could I get him to spill the beans? "You know, Jess, I seriously think your brother might beat you to it."

He leaned back and swung his chair around to face the monitor. "You are so full of it. Ross isn't going to say jackshit about anything."

"Is that why you punched him? To make sure he doesn't say anything?"

"I punched Ross because he took money from my wallet. Now, get lost. I'm busy."

"Sorry, Jess. I'm not leaving until I get some answers." I folded my arms across my chest and waited.

"You're wasting your time, Red," he said as he resumed his game. "What are you going to do, follow me around all day?"

"If I have to."

"What's in it for you? You working for the cops or something?"

"I'm a florist who likes to solve puzzles. But I can't piece this one together without more information."

"Gee, I'm all broken up over that."

I tried to maintain a calm demeanor as I sat there watching his thumbs flying over the controls, his tongue clicking furiously as the race cars crashed and burned on the screen, but I was losing patience fast. Either this jerk's brother or both of them were responsible for a woman's death, yet he sat there acting totally blasé about it, as if he couldn't have cared less.

I grabbed the controller out of his hands. "Talk to me, Jess."

"Give that back," he snarled.

I held it away. "Sybil died because of a stupid prank you guys pulled. She suffocated because she couldn't get the coffin lid open. Doesn't that bother you even a little bit? Don't you care that some innocent person is going to be blamed for her death? The cops are questioning my friend Delilah, Jess, a happily married wife, mother of two kids, a woman who can't even kill spiders, for God's sake. Does *that* make you feel bad? Does *anything* make you feel bad?"

"And here I thought you just liked to solve puzzles. Now, give me back the damn controller."

I held it above my head, as far as the cord would stretch. "Wouldn't it have been enough for Ross to simply make off with Sybil's clothing? Why did he have to close the lid and put that heavy tool chest on top of the casket, too?"

Jess stood up and yanked the controller from my hands. Then he plunked down into the chair and started a new game, completely shutting me out.

"Come on, Jess. Tell me what Ross was thinking. He must have realized Sybil would run out of air—unless that was what he wanted." I waited a beat, then added, "Was that what Ross wanted?"

Jess swiveled his chair to glare at me, running that stud along the inside of his teeth, back and forth, like a jailbird running a tin cup along his cell bars. "If Ross had killed Sybil," he sneered, "don't you think the police would have him in custody by now?"

"Not if your dad used his money to keep him out."

Jess stood up and tossed the game controller onto the countertop, where it landed with a heavy thud. "Then maybe you should talk to my dad and find out." With a final smirk, he strode off.

Crap. I'd wasted almost an hour of precious time on those idiots and hadn't learned a single piece of information that would help clear Delilah.

Chapter Eleven

I hurried down aisle three and around the corner toward my booth, just as Marco came striding out of aisle two toward me. "Why didn't you wait for me?" he asked.

"Because I had this little window of opportunity to talk to Ross and Jess, so I grabbed it—all for nothing, as it turned out. I couldn't get either one to admit to anything. Jess has a solid alibi, and Ross wouldn't talk. The Urbans are so guilty, Marco, but we're going to have a tough time proving it."

"What did you say to them?"

I motioned for him to move away from people standing nearby, to keep anyone from overhearing; then I filled him in on my conversations with both twins. At Marco's look of disbelief, I added, "That's exactly how I felt after I talked to Jess. It's unbelievable that they've been cleared."

"Abby." Marco cupped my shoulders, holding my gaze with his penetrating brown eyes. "You told the Urbans that you believe their prank killed Sybil."

"I know."

"You told them you think they committed a murder!"

"I get it, Marco. But considering the circumstances,

what else could I have done? I know that's not a method you recommend—"

"Not *recommend?* How about forbid? Sunshine, you didn't think this through. And by tipping your hand, you might have put yourself in danger."

"Come on, Marco. Thing One and Thing Two are pranksters, not killers. They're not going to come after me. Besides, now that they think I'm on to them, they'll be on their guard, and you know that people on their guard are more prone to make mistakes. Then all it will take is one slipup, and *whammo.* We've got them. There's no way I could have kept quiet about what they did and missed that little window of opportunity to get them to spill the beans."

"I don't care if you had a garage door of opportunity, Abby. Telling someone you're on to them is a foolish move. You should have waited for me before you questioned the Urbans. You're still a novice at this."

First I was foolish and then a novice? Nothing like adding insult to injury. I folded my arms and glared at him. "So, in other words, I'm incompetent without you."

"That's not what I meant. You're extremely competent—as a florist." He lifted his hands, as though searching for the right words. "Maybe *inexperienced* is a better word. You're still inexperienced when it comes to interviewing suspects."

"And yet you asked me to track down Snuggles the Clown's killer when you were under suspicion for murder, which I was able to do without you, if you will recall. Who's to say my way won't work on the Urbans?"

"I'm not concerned about your way working, Abby. I'm concerned that it will work too well. Do you understand what I'm trying to say?"

"Sure I understand. You think I made a major blunder that's going to get me killed, and how I managed to stay alive this long is a total mystery."

"Listen to me," he said, lifting my chin to meet his gaze. "You know how much I appreciate what you did for me in the clown murder case, but that's a separate issue. It's not about me now. It's about you being safe. I don't want anything to happen to you. Okay?"

I could feel my indignation wearing away like a sand castle in the wind. I knew Marco's angry reaction had come straight from his heart. He cared. And he was willing to risk hurting my feelings to let me know just how much.

"Okay," I said at last. "But next time, could you not use words like *foolish* and *novice*? Because I may have to hurt you if you do."

Marco's mouth lifted at the corners into a ninety-degree tilt, the Salvare version of a full smile. I smiled back—and just like that, there it was, that powerful connection between us. He felt it, too, and his gaze softened. "Do you know where I'm coming from now?"

"Yes." I wrapped my arms around him and laid my head against his heart. "Don't be concerned, Marco. I know how to take care of myself."

He groaned.

At that moment the PA system crackled to life. "Don't miss TV personality Chet Sunday's *Make It Easy* show today at eleven o'clock. That's Chet Sunday appearing half an hour from now onstage in aisle one."

I reluctantly released Marco to check the time on my watch. "We should get a move on. Nikki will kill me if I don't bring back Chet's autograph."

"We've got a lot of ground to cover today. Are you sure you want to waste an hour watching Chet's show?"

"I need to be there only at the end. Remember when Sybil and Chet left after his show yesterday, and he didn't look happy about it? For some reason that's bugging me, so I thought maybe I'd have a chat with Chet after the taping to see what he has to say. 'A Chat with Chet'—ha. It sounds like part of his TV show."

"You're actually willing to consider someone other than the Urbans as a suspect?"

"I'm not a novice, you know." I smiled sweetly.

At that moment Lottie came bustling toward us. "Abby, you and Marco need to get up to the hotel's reception desk pronto. I just came from there, and some slick-dressing, out-of-town lawyer is making a big stink about a phone message he got from Sybil, something about some belongings she wanted to give to him. They're making him wait for the cops before they give out any information, and he's having a hissy fit. If you hurry, you might be able to find out more."

"Let's go," Marco said.

"How will we recognize him?" I called to Lottie as we started away.

"Look for the fanciest ostrich-leather shoes you've ever seen."

Since I'd never seen even a plain pair of ostrich-leather shoes, I wasn't sure that would be much help, not to mention that I was already feeling sorry for the bird.

"Why would Sybil want to give some of her belongings to her lawyer?" I mused, hurrying to keep up with Marco's long-legged stride.

"I'd guess for safekeeping."

"If she wanted to keep them safe, why drag them with her to a convention? Unless . . . Marco, maybe Sybil was afraid something would happen to her, so she left a clue to her killer's identity just in case she died. Isn't that how it happens in the movies?"

"Since this isn't the movies, let's hope the lawyer will enlighten us."

We dodged slow movers and oblivious browsers, hurrying up the main hallway past the phony phone booth and ceiling-high windows, up the ramp into the hotel, through the lobby, and straight toward the reception desk. Halfway there, Marco stopped and pulled me off to one side. "Ostrich shoes at eight o'clock."

I turned to the left and saw a stocky man with kinky white hair, wire-rimmed glasses, nutmeg-colored skin, a tan knit shirt, dark brown trousers, and a pair of bumpy, caramel brown shoes—was that what ostrich skin looked like? He was standing beside a table with a gigantic floral arrangement on it. *Note to self: See what florist the hotel uses.* His arms were folded across his chest, and one shoe was tapping the floor beside his briefcase as he watched the revolving doors.

"How did you recognize the ostrich shoes?" I whispered to Marco.

"I owned a pair once. See those bumps? That's where the feathers were."

"Aren't ostrich shoes expensive?"

"Do you want to stand here discussing shoes, or should we talk to the man wearing them?"

"What are we going to say?"

"Watch and learn, Sunshine."

Using that confident swagger that never failed to stir my "innards," as Lottie would say, Marco strode up to the man in the ostrich shoes and displayed his PI identification card. "Marco Salvare, private investigator and former police officer with the New Chapel PD. This is my associate Abby Knight."

I gave the man a smile that I hoped looked investigator-like.

"Rex Crawford," the attorney said after a moment's hesitation, shaking Marco's hand and then mine, but clearly not sure why.

"I understand you're here regarding some personal property of Sybil Blount's," Marco said as he put his wallet away. "Are you her attorney?"

"I might be. In what capacity are you here, Mr. Salvare?"

"Purely as a private investigator. A friend of mine is being questioned in Ms. Blount's death, and I'm trying to gather as much information as possible to keep her from becoming a suspect."

"Suspect?" His richly textured voice resonated across the room, causing heads to turn our way. He toned the volume down a notch and stepped closer. "Are you saying there was foul play?"

"It appears that way," Marco said. "I'm sorry; I thought you knew."

Crawford looked ready to explode. "All I know is what I heard on the radio this morning, that she died while attending a convention. And the only information I got from those jackasses behind the counter is that her room has been sealed off and I have to talk to the authorities if I want access to her belongings. No one said anything about foul play."

"Then maybe we can help each other." Marco gestured toward a lounge area filled with cozy leather club chairs and a richly appointed bar. "Can I interest you in a cup of coffee?"

The attorney pulled back warily. "Slow down, son. Before we take this discussion any further, what assurances do I have that your friend isn't involved? No offense, but I don't want to be aiding someone who might be responsible for my client's death."

"Our friend," I said testily, "is one of the sweetest, kindest, gentlest women you'd ever want to meet. But *your* client, on the other hand, was a—"

"Abby," Marco said in a cautioning voice, putting a

hand on my shoulder to remind me that I was supposed to be watching and learning.

"Mr. Crawford, our friend Delilah Dove, and her husband, Max, have run a family-owned funeral home in New Chapel for years," Marco said. They have an excellent reputation, and their many friends and customers will testify to her character. Delilah has no credible motive to do your client harm, and any allegations that she does are ludicrous. But there are others attending this convention who do have motives, and if you're willing to work with us—"

"Hold on a minute," Crawford said, holding out his hands. "You're going too fast for me. All I deal with is estate planning and tax concerns—you know, wills, trusts, tax returns, and the like. Except for the message she left me, I haven't heard from Sybil since last April at tax time. I'm not sure how I can be of any assistance to you. And while I appreciate your offer, I've got a dead client here, and if this is, in fact, a homicide, I need to find out what it was my client wanted me to have, because it could be important to the investigation."

"We understand your concerns," Marco assured him, "but would you at least hear us out?"

Clearly unsettled by the turn of events, Crawford glanced at his watch, then back at the door, which was still devoid of any cops. "I suppose I can listen to what you have to say—as long as our conversation is strictly off the record."

That was lawyer talk for *"If anyone asks me, this*

conversation never took place."

The men allowed me to lead the way through the reception area and up two steps into the lounge, where we took seats at a table off by itself. A waitress swooped in immediately, and we ordered coffees all around.

Rex Crawford leaned forward, his gaze serious and intent. "Before we go any further, I'd like to know how you acquired your information, Mr. Salvare, and just to make things easier, let's refer to my client by her first name."

"Certainly," Marco said. "To set the stage for you, Sybil was supposed to give the opening remarks at last night's convention banquet, which Ms. Knight and I were attending. When Sybil failed to show by the end of the dinner, we suspected something had happened to her and initiated a search."

Oh, so now it was *we*. Funny how Marco forgot that *I* was the one who had insisted on looking for her.

"We arrived at the scene shortly after the cops did, so we got a good look at everything before the room was disturbed. We'll share that information with you as well as the names of two men who should be investigated."

I nodded in agreement, ready to explain that I'd almost been a victim of foul play myself, but Marco quickly put a hand over mine and said to the attorney, "First, we need your word that you'll reciprocate by sharing the contents of the message and whatever belongings you find."

Crawford paused as the waitress brought our coffees. "Explain to me again why I should do that."

"Because Delilah is innocent," I said before Marco could remind me again that I was supposed to be his mute apprentice, "and the two guys who should be suspects aren't, and somehow we have to convince the prosecutor that he's looking in the wrong direction."

"And you think whatever it was that Sybil left for me will prove your friend's innocence?"

"We'd like the opportunity to find out," Marco said.

Crawford sipped his coffee while he thought it over. "I'll see what I can do to help you out, but I'd like to ask you a couple of questions first."

"Go ahead," Marco said.

"Was my client's death a clear case of homicide?"

Marco sat back, looking every inch a savvy, confident private eye. "There's not a doubt in my mind. Sybil was found in a storage room inside a closed casket, wearing only her underwear, her clothing—"

"Back up," Crawford said, holding up his hands. "Did you say inside a *casket?*"

"With a heavy tool chest propped on the lid so she couldn't get out," I added.

"Holy stars and bars. Had she been restrained? Were there any ropes on her wrists, any handcuffs?"

"Not that we saw," Marco replied. "Also, there were no visible marks on her throat. I don't know what the autopsy or toxicology reports will show, but at first blush it appears she willingly climbed into the casket."

The attorney's eyes nearly bulged out of his head. "She *climbed* into the casket?" The poor man was starting to come undone.

"I know that sounds off the wall," Marco said, "but bear in mind that this convention is for morticians, and some of their activities are, well, a little out there for the rest of us. The storage room was the holding area for caskets that were entries in a contest, and Sybil was the judge."

"The caskets were supposed to be decorated as different objects," I explained. "You know, like a jet plane or a piano keyboard."

For a moment Crawford simply sat there as though his mind wouldn't accept what we were saying. Then he took off his glasses and polished them with the linen table napkin, muttering, "My, my, my."

"Sybil was supposed to announce the winning entry after the banquet," I said, "but she never showed up."

"Correct me if I'm wrong, but choosing a winning—er, entry wouldn't require her to take off her clothing and climb *into* the casket, would it?" Crawford asked.

"I don't think the people here are that far out," Marco said.

"But there *was* a rumor floating around that Sybil had arranged to meet someone in the storage room before the banquet," I said.

"For what purpose?"

"Supposedly for a tryst," I said.

"A tryst. In a *casket*. Which she then died in." Crawford calmly hooked the wire ends of his glasses over his ears, blinked a few times to adjust his vision, and put his hands on the table, as though performing a normal act would restore his bewildered mind. "I have to agree with your assessment, Mr. Salvare. It seems a clear case of homicide. What about this witness you mentioned earlier?"

"She's definitely way out there," I said.

"Her name is Angelique DeScuro, and her business is called Music of the Soul," Marco said. "Whether she was involved in Sybil's death isn't clear at this point. The only information she provided was her discovery of the tool chest sitting on top of the closed casket and a nylon stocking hanging out of one end. Apparently that stocking was her tip-off—otherwise, she wouldn't have looked inside the casket."

"Is this Angelique a prime suspect, then?" Crawford asked.

"I don't have any information on that yet," Marco said, as though he expected some momentarily. "Angelique seemed very taken with Sybil, almost to the point of idolizing her, so it doesn't make sense that she would kill her."

"Actually," I said, "it does. Angelique told me she wanted to record Sybil's soul music, and she can't do that unless the person is checking out."

"Whoa. Hold on a minute," Crawford said. "What do you mean by Sybil's soul music?"

"According to Angelique, it's the music the soul makes when leaving the body," I explained. "She records the so-called soul music onto a CD for the family of the deceased. It's weird, but that's what she does for a living. She told me Sybil's soul was so unique that it had to be recorded. Make of that what you will."

"Are these people crazy?" Crawford asked.

"It gets crazier," I said. "When the police arrived, Angelique had her tape recorder with her and she was sitting in front of the casket rubbing one of Sybil's nylon stockings against her face. That has to raise a few red flags. And if you think about it, Marco," I said, turning to face him, "Angelique could have held the lid down to keep Sybil from escaping while she did her recording, then positioned the chest on the floor and claimed she found it on top."

Marco shook his head as though my idea reeked. "So you're saying Angelique killed Sybil to get her recording, then called the cops when she was finished? Not likely. How would she have convinced Sybil to get inside the casket?"

"Who's to say Sybil didn't swing both ways? Maybe she was meeting *Angelique* for that tryst."

"So your opinion then is that this Angelique is the killer?" Crawford asked me.

I scratched my nose, slightly embarrassed that I'd painted myself into a corner. Across the table, Marco was waiting to see how I'd get myself out. "Um, well, actually, no, that would be Ross and Jess Urban, or maybe just Ross. But certainly both of them had the strongest means, motive, and opportunity of anyone here at the convention." I went on to explain how the

Urban twins had lured me into the coffin–phone booth, about the prank they'd played on Sybil, and about finding Sybil's clothes on the mannequin.

"These young men wouldn't be Conrad Urban's sons, would they?" Crawford asked nervously, reaching for his napkin.

I nodded. "Do you know Conrad?"

The attorney mopped his forehead. "Do you see our waitress? I need water. Fast."

Chapter Twelve

The waitress had gone behind the bar to fill an order and was standing with her back to us, so Marco called out, "Excuse me, can we have some service here, please?"

She didn't hear him, so I jumped up and grabbed a full glass from a woman at the next table. "Have you had any of this yet?" I asked the startled female, who quickly shook her head.

"Great. Thanks. We'll get you a fresh supply in just a minute."

I put the glass of water in the attorney's hand, and he took a long gulp, then held the cold tumbler against his forehead just as the waitress bustled over.

"She needs a glass of water," I said, and pointed to the bewildered lady next to us.

"I apologize," Crawford said to us. "All this talk about caskets, and soul recordings, and now the Urban family . . . It's a little much for me to absorb."

"No problem," Marco said. "Take your time."

The attorney took a slow drink, then put down the glass. "I'm sorry. Please continue. You were talking about the Urban boys."

"I don't have anything else," I said, "except that I'm absolutely certain Ross and Jess are behind Sybil's death. They pulled a prank that went terribly wrong, and yet the police cleared them."

"They would," Crawford said. "Do you have any idea how much power Conrad Urban wields?"

"He's not from our neck of the woods, and we're not in the funeral business," Marco said. "I'd never even heard his name until yesterday. Had you, Abby?"

"All I know about Conrad Urban is that he owns a big funeral-home chain, makes a lot of money, and has two spoiled-rotten sons," I said.

"*Big* doesn't begin to describe his business," Crawford told us. "Conrad heads the Unified Mortuary Service Corporation, a leviathan chain that covers a five-state area and is still growing. He holds a tremendous amount of political clout. He golfs with federal judges, takes councilmen and state representatives for vacations on his yacht, and throws lavish parties. When he backs candidates, they win. By the same token, his clout would make a district attorney gun-shy were it to come to prosecuting any of Conrad's family members. Trust me on this—without irrefutable evidence, his sons will never be suspects."

"That is so totally unfair," I protested.

"Money talks," he said. "But let's go back to this

142

friend of yours. There must be some reason she's being questioned. How does she fit into the picture?"

Marco explained about the scene Sybil made at the booth and Delilah's run-in with her at past conventions as well as in the storage room before the banquet. "Now the cops are claiming that Delilah was the last person to see Sybil alive, as if that makes it a foregone conclusion that she's the killer."

"Honestly, Mr. Crawford," I said, "Delilah didn't have a problem with Sybil. It was Sybil who had a problem with Delilah, and I'm sorry if this offends you, but I saw Sybil trying to provoke an argument with her."

"Let me tell you a little bit about Sybil," Crawford said. "I got to know her about ten years ago when her husband, Thaddeus, hired me to take care of his estate planning. Sybil was demanding and quick to take issue, but I managed to get along with her. Of course, it helped that I only saw her twice a year.

"About a year before Sybil's husband passed away, she became obsessed with the fear that she was going to be left destitute one day, and after Thaddeus died her fears intensified, even though I assured her that he'd left her well off. Since she had been a cosmetician at the Billingsworth and Blount funeral home—that was where she met her husband—she decided to develop and sell her own line of cosmetics, calling it her retirement fund. I know she aggressively pursued clients, but her business never really took off. I'm sure her personality had something to do with that, but I

143

can't imagine her making any *mortal* enemies from selling cosmetics."

Obviously he hadn't seen any of her products.

"What about the message she left you?" Marco asked. "Do you still have it?"

Crawford pulled out his cell phone, tapped in his code, and handed it to Marco, who held it between his ear and mine.

"Rex," we heard Sybil say, her voice hushed and panicky, "I need to meet with you right away. Something happened and I'm worried, but I can't go to the police and I don't have anyone else I can trust. I'm at the Woodland Convention Center off Route 12, about half an hour north of New Chapel. Please, Rex, I need you to keep some things for me just until I get back into South Bend next week, so call me the minute you get this. I wouldn't ask you to come all this way if it wasn't urgent. I'll explain more when I see you."

The message ended and Marco handed the phone back. "Do you have any idea what she wanted to give you?"

"Not a single clue, so I'm not sure I'd know them if I saw them. As I said, I haven't spoken with her in months. This call came completely out of left field, and unfortunately, my cell phone was off all weekend while we attended a family wedding in Ohio—my wife has a rule about cell phones at family events and I've learned not to break it, for harmony's sake. So I received the message only this morning. Now that

144

you've heard it, you can understand why I came straight here."

"What do you think she meant when she said she couldn't go to the police?" Marco asked.

"Son, I wouldn't want to speculate on that."

That was more lawyer talk. This time it meant, *My client might be involved in something illegal, but I can't say so.*

"I'd like to get into her room and have a look," Crawford told us, "but I know I'll be fighting an uphill battle to get the police to let me in."

"We know ways around that," I told him, only to have Marco throw me a glance that said, *That's not what you admit to a lawyer.* Okay, so there was another reason why I hadn't passed my law school exams.

"Have you checked with the front desk to see if Sybil left an envelope or package for you?" Marco asked.

"She didn't, nor did she mail anything. I had the clerk check as soon as I arrived. Since it's a weekend, nothing went out. So either she didn't feel as though she was in any immediate danger or she did but never got to take steps to ensure the items reached me."

"What time was her message sent?"

Crawford checked the screen on his cell phone. "Three fifteen yesterday afternoon."

Obviously whatever had prompted her distress call had happened well before she met the killer in the storage room. I tried to recall what had been going on at three fifteen. Lottie had arrived at two o'clock, and not long after that Sybil had come around with her checklist. What could have triggered her panicked phone call? Had she been threatened by someone as she made her way around the hall? Would security cameras have recorded her movements? I'd have to remember to ask Marco later.

"Are you aware of any personal relationships that might have placed your client in danger?" Marco asked.

"I never probe my clients' personal business."

"What about inheritance problems? Did she have any children or stepchildren?"

"None."

"What do you know of her husband's family?"

"They predeceased him. Thaddeus had one close friend whom he treated like a brother, and that was Walker Billingsworth, his partner in the funeral-home business. I handled Walker's estate for awhile, but after Thaddeus died, the colonel retired and decided to take care of his finances himself."

Marco glanced at me to see whether I had anything to add, but I was fresh out of ideas.

"Did you have anything else to ask us?" Marco said.

"Not at present. My next step is to try to talk the police into letting me into Sybil's room—if they ever show up." He pulled out a business card and wrote his cell phone number on the back. "Will you let me know if there are any new developments?"

"Be glad to, if you'll do likewise." Marco took out

one of his own business cards and gave it to the attorney. At that moment, a hotel employee in a burgundy coat came into the lounge accompanied by an officer from the sheriff's department. He pointed to Crawford.

"Looks like the authorities have finally arrived," Crawford said, springing up. "Let's see if I have any luck."

"Attorney Rex Crawford?" the cop asked, striding toward us.

Crawford tapped the face of his watch. "It's about time you got here. I've come all the way from South Bend to pick up some items my client insisted I keep for her, only to find that the hotel won't let me access her room."

It was great posturing, but it didn't do him any good. The cop said gravely, "Mr. Crawford, your client is dead. We've sealed off her room."

"I'm well aware of the circumstances, Officer, but she didn't die in her room, did she?"

"No, sir."

"Then it's not a crime scene. Why is it sealed?"

"Because her death is under investigation."

"But she didn't die in her room."

"As you know, sir, there's always the possibility that evidence may be contained in a victim's room."

"Was a search of the room conducted?"

"I believe so."

"So, legally, Officer, there's no reason to keep me out, is there? So how about letting me inside to take possession of the belongings she set aside for me; then you can seal it up again?"

The cop looked flustered. "I can't go against orders, sir."

Crawford heaved a big sigh, looking very disheartened. "In other words, I'll have to get a judge to give me an order saying you have to let me in, and then you'll have to come back out here and do what you could do right now, on the spot. Why go through all that rigamarole?"

"Because I have orders, Mr. Crawford."

"Then I'll just have to see the judge in the morning."

"That would be fine, sir. Is there anything else I can help you with today?"

Crawford cast us a quick glance, then rocked back on his heels. "You can tell me who your suspects are."

"I can't do that, Mr. Crawford. You'll have to take it up with the DA."

"Then I guess there's nothing else you can help me with."

As the cop strode away, Crawford turned to us and shrugged. "It was worth a shot. I'll have to file a petition with the court in the morning so I can get a hearing set on the matter, although to be quite frank, the judges in this county don't know me from Adam, so they may not be inclined to rule in my favor. By that I mean don't hold your breath." He put a five-dollar bill on the table. "That should cover my coffee and a tip." He held out his hand. "It was a pleasure to meet you both. I'll let you know what happens in court."

As we watched Crawford stride out of the lounge, I said, "Marco, we can't wait for a court order that might not even happen. We're going to have to get inside Sybil's room ourselves."

"Yep," he said, standing to stretch his legs, "I came to that same conclusion."

Chapter Thirteen

How are we going to get inside Sybil's room?" I asked Marco as he steered me toward the bank of elevators. "We don't have her key card, and the door is probably sealed with yellow police tape."

"It won't be a problem. Watch and learn, Sunshine."

That was quickly becoming my least favorite saying. We stepped into an empty elevator car, and Marco pressed the button for the fourth floor. "What's your take on Sybil's message?" he asked.

"That she had things in her possession she shouldn't have had, something illegal. Otherwise, why not go to the police if she was worried about them? Maybe she was selling drugs and used her cosmetics line as a front."

"That doesn't fit her style."

"And you know her style because . . . ?"

Marco kept his gaze fixed on the changing floor numbers. "Because I excel at sizing up women."

"Oh, really? And how do I size up, Mr. PI?"

He gazed down at me, his dark eyes igniting with sudden heat at my challenge. It didn't take much to light Marco's fire. Of course, it didn't take much to light mine, either, because when one corner of his mouth curved up ever so slightly, my core temperature rose at least ten degrees. It was still climbing when he dipped his head toward mine. But just as our lips touched, the elevator doors opened, and five people stood outside, staring at us.

I blinked at them in surprise, then glanced up to see whether we were on the right floor. Apparently we were, because Marco took my arm and ushered me out. Across from the elevators a large brass wall plate indicated room numbers. I stood in front of it, trying to remember which way we'd gone the evening before. "Is Sybil's suite number 412?"

"This way," he said, turning my body toward the right. He knew that elevator rides left me directionally disabled.

According to what Delilah had been told, most of the conference attendees had single or double rooms on the second and third floors. But some, like Sybil, had chosen a more expensive suite on the fourth floor.

"I'll bet Sybil reserved a suite up here to give her more privacy," I said as we strode up the long hallway. "Maybe she squeezed in a few other liaisons besides the one in the storage room. That bellboy-toy crack we heard at the banquet might not have been too far off. She could have even brought Chet up here."

Marco looked doubtful. "Chet would have to be awfully careful to maintain his wholesome reputation, especially in a place this public."

"You'd think so, yet Max said Sybil was the one who arranged for Chet to attend the convention, so they must have had some kind of relationship. Oops. That reminds me." I checked my watch. "Chet's show ends in fifteen minutes."

We rounded a corner to a shorter hallway, and Marco stopped with a muttered, "Damn." Down the hall I could see a door sealed with two strips of yellow DO NOT CROSS tape. "What's wrong?"

"I thought the maids would be cleaning down on this end. I didn't see their carts at the other end."

"They won't be cleaning Sybil's room anyway," I said as we turned around and headed toward the elevators.

He gave me a look that said, *No kidding.* "Let's go back to the lobby. I'll check at the front desk to see what time they clean this floor."

"What are you going to do? Steal a key card from one of them?"

"Do you know a better way to get in?"

"Well . . . you're always bragging about the power of your famous Salvare charm. Why don't you use it to dazzle one of the maids into opening the door for you?"

He gave me his heart-melting grin. "Only if I want to take the easy way out."

"Someone's certainly full of himself."

"You were the one who brought it up." We stopped in front of the elevator bank, and Marco pushed the DOWN button. The door slid open and he held it so it wouldn't close on me. "So you like my charm, huh?"

"Among other things," I said with a flirtatious smile, taking my place beside him.

"Want some time to elaborate on those other things?" He pointed to the red button marked STOP. "There is such a thing as an elevator getting stuck between floors."

Hmm. Stuck between floors with a very sexy guy. Now *there* was something I'd never experienced before. Well, actually, I *had* been stuck on an elevator once, but not with Marco . . . and not on purpose.

Still, with my claustrophobia, could I stand the furious heart pounding and breathless sweatiness that was sometimes accompanied by a near faint whenever I felt trapped? No problem. Marco had that effect on me anyway. Of course I wanted to be stuck with him. Was I kidding? With the hot look he was giving me? "Let's go for it," I told him.

I had one hand on the top button of my blouse when I heard, "Hold the elevator, please."

Hey, *I* was supposed to say that! I peered out to see Colonel Billingsworth striding toward us. So much for the sweaty elevator interlude.

"Thank you," he said, stepping in beside us. As usual, the colonel looked dignified in his dark suit, white shirt, and solemn tie, his Purple Heart medal pinned to one lapel. "It's hard to get an elevator at these conventions. Too many people wanting to use them at the same time."

As the elevator began to descend, I said, "I see

you're one of the lucky ones to have gotten a room on the fourth floor."

"To tell you the truth, I got it by chance. Some sort of mix-up at the front desk. I told them I didn't mind." He chuckled.

"Are you anywhere near Sybil's suite?" I asked, trying to figure out whether he could help us get into her room. An adjoining suite would be ideal. There was usually a connecting door.

"Opposite end of the building."

That was no help. The elevator stopped to pick up passengers, so I shifted to the back of the car to make room and happened to spot a security camera in the front corner. If there were cameras in the elevators and a camera in the bar area, there would have to be more all over the hotel, so why not in the convention center, too? I nudged Marco and pointed upward. He nodded that he'd seen it, too.

As soon as we exited into the lobby, I pulled Marco off to the side. "Maybe there's a videotape that shows Ross with Sybil in the storage room."

"I thought of that, too, but I'd bet any money the police already confiscated the convention-center videos. After all, they have the bar video that cleared Jess." He paused to think. "The security manager might have backup tapes, though."

"Let's find out."

First we stopped to ask when the maids would be cleaning the fourth floor and learned they would be there between noon and three o'clock, a pretty wide window. Next Marco asked to see the security manager, and a few minutes later a scowling, beefy guy in a short-sleeve white shirt and a buzz cut stepped through a door marked PRIVATE.

"Uh-oh," I said softly. "He doesn't look user-friendly."

"Not a problem," Marco murmured out of the side of his mouth. "See that tattoo on his right forearm? Navy SEAL."

Ah! The brotherhood of the Special Forces. Being a former Army Ranger, Marco would know just how to get the man's cooperation.

Marco checked his watch. "It's almost noon. Why don't you go chat with Chet, and I'll see what I can do here? I'll meet up with you at your booth later."

"What about lunch? I'm getting hungry."

"Don't wait for me. I may get to see the tapes now."

Marco left to talk to the security manager, so I headed for the convention hall to get the autograph for Nikki and see what information Chet would give me. I made it to his booth with five minutes to spare, and because the crowd was thinner, I nabbed a seat in the last row just as the *Make It Easy* star was wrapping up his show.

"So you see," Chet said to the audience, unbuckling his tool belt, "you have no reason to toss your old tapes or reel-to-reels and lose all those precious memories. Remember, there are always ways to"—the theme song started in the background—"make it easy on yourself."

It was smarmy, but the crowd ate it up, applauding wildly as the music swelled behind him. He hung up the tool belt; then, after the director gave a signal, he walked to the front of the stage and sat on the top step to sign autographs as the production crew began to shut down the set behind him. Digging for my notepad, I hurried to get in line.

"Isn't this exciting?" asked a very tall, attractive woman with auburn hair, golden brown eyes, and a wide, full mouth, smiling down at me from her towering height. She had on a hot pink V-neck sweater and a tight black skirt. There were smudges of hot pink lipstick on her front teeth, but I didn't have the heart to tell her. Plus, her eyeteeth looked like viper fangs, so I thought it was best not to rile her.

"My name's Sue Antioch," she said, sticking out her hand. "I'm with Jasper and Krebbs Mortuary in Chicago."

"Abby Knight," I said, shaking the offered hand. "I own Bloomers Flower Shop in New Chapel, Indiana."

"Never heard of it. Omigod, look at Chet up there. Don't you think he's the sexiest man alive? I just love his captivating Russian accent."

That captivating accent was so minimal, you'd miss it if you were chewing. "I thought he was from Croatia."

"No, Russia."

"Are you certain? I read in *USA Today* that—"

"Russia." Sue narrowed her golden eyes at me. Were her pupils vertical? Didn't snakes have vertical pupils?

I forced a smile, then looked away, glad I hadn't mentioned those lipstick smudges. I glanced at my watch again and saw it was already past noon. I had less than five hours before the convention ended. Why wasn't the line moving faster?

With only one person ahead of her, Serpent Sue experienced a sudden moment of panic and quickly pulled out a silver lipstick tube, then doused her mouth with a fresh layer of slick color. She pressed her lips together twice, then turned toward me, baring her fangs once more. "Did I get any on my teeth?"

"Not a problem." And that wasn't a lie. Considering how far down that V-neck sweater went, I doubted Chet would notice anything above her larynx anyway.

"Hello," the *Make It Easy* star said to her, his brows lifting as his gaze moved to the point of the V, proving that even wholesome types could be tempted by the right letter of the alphabet.

"Oh, Chet," she breathed, "I adore your show. I wouldn't miss it for anything."

"Tank you," he said, taking the pen she held out for him. Since she didn't offer any paper, he asked, "What would you like me to sign?"

She leaned down to whisper in his ear, then pulled back to say in a purr, "But maybe we should meet up later for that."

He laughed uneasily. "I tink we might be arrested if I tried that."

Oh, ew! That Sue had a lot of nerve.

When my turn finally came, I handed Chet my

notepad and pen and said, "Would you make that out to Nikki, please? That's *N-I-K-K-I*."

He scribbled a few words, handed me the notepad, and said, "There you are, Nikki."

"I'm Abby, Nikki's roommate. But thanks for the autograph."

"Okay, Nikki," he said with an exaggerated wink, as if he were in on my secret. "Tell your *room*mate I said tanks for stopping by."

My eyebrows came down like falling bricks. Whether Chet was a TV star or not, I didn't like having my word doubted. Pulling out my wallet, I flipped it open so he could see my driver's license, then pointed to my name. "See there? Abby Knight. Not Nikki."

He barely glanced at it and instead looked around to see whether anyone else was waiting to see him. Since I was the only one left, he stood up and gave me a well-rehearsed smile. "Tanks for stopping by, Nikki's roommate."

Suddenly, over the PA system, we heard, "A reminder that there will be a memorial service for Sybil Blount at one o'clock this afternoon in the Redenbacher Room. Please make time in your schedule for a short tribute to our late chairperson."

Chet had paused to listen, and as he turned away at the end of the announcement, I heard him say under his breath, "No, tank you."

Not exactly something a friend would say—and yet Max had told me that he'd come to the convention as a favor to Sybil . . . or so she had said. It made me a little suspicious of their purported relationship.

"Isn't it tragic about Sybil?" I called as he started across the stage toward the back of the set.

"Very," he called back.

I jogged up the steps after him and picked my way around electrical cords and equipment. "You were a friend of hers, weren't you?"

"Not really, no," he called over his shoulder.

"But didn't she arrange for you to appear here?"

Chet stopped and turned to face me, clearly exasperated by my pestering. "Yes, she arranged it. That doesn't mean we're friends. Are you friends with everyone you talk to?"

"But I saw you two leaving together after your show yesterday."

"So?"

"So that's why I thought you and she were—"

"Listen, Nikki's roommate," Chet said, "I'm flattered by your interest in me, but the only connection I had with Sybil was a business one. We went to the hotel's lounge so she could give me a check for my appearance. She wanted to do that in private. Do you get it now?"

"She paid you to come here? I thought you did it as a personal favor."

"Sybil preferred that everyone believe I came as a favor, so I played along. It was her moment of glory. As long as I get paid, what do I care? So, you see? No reason to be jealous."

Jealous, ha! Clearly this minor television star had a major ego problem—and apparently no personal ties to Sybil. "You didn't seem happy about getting your check, though."

"She interrupted when I was signing autographs. My fans weren't happy, either. But it all worked out."

As Chet started to walk away, I had another question for him. "Doesn't Habitation Station pay you to make appearances?"

He stopped again and turned with a sharp sigh. "Not that it's any of your business, but my contract calls for me to make ten appearances a year. After that, I'm a free agent. I choose where and when. God only knows why I chose this one. It certainly won't happen again."

At that moment, his cell phone rang, playing the *Make It Easy* show's theme song. Chet immediately pulled his phone from a holder clipped to his belt, checked the screen, and before answering, said sardonically to me, "Was there anyting else you wanted to know, or may I take this call now?"

Just to annoy him, I pretended to ponder my answer, making him wait several seconds longer than necessary. "If I have anything else, I'll come back."

I stopped at the Pretzel Station to pick up a six-pack with cheddar cheese sauce, then headed for my booth, where I found Lottie talking to several browsers. Across the aisle, Grace was seated on a chair beside Angelique, listening intently to something through headphones.

"Did you find the lawyer?" Lottie asked as soon as she was free.

"Found him, talked to him, and really appreciate your tipping us off. Have a pretzel and I'll tell you all about our conversation."

"No, thanks, sweetie. Gracie and I weren't sure when you were coming back, so we ate about fifteen minutes ago. By the way, did you hear the announcement about the memorial service?"

"Yes, and I should probably attend. It'll be interesting to see who shows up and who doesn't."

"Grace wants to go, too, so I'll stay at the booth. It's been pretty dead today anyway." She clapped a hand over her mouth. "Lordy, I have to stop talking like that around here."

"Why does Grace want to go to the service? She didn't even know Sybil."

"Maybe not, but she sure has been asking heaps of questions about her." Watching the pair across the aisle, Lottie shook her head. "I don't know how Grace can stand that music—if that's what you want to call it."

"Maybe she's considering signing up for a soul recording. You know Grace. She isn't afraid to try anything."

"Nah. She's just over there to win Jolly Roger's trust."

"Two questions. Why do you call Angelique *Jolly Roger*, and why does Grace need to win her trust?"

"I call her Jolly Roger after the pirate flag—you

know, white skull and crossbones on a black background? And Grace is over there so she can find out why Angelique had her tape recorder with her in the storage room."

"Why does she need to know that? You'd think she was conducting her own investigation."

Lottie glanced at me askance. "You mean you just figured that out?"

"Grace is investigating? Doesn't she trust Marco and me to do it?"

"Honey, you know Gracie better than that. This is just her way of helping Delilah. Now, why don't you tell me what you learned from Ostrich Shoes?"

There was so little traffic in our aisle that after I'd filled Lottie in on our conversation with Crawford, she decided to take a stroll to stretch her legs. I stayed at the booth, munching on pretzels and waiting for Grace to finish schmoozing with Angelique so I could find out what she was planning. I still couldn't decide whether I was grateful for the extra help or offended by it. Whichever it was, I wasn't comfortable.

My cell phone rang. It was Marco sharing good news and bad news. On the good side, the hotel had backup security tapes of the bar, the elevators, the exits, and the convention hall, and the security manager had agreed to let him view them during his lunch hour from one to two o'clock. The bad news was that there was no camera in the storage room, and hence no tape of Sybil's final rendezvous.

"At least we'll be able to verify Jess's alibi," I told him.

"I've got forty-five minutes before I can view the tapes, and there's no sense wasting that time, so I'm heading up to the fourth floor right now to see if I can get into Sybil's suite. Why don't you meet me there? With any luck I'll be inside by the time you arrive, so make sure you don't draw any attention to yourself on your way in."

Don't draw *attention* to myself? "So the pom-poms and noisemakers are out?" I asked, but the line was already dead.

Grace came back to the table just then, but there was no time to quiz her. I explained our plan, then dashed through the convention hall toward the hotel. As I passed the phony phone booth and thought of the Urbans, I crossed my fingers and wished really hard that whatever Sybil had left for her attorney would serve as a big neon sign pointing directly at them.

I stepped off the elevator onto the fourth floor and looked both ways, trying to remember which way we'd turned before. The hallway stretched way down to the left and was empty except for a cleaning cart at the far end. To the right the hallway wasn't as long, and turned a corner. I finally gave up, checked the big brass sign, and headed right.

When I rounded the corner I was surprised to see Marco striding toward me. Behind him, a cleaning cart filled with towels, sheets, and other supplies stood in front of an open door directly across from the door marked with yellow police tape. Marco motioned for me to back up, and in my haste to comply, I nearly tripped over a room-service tray someone had placed on the floor against the wall. Nothing like almost drawing attention to myself.

"Why aren't you in Sybil's suite?" I whispered as we moved back into the main hallway.

"There's been a hitch."

"What happened?"

"I couldn't get inside." He didn't elaborate, but by the frustrated frown on his face I had a feeling his Salvare charm had failed to work its magic.

He said close to my ear, "There's a housekeeper cleaning at the other end. Let's head that way. Maybe I'll have more luck with her."

At the far end of the hall we stopped beside the cleaning cart. "What's the plan?" I whispered. "A little Salvare magic or something more mundane, like picking her pocket?"

"Watch and learn, Sunshine."

That phrase was really getting on my nerves.

Pausing outside the door to give me a thumbs-up, he strode into the room. I crept as close as I dared, trying to hear what Marco was saying, but I could make out only his low murmurs, then a high voice speaking some very rapid Spanish, followed by more low murmurs followed by faster, and now angrier, Spanish.

A moment later Marco came striding out of the room, passed me by, and kept going, so I hurried after him. He didn't stop until he had gone past the elevator bank to the corner before the short hallway, where he began to pace back and forth, glowering.

"That magic just ain't happening today, is it, Houdini?" I said, trying to keep a serious face. He cast me a look that said, *Not funny.*

I studied my fingernails. "You might actually have to steal a master key card."

"Can't. The cards are kept on chains hooked onto their belts."

No Salvare charm and no key card? No good. How the heck were we going to get into the suite? I peered around the corner and noticed that the cleaning cart was now farther down the hallway. The maid had moved on to the next room.

Marco sighed in frustration. "Let's go. We're going to have to wait until Crawford can get Sybil's belongings."

"That could take days, Marco. We've got to know what those belongings are now."

"What do you want me to do? Scale the building and break a window? I wasn't able to talk my way in or bribe my way in, and I can't get the key card off the chain unless I bring a pair of bolt cutters, and the maid might catch on if I tried that. There's nothing left to do other than break down the door, and I think someone might notice that, too. So we'll have to wait."

"So you're just going to give up?"

"We. Can't. Get. Into. The. Room," he said slowly, as though I just wasn't getting it, a sure sign he was *mega*frustrated. "Come on. Let's get out of here."

"Wait a minute." I peered around the corner again, thinking hard. Was there any way to convince the maid to let me into a room that wasn't mine? What if it *was* my room? What if I'd locked myself out?

Ha. I had it. I turned back to Marco. "I can get in."

He crossed his arms and gazed at me skeptically. "How?"

I drew a square in the air and pretended to hand it to him. "Here's a box. Think outside it. And I'll need five bucks. I left my purse at the booth." I held out my palm.

"I already tried bribery," he said, reaching for his wallet.

"I'm not going to bribe her."

He handed me a five-dollar bill. "Then, what's the plan?"

Boy, was I hoping he'd ask that. With a sly smile I tucked the bill into my pants pocket. "Watch and learn, Houdini."

Chapter Fourteen

I took off my boots and shoved them into Marco's arms, then took the clip out of my hair, bent over at the waist, and ran my fingers through my blunt bob, shaking my head until my locks looked like a pile of red straw. I stood up to brush the hair from my eyes and said to Marco, "You'll need to stay out of sight. Oh, and make sure you don't draw attention to yourself."

He glowered at me, but I merely smiled sweetly and stepped around the corner. Good thing he couldn't see me now, because I was sporting quite the smug grin. It felt glorious to be the one giving the orders for a change.

I picked up the room-service tray and walked up the hallway, placing it to the side of Sybil's door. Next, I carefully pulled off a strip of yellow police tape and placed it in the same position across the door of the room next to hers. I did the same with the second strip, crossing my fingers that the busy housekeeping staff hadn't paid close attention to which room had been sealed off. I was also hoping that the occupant of the other suite wouldn't return to find his door sealed.

Okay, Abby, you're on.

I took a few quick breaths, put on a worried expression, then hurried to the open doorway, where I saw a thirtysomething Hispanic woman in a gray dress and white apron vacuuming beside the bed. "Hello?" I called frantically, knocking on the door. "Excuse me?"

The woman glanced over her shoulder, saw me, and shut off her vacuum. "Jes? May I help jou?"

"Oh, I truly hope so. I came outside to set my food tray in the hallway, and the door shut behind me. I feel like such an idiot. My key card is in the room, and look at me. I haven't fixed my hair yet, and I don't even have my shoes on—and I'm supposed to be at a business meeting in ten minutes. I haven't even started to dress for it. I really don't want to go down to the lobby looking like this. Would you mind letting me in? There's a five-dollar tip in it for you as soon as I can get to my purse."

The maid glanced at my hair, then at my feet, then left her vacuum cleaner so she could walk over to the doorway to peer down the hall. I followed close behind, watching as a perplexed look flashed across her face when she spotted the tray on the floor outside Sybil's room. What if she had a better memory than I thought? What if my ruse didn't work?

I tapped the face of my watch, hoping to put some pressure on her. "Twelve twenty? There's no way I'll make the meeting on time now. I can't believe my door shut behind me. That will teach me to order room service on a busy day. You know, they really should make these doors with some kind of safety on them. I'll bet this happens a lot, doesn't it?"

At that the maid relented. She pulled the chained key card from her pocket, walked to Sybil's door, ran the card into the slot, and turned the handle. "There jou go."

"Thank you so much!" I gushed, stepping inside. "I'll be right back with your tip."

I made sure she heard me open the closet door just inside the short hallway so she'd think I was retrieving my purse. But when I glanced up, two human heads were staring down at me from the closet shelf overhead.

I clapped a hand over my mouth to squelch a yelp of surprise. Once my heart started beating again, I realized that they weren't human at all, but dummy heads in wigs and makeup. Sybil must have kept them as spares for her cosmetics display.

Quickly, I shut the closet, pulled Marco's five out of my pocket, then stepped back outside and handed it to the maid. "Thank you again. You're so kind."

"Jou're welcome," she said with a big smile, and went back to finish her vacuuming.

I held the door open and a minute later Marco slipped inside. I shut and locked it, then turned to give him a curtsy. "Hold your applause, please."

He rolled his eyes in mock exasperation as he handed me my boots. "I suppose I'll have to live with this for the next hundred years."

"At least that long. Okay, what should we do first?"

"Set your cell phone to vibrate."

While I did that, Marco pulled two sets of latex gloves out of his jacket pocket and handed me a pair. "We don't want to leave fingerprints."

"You carry gloves with you?"

His expression said, *I'm a PI. Do you really need to ask?*

"What are we going to do about my fingerprints on the yellow tape and the closet door—and the door lock?"

"We'll have to remember to smudge them all when we leave."

"So?" I said as I tugged the stretchy material over my hands. "Did I do good? I'm not feeling the love yet."

"You did great, Sunshine. Smart thinking."

It wasn't as satisfying as a really hot kiss, but it would do for now.

Marco turned to give the suite a visual scan. From where we stood we could see the sitting room, a small space furnished with a beige tweed love seat and matching chair, end tables and a tall armoire in cherry wood, and a table and four chairs in front of a window that looked out on the woods behind the hotel.

"Okay, let's do this quickly and get out of here," Marco said. "I'll take the closet and sitting room. You check the bedroom and bathroom."

"Gotcha." As I started for the bedroom, I called, "I wish I knew what we were looking for."

"Probably an envelope or a wrapped package."

I heard him open the closet door and suddenly remembered the dummy heads. "Wait, Marco! There are—"

"Shit!"

Too late. I peered around the corner at him. "I see you found the heads."

"Thanks for the warning."

While he pulled out two large, rolling garment bags, I headed for the bedroom, where I paused to take stock. There was a king-size bed covered by a floral-patterned bedspread, two cherry nightstands, another cherry armoire opposite the bed, and a doorway leading to a bathroom. On the bed was a large leather purse, which I immediately opened, but all that was inside was a wallet with credit cards and money intact, lipstick, a pack of tissues, breath spray, and a lint-covered cough drop.

I looked under and behind each piece of furniture,

then opened the drawer of the nearest nightstand and found the usual writing tablet, spare pen, hotel brochure, Yellow Pages phone book, and green Gideon Bible. The other nightstand held a similar selection. The armoire contained a television, a keypad, a game controller, a VCR/DVD player, and three drawers. I pulled the television out far enough to look behind it, then lifted the electronic equipment to glance beneath.

In the first drawer I found a bunch of brochures advertising Sybil's cosmetic line and a number of small shiny black cardboard boxes imprinted with her red rose logo, all scattered across the bottom. Because I wasn't certain what I was looking for, I opened each box, but all they held were various types of makeup, and I was pretty sure she wouldn't be giving that to Crawford.

The second drawer contained at least a dozen pairs of black lace panties, black push-up bras, garter belts, several black teddies, and a stack of unopened packages of fishnet stockings, all jumbled as though she had been rooting through them. I doubted any of those items were for Crawford, either. The third drawer was also in disarray, holding what appeared to be workout clothes, exercise bands, and a purple yoga mat.

"Nothing in the garment bags," Marco called.

"Nothing in the bedroom, either."

Next I headed to the bathroom and felt inside for a light switch, turning on a row of bright bulbs over the mirrored wall above the sink and marble countertop. I looked over the items on the counter—the usual assortment of lotions and mouthwash—and spotted a perfume bottle with a Gucci label. Unable to resist a sniff, I uncapped it, then sprayed a little on my left wrist. Wow. Very tart. That was Sybil's scent, all right. I checked the label to see what it was.

"Envy Me," I read aloud. That figured.

"Are you talking to me?" Marco called.

"No," I called back, catching sight of the messy-haired, freckle-nosed redhead in the mirror. Boy, were those lightbulbs unkind.

I ran my fingers through my tousled strands, trying to tame them into some semblance of a bob, then leaned closer to the mirror to examine my face. Why was I cursed with freckles? It didn't matter how many people told me they were cute, I had never yet met a woman who didn't try to hide them.

I spotted an aluminum fold-out makeup case next to the sink, so I opened it and found an assortment of Sybil's Select cosmetics inside, including bottles of thick, shiny base makeup, containers of loose powder, several shades of creamy blush, tubes of dark lipsticks and lip liners, and various makeup sponges and brushes—but no envelope or package. The only sur-prise in the kit was how untidy the contents were, as though she had rooted through them, too. I was begin-ning to see a theme.

I uncapped a jar of loose powder, and dipped my finger inside to dab some on my nose. "Envy *that,*" I told my doppelgänger.

I looked behind the shower curtain and inside the toilet tank, then headed back to the sitting room. "Find anything?" I asked Marco as he checked the armoire.

"No. Were you talking to yourself in the bathroom?"

"Maybe." I sat down on the love seat and gave him a smile.

"I just wanted to be sure it was you and not those heads in the closet."

"Creepy, aren't they?"

"How about checking under the sofa cushions?"

I got onto my knees and lifted the cushions, then dropped down to feel underneath. I even crawled around behind the love seat to see whether the backing was loose. I checked the chairs next, then stood with a sigh. "Nothing."

Marco closed the doors of the armoire and turned to look at me. "Well, this was a bust."

We plunked down on the love seat and sat there gazing around the room, wondering whether we'd missed anything. Suddenly, Marco sniffed the air. "What's that odor?"

"What kind of odor?"

"Like musky lemon oil." He leaned over to sniff my hair.

"It's not my hair." I held my wrist under his nose. "Is this it?"

He took a whiff and immediately pulled his head back. "What the hell did you put on?"

"Sybil's perfume. Envy Me."

He rubbed his nose as if it burned. "No envy here.

And no envelope or package either, unless we over-looked it."

"Was there a safe in the closet?" I asked.

"Nope."

"Anything other than those heads on the shelf?"

"A steam iron."

"Did you check the pockets of the clothes hanging in the closet?"

"Yep. Did you look under the bed?"

"Sure did. And her drawers and makeup kit and a purse." I paused, thinking about the drawers and makeup kit. "Did Sybil strike you as a sloppy person?"

"I haven't really thought that much about Sybil."

"Well, think about her now. Wrap dress, perfect hair, clipboard, schedules. I see her as extremely well orga-nized, yet her things were all jumbled together in the drawers. Even her makeup kit was messy. That raises a red flag in my mind."

"The police went through everything. They're noto-rious for leaving a mess."

It was plausible. I ran my heel over a stain in the rug. "Could there be anything hidden under the carpets? Any loose corners that could have been pulled up?"

"I didn't see any telltale bubble in the carpet."

I hurried back to the bedroom to check there, even dropping onto all fours to peer beneath the bed. "Nothing," I said, returning to sit beside Marco.

"That's it, then," he said, slapping his knees. "Sybil didn't leave Rex's package here."

"Where else would it be? At her booth? She wouldn't leave anything there that she wanted to protect. She didn't give them to the hotel for safekeeping, either, so they have to be here. We're just not looking in the right place."

Marco rubbed his eyes. "Could she have taken it with her to the storage room?"

"For her rendezvous with one of the Urbans? Not on your life."

"You're sure about that?"

"Women know these things, Marco."

He glanced at me but didn't argue. "What about her car? If she drove here, the package could be in the trunk."

"I don't think she'd take that risk. A thief could break into her car."

Marco got up and pulled out his phone.

"Who are you calling?"

"Someone who'll know." He walked over to the window to talk.

Marco had never revealed the name of his police source to me, and I never asked because I knew it would be pointless. He wouldn't dream of putting his source in jeopardy. A few minutes later, he shut the phone and came back. "No car. She hired a limo."

I rubbed my temples, trying to stimulate some thought. "Okay, if I were Sybil, where would I hide important items?"

Marco drew a square with his fingers and pretended

to hand it to me. "Here's your box back if you want to think outside it."

Funny man.

I got up and opened the closet for another look, craning my neck to see the shelf above the clothes rod. "Marco, would you get those heads down for me?"

We each took one, removing the wigs and checking to see whether the stands were hollow, but that idea was a bust, too—not to be punny or anything.

"Okay, let's think about this," I said. "Sybil brought these mysterious belongings with her when she came to the hotel, which means she would have carried them into this suite either in her purse or her bags, and I checked her purse. We know nothing was left in a car or at the front desk, and we've searched these rooms thoroughly. So maybe we should check the garment bags again."

I pulled out one of Sybil's bags, zipped it open, and found a removable center lining that had multiple compartments in it, but all were empty. There was another pocket on the outside of the case, but it contained only more of her cosmetic brochures. "I feel something in here," I said, pressing my palm against the back of the suitcase.

"That's the compartment for the retractable handle."

"Is there a way to get to it?"

Marco crouched beside me. "There's a way in through the main compartment. I checked both of them already, but we can try again."

Marco reached for the other bag and unzipped it,

while I spread my bag flat on the floor, then removed the middle lining. Beneath that was a smaller, snap-out compartment that looked like it had been divided to hold shoes. I removed it, leaving only the heavy interior lining attached to the garment bag frame. "Are you sure there's a way to get to the handle?"

"Pull up on the corner of the lining at the bottom of the case. It's held to the frame by Velcro."

I did as he suggested, and sure enough, the Velcro peeled apart. I reached a hand inside, but all I felt was the metal telescoping handle. *Damn.*

"Well, it was worth a try," I said, pressing the Velcro together.

"I've got something." Marco's hand was inside the other bag's handle compartment.

I crawled over beside him, watching anxiously as he removed a bulky manila envelope. He turned the envelope over, and we saw a pink sticky note stuck to it with *REX* written on it in big letters. Underneath was written, *Hold for me. Do not open. Thx, S.*

"That's it!" I cried. "We found it."

Marco ran his fingers across the envelope, pressing against it to bring forth the outline of a long, rectangular box. "It feels like a videotape." He tried to lift the end flap, but it was glued tight. "We'll have to steam it."

"Shouldn't Crawford be the one to open it?" I asked as he handed the envelope to me so he could put the garment bag back together.

"Once we hand it over, there's no guarantee he'll

share it with us. He could very easily change his mind after he sees what's inside."

"But you shook on it."

Marco rolled the bag into the closet. "He's a lawyer. Do I need to say more?"

"Hand me the steam iron."

Marco glanced at his watch. "Forget it. We've been here too long as it is, and I need to get down to the security manager's office before he leaves for lunch. We can open the envelope afterward."

"Marco, wait," I said as he tucked the package under his arm and started for the door. "If we take it out of the room, we'll be guilty of tampering with evidence." It was one of the lessons that had stuck with me from my law studies.

"Sunshine, we've already broken into Sybil's room. Do you really think that matters now?"

He did have a point. As Lottie liked to say, in for a dime, in for a dollar. "We'll have to figure out a safe place to open it, then, because we'll need steam and probably a TV and a VCR."

"Leave everything to me. I have a plan."

"You're not going to use your charm again, are you?" I teased.

"I learned my lesson. Will you be able to put the yellow tape back?"

"Piece of cake."

"Don't forget to smudge everything you touched with your bare hands to erase your fingerprints." He gave me a wink, then slipped out of the suite while I closed the remaining garment bag and returned it to the closet. I made sure the bathroom light was out and everything was as we found it; then I put on my boots, opened the door just a slit and peered into the hallway to be sure it was safe. All I needed was for the maid to see me.

At that moment, one of the couples who'd sat at our banquet table, Alicia and Walter Tyler, came around the corner and stopped in front of the door with the yellow tape across it.

"Isn't this our room?" Alicia asked, looking bewildered.

Her husband pulled his key card envelope from his jacket pocket and checked the number. "It's our room all right. What the hell is going on here? Why is there police tape on our door? What kind of hotel are they running here, anyway?"

"Calm down, Walt. There's a housekeeper down the hall. I'll go get her."

"She won't be able to do anything about it." Her husband reached into his suit coat pocket and pulled out his cell phone. "I'm calling the police."

Terrific.

Chapter Fifteen

If I didn't stop that phone call, I'd be caught for sure. Short of wrapping myself up in a sheet and running out of the suite screaming like a banshee, hoping to frighten the people half to death, all I could do was try to send them a telepathic message, not that it had ever worked before. I scrunched my eyes shut and concentrated: *Please don't call the cops please don't call the cops please don't call the cops please—*

"Don't bother phoning the police," Alicia told her husband. "Hotel security will be faster."

My eyes flew open. Wow. That was impressive.

"And just how am I supposed to call hotel security when the phone numbers are in our room?" Walter shot back.

"Will you hush? There's a house phone on the table across from the elevators."

Grumbling as he folded his phone and slipped it into his jacket pocket, Walter followed his wife up the hallway toward the corner. I eased the door shut and stood with my back against it, my heart pounding furiously. Now I had to get the tape off their door and back on this one before they returned. But how would I get away afterward without them seeing me? If someone from security, or the cops, figured out that Sybil's room had been entered, I sure didn't want anyone remembering me up here.

Aha! The stairs. I checked the emergency exit map on the back of the door and located the nearest stairwell, but it was on this side of the bank of elevators. I'd still be in plain view, and the Tylers would surely remember me from the banquet. My red hair was a dead giveaway.

Use your head, Abby. Hurry!

"Easy for you to say," I told that nagging voice in

my ear. I eyed the closet, wondering whether I should just hide until night fell and pray that the cops didn't check the room in the meantime.

Wait. The closet. Sybil's wigs!

I opened the closet door and stretched to reach the high shelf, but I was barely able to touch the base of one of the stands with my fingertips. I grabbed a hanger and used it to scoot the stand to the edge of the shelf, then tipped it over and caught it. I pulled off the stiff wig, then jumped up to shove the stand back onto the shelf.

I held the phony hair with some trepidation—the thought of wearing a deceased woman's wig made me shudder—but there was no time to be squeamish. Scrunching my eyes shut, I whispered, "Forgive me, Sybil." Then I twisted my hair into a bun and tugged the wig on over it.

Using the mirror on the closet door, I adjusted the wig, which was a little too big and nearly hid my eye-brows, then tucked in a few stray strands of red hair. How was *that* for using my head?

I took a deep breath, then opened the door. The hallway was clear, so I dashed to the next door, pulled off one strip of tape and flew back to Sybil's door, stuck it in place, then repeated the process with the second strip. I had barely attached the last end when I heard voices coming my way. Oh, no! There was no time to wipe off my fingerprints. I had to pray that the latex gloves had smudged them for me.

Quickly, I hid my hands behind my back, put my

head down, and strode purposefully forward, rounding the corner just as the Tylers came around it from the other direction. They were still arguing about whether they should have phoned the police, so they barely noticed me as I slipped past. Once out of sight, I ran to the stairway exit, reaching it just as the elevator doors opened and two men stepped out, one the beefy security manager and the other a cop. They were in the midst of a discussion.

"—found a new piece of evidence, so with any luck the investigation should start to fall into place—"

I stopped. A new piece of evidence? In Sybil's case? Wait. I knew that voice.

I darted a glance at the man in uniform. *Crap.* It was Reilly. I grabbed the metal door handle to give it a push and realized I still had on the latex gloves.

I let go of the handle and tucked my hands under my armpits just as he glanced my way. He gave me a cordial nod, and our gazes locked for a split second, just long enough to make him pause—and my insides quake.

Please don't recognize me please don't recognize me please don't recognize me. Using my shoulder, I pushed against the door and let it slam behind me as I sped down the concrete steps to the ground floor. I stopped just before entering the lobby to make sure there weren't any footsteps coming down the stairs after me; then I peeled off the gloves, yanked the wig off my head, rolled the whole works into a furry log, and tucked it under my arm. I walked out into the lobby, made sure none of the hotel guests or staff were paying any attention, and headed for the ladies' room near the bar.

Just my luck—a woman was standing in front of a sink applying lipstick, so I shut myself into a stall, put the toilet lid down, and collapsed onto it, breathing a huge sigh of relief. It was a miracle I'd made my escape without being caught, which just went to prove that I was totally not cut out for espionage work. The CIA had no worries about me ever applying.

I stared at the wig log, wondering how to dispose of it. The toilet? No chance of flushing that sucker. It was bad enough that Reilly was on the fourth floor right now, probably trying to remember where he'd seen my face before. Of all people to get off the elevator at that moment, why did it have to be Reilly?

I closed my eyes, trying to recall the snippet of conversation I'd overheard. Something about finding new evidence. Damn. There was no way I could ask him about it without giving myself away.

I waited until the washroom was empty, then crept out, grabbed a handful of paper towels, and rolled the gloves and wig into them. I stuffed them deep into the waste bin, trying not to gag as I pressed them as far down as they'd go. As I washed my hands, I glanced into the mirror, saw the mess I'd made of my hair, and quickly tamed it with my damp hands.

I checked my watch. Yikes. The memorial service had started ten minutes ago.

I hurried to the mezzanine level, located the Redenbacher meeting room, and quietly opened one of its two rear doors. The room was twice the size of a regular classroom and filled with ten rows of folding chairs. At the front was a podium where a woman was singing, "Be Still My Soul," accompanied by a very somber Angelique on her harp, playing with her eyes shut, her face aimed toward the ceiling. Seated behind the singer was Colonel Billingsworth.

The last four rows were empty, so I sat down on the nearest chair and tried to catch my breath as all kinds of questions raced through my mind. Did Marco, who was supposed to be viewing the security tapes, know the security manager had been called to the fourth floor? Did he know Reilly was there, too? Were they right now at Sybil's door? Would they be able to tell the police tape had been removed and put back? Would anyone realize one of Sybil's wigs was missing? Would the missing wig be discovered when the bathroom trash was emptied? Could they get my DNA from it? And, of course, what kind of jail time was I looking at?

Don't borrow trouble, Abby. Think about why you're here.

Why was I there? Oh, right. To see who wasn't. I scanned the people in the room. Billingsworth and Angelique: present. Urbans: absent. No Chet, either, although that didn't surprise me. Five rows in front of me I spotted Grace with two empty chairs beside her, so while the singer finished her song I crouched low and moved up the side aisle to join her.

"Where were you?" Grace whispered as the colonel stepped up to give his eulogy. "I was beginning to worry."

"I'll tell you later. Did you notice that the Urbans aren't here?"

She nodded, then pressed a fingertip to her lips.

"Friends," the colonel began, "thank you for joining me here today to pay tribute to Sybil Blount, the woman who made our annual convention possible through her organizational talents and persistence"—he paused to rock back on his heels—"and there was no one more persistent than Sybil."

At that there were chuckles from the audience.

"Truthfully, I consider Sybil's passing to be a personal loss because, as many of you know, her husband and I were more than just business partners; we were also brothers in blood, having served together in Vietnam. It was Thaddeus Blount who helped me build this association into the powerful group it is today, but it was Sybil who worked tirelessly behind the scenes—"

Behind the scenes? More like under the covers.

"—so much so, in fact, that I had to consider her a silent partner. . . ."

As the colonel continued his discourse, praising his own accomplishments as much as Sybil's, I glanced around the room and saw others trying to hide yawns. The man in front of me appeared to be nodding off—either that or his toupee was on the move.

As my thoughts wandered, I noticed that an open

casket had been set up in front of the podium as a memorial to Sybil, but unfortunately the only things they had to display were her clipboard propped on a small easel, her red marker, a convention brochure folded back to show a very grainy photo of her, and a shiny aluminum makeup case similar to the one I'd seen in her room, only much larger, probably taken from her booth. The case top had been opened to display the many bottles and containers of her private potions. I was a little disappointed that they hadn't included one of her fishnet stockings.

Grace motioned for me to lean closer. "Are you wearing perfume?"

I nodded, and she gave me a quizzical look. She knew I rarely used fragrances other than a light spritzing of body mist. I didn't like anything interfering with the bright, fresh floral bouquets of my flowers. Plus, I couldn't afford the really nice stuff.

"What kind is it?" she whispered.

"Gucci." I held my wrist to my nose to see whether the scent was as strong as before. Whoa. Was perfume supposed to get stronger as the day went on?

"When did you start wearing Gucci perfume?"

I pointed toward the casket, and Grace's eyebrows pulled together. "It's Sybil's? Where did you find it?"

I shrugged. No sense advertising our little break-and-enter.

"Did you get into her room, then?" Grace whispered.

I held a finger to my lips. I didn't want to take any chances of being overheard.

"Were you able to find the package Sybil left for her solicitor?"

Was Grace missing my signals? I glanced around to be sure no one had taken a seat behind us, then whispered, "It's an envelope. I'll tell you about it later."

My cell phone began to vibrate, so I eased it out of my pocket to check the screen. Blast. It was Reilly. Had he discovered my charade? I quickly slid it back into my pants pocket.

"In closing," the colonel said, "let us bid Sybil a fond farewell as she embarks on her greatest convention, and then let us observe a moment of silence while we remember the woman whose dedication to our association shall always be an inspiration to us all."

The room went absolutely still as Colonel Billingsworth came down from the podium and carefully closed the casket. Then, as everyone rose from their seats, the casket was lifted and carried down the center aisle by six sturdy men in a procession led by the colonel, who marched with the solemn dignity of a grand marshal leading the Veterans' Day parade.

As people gathered in the main hall outside the room to talk, Grace pulled me off to the side. "You found an envelope containing Sybil's belongings?"

"Yes, but we don't know what's in it yet because it was sealed. It felt like a—"

By the way Grace shifted her gaze, I knew someone was near enough to overhear. Looking over my head, she said, "What a lovely eulogy, Walker. You did a smashing job on such short notice."

186

I turned as the colonel moved into our circle, beaming at her. "Thank you, dear lady." He gave me a polite nod, but I could tell his focus was on Grace. "The service went well, I thought."

"And the music was lovely, too," Grace said, patting his arm. "Excellent choice."

Feeling as though I should contribute something to the conversation, I said, "That Angelique really knows how to pluck a harp, doesn't she?" At Grace's pained expression, I threw in, "We're fortunate to have her here—with her harp—plucking."

Grace rolled her eyes.

"Yes, we are fortunate, indeed," the colonel said. "Angelique has been so overwrought since Sybil's death that I was astounded she managed to hold herself together today. It was actually her idea to participate in the service. She felt quite strongly about it. Angelique truly admired Sybil."

He leaned closer to say in a low voice, "And, frankly, Sybil wasn't someone people usually admired. In fact, she was intensely disliked by the majority of our members. But there's no accounting for taste, is there?"

I was amazed that the colonel would admit such a thing about his friend's wife, especially after the glowing eulogy he gave Sybil. It made me think he might be persuaded to share what he knew about Sybil's behavior with us.

"If I might ask, colonel," I said, "did Sybil strike you as the type to get involved in anything illegal?"

He gave me a stunned look. "Why would you ask me that?"

"Well, you were a friend of her husband's, so I thought you might have an opinion."

The colonel turned beet red as he blustered, "It's true I was Thaddeus's friend, but as far as having any knowledge of Sybil's activities, legal or otherwise, that isn't something Thad would have discussed with me."

Before I had a chance to press further, Grace switched the subject back so smoothly that it was as though I'd never opened my mouth. "I believe it's not so much admiration that is causing Angelique's distress as it is a sense of responsibility. After all, she did find Sybil's body, didn't she? Now, perhaps we should move on to a more pleasant topic. Will you be staying until five o'clock today, Walker?"

"I'll be here," he replied eagerly, "long after everyone else has packed up, no doubt, now that I've assumed the chairperson's duties."

"How very noble of you, Walker," Grace said, giving him a smile. "Would you be available to have a cup of coffee with me sometime this afternoon?"

The colonel straightened his tie. "I'd be delighted to join you, Grace."

"Shall we say Starbucks in fifteen minutes, then?"

My cell phone began to vibrate, so I checked the screen. *Rats!* Reilly again. "Excuse me," I said to Grace and the colonel, and stepped away to answer it.

Trying my best to sound virtuous, I said, "Hey, Sarge. What's up?"

"Abby, where are you?"

That is a question most often asked if the other person thinks you are somewhere you shouldn't be, like near a suite that has been broken into. Quickly, I cupped my hand over the phone so he'd think I was in a quiet room. "At Sybil's memorial service," I whispered.

"Were you up on the fourth floor of the hotel about half an hour ago?"

I checked my watch. Whew. Saved by a technicality. Half an hour ago I was tearing down the stairs *from* the fourth floor. "Nope," I whispered. "Wasn't me. Why?"

"I'm on the fourth floor right now, looking into a matter for some hotel guests who say there was yellow crime-scene tape across their door, and now it's back on the door next to theirs, which happens to be the vic's suite. Any idea how that happened?"

"Um, right off the top of my head I'd want to know if they'd been drinking."

"They haven't been drinking," he growled.

"Then I'm fresh out of ideas. Sorry."

"Here's the thing. I've got a witness from a room up the hallway who described you perfectly, down to your freckles. Seems she heard voices and looked out of the peephole on her hotel room door and saw a shoeless redhead talking to one of the housekeepers. And guess where they were standing? Right in front of the vic's suite."

"I hate to disappoint you, Reilly, but my feet are

covered. Must be a case of mistaken identity."

"Yeah, right, like there are other short, freckle-faced redheads running around here."

"They say everyone has a double. What are the odds of my double turning up here at the same time as me? Listen, Reilly, the service is about to end, so I've got to hang up now." I shut the phone and breathed a sigh of relief. It wouldn't hold him off forever, but it would stall him for awhile.

I joined Grace just as the colonel said to her, "I'll see you soon," and wiggled his eyebrows as though she'd just set up a daring rendezvous.

"Shall we head back to our booth, then?" Grace said to me. "Lottie's been by herself far too long. She'll be wanting a little stretch now, won't she? Who rang your mobile?"

"Sgt. Reilly. Not important. Why did you change the subject after I asked the colonel about Sybil?"

"I could see how uncomfortable the topic made him. And as long as we're discussing the matter, why did you ask him if he knew whether Sybil had been involved in something illegal?"

"Because the colonel was close to Sybil's husband. It was a long shot, but I figured if there was anything fishy going on in her life, her husband might have known about it and confided in his army buddy. I guess men just aren't as chatty as women."

"What gave you the idea she might be involved in something illegal in the first place?"

"In her phone message to Crawford she said she

wanted him to take possession of certain belongings because she couldn't go to the police. Doesn't that sound like she had something illegal in her possession?"

Grace's forehead wrinkled as she pondered the possibility. "I see."

We entered the lobby and found it jammed with people checking out, so we had to pause our conversation as we wove through the crowd and headed up the corridor that connected the two buildings. We kept going until we reached the exhibition hall, but there our path was blocked by the huge crowd at Chet Sunday's *Make It Easy* set.

On one end of the stage, Chet was seated behind a table autographing glossies of himself for a long line of women. On the other end of the stage, representatives from Habitation Station, wearing neon green vests and matching baseball caps, were handing out neon green tape measures to promote their casket kits to the men who had taken a pass on the autograph queue.

"I'm surprised Chet Sunday didn't attend the memorial service," Grace remarked as we tried to squeeze past. "I thought I heard that he came here as a favor to Sybil."

"That's what Sybil wanted people to think. I had a little chat with Chet earlier, and he set me straight. The truth is, she paid him to be here."

"Really? Habitation Station didn't pay him?"

"They pay him for ten appearances a year, and this isn't one of them."

"A busy television personality wouldn't come cheaply, would he? How much do you think it took to buy his appearance for two days?"

"I don't have any idea," I said as we broke free of the crowd and started toward aisle two, which was wide open. Not a shopper or browser in sight. The convention seemed to be waning quickly. I had to hope the Urbans didn't pack up and take off before I had a chance to prove their involvement in Sybil's death.

"It seems odd that Sybil would pay for Chet to appear here," Grace said. "Conventions are expensive to put on. Budgeting in a television personality would be costly, and from what I've learned about Sybil, she was remarkably frugal."

"True, but scoring Chet's appearance was a feather in Sybil's cap. It made her look important, and she was all about looking important. Maybe she paid him out of her own pocket so his appearance fee wouldn't show up in the convention's records. Besides, Chet wouldn't have done something as reckless as putting Sybil's clothes on that dummy. As far as I'm concerned, Chet is off the list."

"Perhaps you're right." Grace glanced at the watch pinned to her bodice and clucked her tongue. "Oh, dear. I should have made my coffee date in half an hour instead of fifteen minutes."

"You realize the colonel has a crush on you, right?"

"I sincerely hope so. I've certainly tried my best to foster it."

"Grace!"

"Heavens, dear, don't look so shocked. It's for our investigation."

"*Our* investigation?"

"You don't mind my poking around, do you? Two brains are better than one, as the saying goes—or three brains, in this case. And as I explained before, Delilah is my friend, too. I certainly don't want to see her charged with murder."

"I appreciate your help, Grace, but Marco and I are pretty good at finding killers. Remember Snuggles the Clown? Remember the Jack-in-the-Pulpit murder? Or the time you were attacked at your house in your Elvis room?"

"In other words," Grace said with a wounded sniff, "you prefer to handle this investigation yourselves."

"You know I love you, Grace, and always appreciate your help, but you have to admit we do have more experience." Was I starting to sound like Marco?

"Have the two of you found anything to clear Delilah?"

"Well, no, not yet, but we haven't opened the envelope."

"Do you have any idea what's inside?"

"Possibly a videotape."

"I see. And if this videotape fails to deliver your suspect, the convention will be over in a few short hours and all your witnesses and suspects will be gone. What then?"

I scratched my nose. What then, indeed?

Grace studied me with a shrewd eye as we drew near our booth. "You're not afraid I'll find the killer before you, are you?"

"What? No! This isn't a contest."

"Then what is your problem, dear?"

What *was* my problem?

The best defense is a good offense, my dad always told me. "Why don't you tell me what *your* investigation has turned up so far, Grace."

"I'm glad you asked. For beginners, after spending more than an hour with Angelique, I can earnestly say I don't believe that young lady had anything to do with Sybil's death other than discovering her body. Apparently Angelique had overheard Sybil arranging to meet someone there before the banquet, and when Sybil failed to show after a reasonable amount of time, Angelique ran straight to the storage room. The door was shut and no light showed beneath, but then she spied a red rose petal on the floor and thought she detected Sybil's perfume, so she decided to investigate. She firmly believes that the rose Sybil wore yesterday is still in the killer's possession."

"Did you explain that whoever killed Sybil isn't likely to keep the rose because it would be evidence?"

"It would have been a waste of time. Angelique's mind is made up, and I think we can agree that she's rather eccentric."

"Is that how you explain those weird musical terms she uses?"

"Angelique thinks in those terms, dear. She sees

people as a collection of notes, each person giving out different vibrations—some gentle, some fierce, some dull, some lively."

"Some short and disconnected."

"Yes, well, *que será, será.*"

What will be, will be. That was Grace's way of telling me to get over it.

"Angelique was absolutely fascinated by Sybil's aura," Grace continued. "She said Sybil was a unique individual with a dark, narcissistic dissonance the likes of which she'd never encountered before. Angelique had no desire to hasten her death. Quite the contrary. She felt compelled to study Sybil and truly wanted to get to know her better."

"Did you ask why she had her tape recorder out if it was evident that Sybil was dead?"

"First, you must understand that the portable tape recorder goes wherever Angelique goes. It's always in her bag, charged and ready to record. She gave me the name of a woman in her employ who can verify that. When Angelique opened the lid and saw Sybil's blue lips, she pulled out her mobile phone to call for a medic, then removed her tape recorder in the hope that Sybil's soul hadn't yet left the body. Unfortunately, it was too late, and poor Angelique was so distraught by the thought that if she'd been there sooner she might have prevented Sybil's death that she collapsed onto the floor in a state of shock. Having lost many that were dear to me, I can distinguish genuine grief from a phony act in a second, and I say with absolute sincerity that Angelique is genuinely grief stricken. I think we can safely rule her out as a suspect."

"So Angelique is out, and Chet is out. That leaves us with the Urbans—who, by the way, were my original suspects. I'm glad you agree with me on that, Grace."

"Actually, there's someone else I'd like to investigate."

"Please don't say Eli Cotton."

"Goodness no, the man's a flake. His beef is with the morticians' association, not with any one individual."

Grace had certainly been thinking a lot about this case. "Who, then?"

"Will you look at that?" She pointed to our booth, where we could see Lottie sitting in a folding chair with her feet propped up on the table, her head drooped to one side, and her mouth open. She was snoring loudly.

"Good thing we have no customers," Grace said, hurrying up to our table.

She started to reach across to wake Lottie, but I caught her sleeve. "You didn't tell me who you're going to investigate."

"Didn't I? It's Walker Billingsworth, of course."

I gaped at her. "The colonel?"

Lottie woke with a snort, and her head snapped up. "I'll have some chicken." She glanced at us in confusion. "What? Didn't one of you just say you were going to order Kentucky Fried Chicken?"

Grace sighed. "I'll be at Starbucks if you need me."

"I'll be right back," I said to Lottie, and hurried after

Grace. "You think the colonel is involved in Sybil's death?"

She motioned for me to follow her. We stood against the back wall, well away from people heading toward the food court. "Let me ask you something, dear. These premonitions you get—you call them gut feelings—do they hit you right here?" She put the tip of her finger against her abdomen, just below her rib cage.

"That's the spot."

"Yes, I thought so."

"But, Grace, the *colonel?* The Vietnam war hero?"

"Walker is not a colonel, Abby. He's an impostor."

Chapter Sixteen

What are you saying, Grace? The colonel—er, Walker—lied about Vietnam?"

"He didn't lie about serving in Vietnam. You see, this all came about because of my, well, *gut* feeling, so I stopped at the Internet café to do some research and discovered that he never went above the rank of captain."

"It's not unheard of for former military men to call themselves colonels. You can't accuse a man of murder because of that."

"I'm not accusing, only questioning. There's a big difference. We cannot dismiss the fact that Walker lied about his rank. If he lied about that, he could well have lied about other things, such as where he was at the time of the murder. As Aristotle once said, 'Liars when they speak the truth are not believed.' "

"But I saw the colonel—er, Walker—oh, hell, the colonel—at the banquet. He gave the opening remarks. And he arrived at the storage room *after* Marco and I did."

"What time did Walker give his remarks?"

I had to think back. "Maybe seven twenty? Okay, I see where you're going with this. He could have killed Sybil before the banquet. But why? He had to have a motive. And what about her clothes being on the dummy? That prank was definitely not the colonel's style."

"Didn't you tell me that Walker barely tolerates the Urban twins? And that he'd love nothing more than to have them banned from future conventions? What better way to get rid of them once and for all than to manipulate events so that they're charged with a crime? It's possible Angelique wasn't the only one who heard Sybil setting up her tryst. Perhaps Walker saw an opportunity to make those two young men appear to be culprits, and he took it."

"But to murder someone just to get the Urbans banned from conventions? That's pretty extreme, Grace. Plus, it would take very careful planning."

"He was a leader in Vietnam, dear. Battle strategies, and all that. Believe me, Abby, I am hoping for nothing more than to find out that Walker is perfectly innocent, but until I know, I can't rule him out."

"I still don't buy it. Sybil's husband was the

colonel's friend. Do you honestly think he would kill his friend's wife as revenge against two young jerks who liked to pull pranks? Remember how he praised Sybil in his eulogy?"

" 'False words are not only evil in themselves, but they infect the soul with evil.' Those were Plato's thoughts on the subject, and that's all I have to say until I know more."

My phone began to ring, so Grace said, "You get that, and I'll be off, then."

"Wait a minute, Grace." I checked the screen to make sure it wasn't Reilly calling again, then flipped it open and heard Marco grumble, "One hour of scanning a whole day's worth of videotapes and my eyes are killing me. I'm just leaving the security manager's office now."

"Hold on a minute." I held my hand over the phone and said to Grace, "Be careful. Don't let the colonel know what you're up to. And remember not to—"

"I'm not a fool, dear, but thank you for your concern."

I watched her go, then remembered Marco on the line. "Sorry. I was trying to talk Grace out of playing detective."

"Why do you want to talk her out of it?"

"Because *we're* working on the murder."

"Sunshine, at this stage of the game, the more the merrier."

"But she doesn't have our experience."

"You don't have *my* experience. Has that ever stopped you?"

"Oh, sure, like you've never tried to talk me out of it."

Marco didn't like to argue with me—or debate, as I preferred to call it. Unlike me, who could debate for hours. So he simply changed the subject. "Do you want to hear what was on the security video?"

"Sure. Is it anything that will help Delilah?"

"We'll talk about that afterward."

That didn't sound good.

"The videotape of the lounge area showed one of the Urbans seated at the bar from six oh-three p.m. until six forty-seven p.m. He was dressed in a dark suit and tie with neatly combed hair, but there's no way to tell which twin it was. If you'll remember back to the banquet, both of them wore dark suits."

"That would be the one time this entire weekend that Jess's hair was combed. His tongue stud would be a dead giveaway, but I don't suppose he opened his mouth wide enough for a view of that."

"There are no close-ups of his mouth at all. The angle is wrong, and the tape wasn't that clear anyway. But here's the bigger problem. I just got off the phone with my source at the police station and found out that Ross claimed *he* was at the bar during that time. He swears that's him on the videotape, not Jess."

"They're both using the same alibi?"

"You've got it. And since the cops can't tell which one of them was actually there, without hard evidence to prove otherwise, they're both off the hook."

"No way."

"I'm afraid so. Using the same alibi is clever—almost too clever for Ross and Jess. I'm betting their father's lawyer has been advising them."

"Great. Now, how are we going to find out which one is telling the truth?"

"Get one of them to point the finger at the other."

"I tried that with Jess, but he wouldn't crack. If their lawyer is advising them, I'll bet Ross has been told not to talk, too."

"Then we better hope that whatever is in the envelope does the finger-pointing for us."

"What if it doesn't, Marco? What if all we find inside is a watch?"

"It's not going to be a watch. Remember, whatever it is, Sybil couldn't go to the police with it."

"Maybe it's a stolen watch, then. You know what I mean. What are we going to do if what we find inside is totally useless?"

"Let's just take it one step at a time. Hold on a minute. I'm cutting through a crowd by Chet Sunday's set."

I glanced down the back of the hall, where I could see round tables and chairs set up for Starbucks's customers. Grace and the colonel were seated at one.

"Okay, I can talk now," Marco said. "And by the way, the security video confirmed that Chet was with Sybil in the lounge area at a little past noon, which is approximately the time we saw them leave his set together."

"That matches what he told me."

"Did he also tell you he and Sybil took the elevator to the fourth floor of the hotel afterward?"

"No way. Were they caught on camera?"

"They sure were. The elevator ride could be a coincidence, but I wouldn't cross him off the list yet."

"Still, I can't see him putting Sybil's clothes on the dummy. It's too childish. And honestly, Marco, would a popular, good-looking TV personality who plays up his wholesome image really take a chance of being seen going into Sybil's suite?"

"Maybe she paid him for that appearance, too."

"If he came for the money and the exposure, that would cover both, wouldn't it?" I had a sudden picture of Sybil and Chet getting horizontal in her bedroom and couldn't help but snicker. "I wonder if Chet keeps his tool belt on?"

"Abby, stick to the subject."

I started to giggle. "Tape measure, anyone?"

"Will you stop that?" he asked, trying not to laugh himself.

"Sorry. I think it's stress related. But seriously, Marco, if Sybil paid Chet for his, well, appearances, then what's his motive?"

Marco was stumped, and whenever that happened, he didn't waste time pondering. He simply moved on. "I picked up a few other details from my source. The preliminary autopsy report showed that Sybil died between six and seven o'clock, most likely around six thirty. The cause was asphyxiation, and the only identifiable fingerprints were Angelique's, which were found on the outside doorknob and the casket lid. The detectives are attributing that to her opening it. All of the other surfaces they tested either had been wiped clean or were smudged with too many prints to get clear impressions."

"Someone wiped the surfaces? That doesn't sound like a prank that went wrong. I hate to sound supportive of my main suspects, but if the Urbans had shut Sybil inside as a joke, they wouldn't have bothered to wipe off the fingerprints."

"Unless they wanted her to die."

"Premeditated murder? I hadn't thought of that. Maybe the prank they pulled on me was for practice."

"At any rate," Marco said dryly, not buying my theory, "the police investigators are still combing through the evidence, hoping to find a hair or something to get some DNA. It doesn't appear that whoever met Sybil in the storage room stayed long enough for a tryst. No evidence was found on or inside her body."

"So no rockets went off for the mystery man?"

"If one lifted off, it didn't touch down; otherwise, the cops would have found DNA. There were also bruise marks in the shape of hands on Sybil's chest, most likely male, probably made when the killer pushed her down inside the casket to shut the lid."

"That would definitely eliminate Angelique, with her tiny hands." Which meant that Grace had figured that one correctly. Score one for Grace.

"That's what the detectives have decided. She's out

of the running. But here's the bad news. They won't rule out Delilah."

"But you said the handprints were male."

"*Most likely.* Delilah is a strong woman, with strong hands. The cops have photographed the marks and are going to try to match them to her handprints."

"That's still pretty flimsy as far as evidence goes. I mean, no fingerprints, no DNA—"

"Maybe DNA."

I had a sudden flutter of anxiety. "Maybe?"

"The cops recovered a smock that Delilah identified as the one she'd used to protect her dress when she went to the storage room to fix her contest entry."

"But Delilah freely admitted she was there. So big deal if her smock was there, too."

"That's the tricky part. She stated that she folded the smock and left it on a shelf by the door. But the cops found it in a trash can outside the building near the back exit."

"So it ended up in a trash can. That's not so bad."

"There was a red rose rolled up inside it."

Chapter Seventeen

That anxious flutter turned into a rapid pounding. "Are the cops sure it was Sybil's rose?"

"They're checking her DNA against epithelials from the stem. The new theory is that Delilah wiped off her fingerprints with the smock, then hid the rose inside and disposed of both."

"That's crazy. Delilah wouldn't have taken Sybil's rose, and she certainly wouldn't have put it in her own smock to get rid of it. She'd be incriminating herself."

"Look at it from the detectives' point of view, Sunshine. If Delilah shut Sybil in the coffin, then she'd be in a hurry to hide or clean anything she handled and get out of the storage room before she was discovered. So she would use whatever was handy—her own smock, if necessary—then ditch it outside the building, where, hopefully, it wouldn't be found."

"Has anyone thought of the possibility that Delilah was set up?"

"How would the killer know that Delilah would be in the storage room at six o'clock? Or that she would leave her smock there? I think Sybil's death was a spur-of-the-moment decision. Someone shoved her down inside the casket and slammed the lid, then quickly looked for a way to cover his tracks."

"I hate to say this again, but the way you describe it, I sure don't see it as an Urban prank. Then again, who else would dress the dummy in Sybil's clothing?"

"Someone who wanted the cops to think it was the Urbans."

"Who but Ross and Jess would take the chance of being caught?"

"Hold on a minute. I'm at the back exit. I'm going outside to take a look at something."

While I waited for Marco to return, I paced down to aisle one and back, nervously glancing at my watch. The afternoon was passing quickly, and we still had no solid leads. I couldn't help but worry that the contents of the envelope would produce a dead end.

I turned around to see whether Grace was still having coffee with the colonel, but their table was empty. I turned to glance at our booth, but only Lottie was there. Where had Grace gone?

"Well, that answers my question," Marco said. "There's one video I wasn't able to view because I ran out of time. It's from a camera positioned at the back exit that I was hoping could show us who put the smock in the trash can. But I just checked and the trash can is around the corner. There's no way the camera could view it."

"Okay, now I'm really worried, Marco. If whatever is inside that envelope doesn't point to someone besides Delilah, what are we going to do?"

"Don't panic yet. The video of the back exit will still show who used that door yesterday evening. The only problem is that I can't view that video until the manager takes his dinner break."

"That still won't help Delilah. She left the building to go out to the van for more glue, remember? She'll be on the tape."

"And so will everyone else who used the door. Hopefully one of the Urbans will show up on it."

"And if they don't?"

"Let's not cross that bridge yet."

"We'd better open the envelope soon, Marco. It's already after two o'clock."

"How about in five minutes?"

"That works for me. Where are you now?"

"Turn around."

I swung around and there at the Starbucks counter was Marco, in his black leather jacket, snug blue jeans, and black boots, that gorgeous male, who, under normal circumstances, rang my chimes. Today, unfortunately, I wasn't hearing the music.

A few moments later he came toward me carrying a tray with four coffees on it. "I thought we could all use a little pick-me-up."

"You've got a spare one, then. Grace isn't here."

Lottie saw us coming and jumped up to meet us. "Bless your heart, Marco," she said, removing the lid from her cup to inhale the fragrant aroma. "I was starting to fall asleep."

"Starting?" I reached for a cup. "You were snoring soundly about ten minutes ago."

"I've never snored a day in my life. And where did Gracie rush off to?"

"She had a coffee date with the colonel, or I guess I should say the *captain,* because, as it turns out, he's not a colonel after all."

"What?" Marco said, looking seriously disappointed.

"Grace found out that the esteemed Colonel Billingsworth never made it above captain. So now she thinks that because he lied about his rank, he should be investigated. She's off playing detective right now to prove she's right."

At my eye roll, Lottie said, "Don't discount Grace.

She's a smart gal. Look at her careers—nurse, legal secretary, school librarian. Our Grace isn't a dummy, that's for sure."

"She isn't a detective, either," I reminded Lottie.

"She could be if she set her mind to it."

"Grace could be a bagpipe player, too, but that doesn't mean she's cut out for it. After all, PI work is dangerous. It takes someone who's young and agile. Right, Marco?"

"Actually, ninety-five percent of the work is done sitting behind a computer, researching and following paper trails. Pretty dull stuff."

"Thanks for the assistance," I muttered.

"Why don't you want Grace to help you, sweetie?" Lottie asked. "You haven't minded asking her to do research for you."

Marco perched on a corner of the table and sipped his brew, watching me with amused eyes. "Yes, tell us, Abby."

"I'm getting a little tired of everyone harping on this subject."

Lottie held a hand to the side of her mouth to say to Marco, "That's what people say when they don't have an answer."

"I have an answer," I said testily. *Just not a good one.*

"Let's hear it," Lottie said.

"Okay. Here it is. I don't think it's becoming for Grace to snoop."

Lottie threw back her head and let loose with a big

laugh. "Becoming? See, if I was Grace, I'd have a fancy quote for you on that lame excuse. Since I'm not, I'm gonna pass on my mama's favorite saying. 'What a load of beetle dung.'"

At that moment Angelique returned to her booth, pushing a cart on which she had placed her harp. Ever the gentleman, Marco put down his cup and slid off the table to go help her. "I'll be back in two minutes. Settle this while I'm gone, okay?"

Lottie put her coffee aside and leaned toward me. "You want to give me an honest answer now that your honey bun is gone?"

"I gave you my answer."

"You gave me *an* answer. Now give me the real one. You know you can tell me anything. Between my four hell-raising sons and my own misspent youth, I've heard it all, seen it all, and done it all. Nothing will surprise me."

"Your misspent youth?"

"I'm a product of the seventies, Abby. A member of the radical, bra-burning, pot-smoking, protesting, hear-me-roar generation."

Thinking of the forty-two dollars I had just plunked down for a decent underwire, I said, "I can't believe you burned a bra."

"It was symbolic, to show how we were going to turn the world on its ear by defying the stuffy conventions of our parents. Oh, yeah, we were something back then." She sighed wistfully, as though she couldn't believe she had once been that rebellious.

Then she patted the chair next to her. "Confession time, sweetie. Put your buns down here."

I wavered between sticking to my lame answer and being up front about my selfishness. Finally, I sank down beside her and put my head in my hands. "I know I'm being totally self-centered, but I'm afraid Grace will solve the case."

"What's wrong with that?"

"She *always* succeeds, Lottie." I felt so horrible admitting it that I wanted to crunch myself into a ball and fall into a trash can. "Never mind. Forget I said that."

Lottie put a comforting hand on my shoulder. "I get what you're trying to say. You're afraid that if Grace succeeds, then you've failed."

"Again."

"Sweetie, you know that's not true."

"Think about Grace's past. How many women can go from being an army nurse to a horse walker to a tattoo artist to a school librarian to a legal secretary and succeed at all of them? Then there's me. I was a complete flop at learning to play the piano, I wasn't coordinated enough to be a cheerleader, I couldn't hack math or science so I had to forget about med school and try law instead, and I couldn't cut it there, either. Now I finally find a career I love, yet it's a constant struggle to keep Bloomers operating in the black. But I *have* helped solve five murder cases, and I'm learning more with each one. If Grace solves this case with no training, then what does that say about me? What will Marco think?"

"Abby, everybody fails sometime or another. If you want to talk about failure, take a gander at yours truly. Remember, you bailed me out when you assumed the mortgage for Bloomers. And I'll bet if we asked Grace, she'd have plenty of stories about her own goof-ups. As for your being selfish, I think it has more to do with your self-image. You have to erase that little mental neon sign on your forehead that says 'Loser' and replace it with one that says 'Not afraid to try.' You know that's how we see you, don't you? And how Marco sees you?"

"Really?" I felt a sting of tears beneath my eyelids and quickly scrubbed them away. I hadn't thought of it that way before, but if I hadn't tried the piano, or cheerleading, or even law school, how would I know whether I could do them or not? One thing I'd never been was spineless.

"Let's borrow one of Gracie's sayings and not put the cart before the horse," Lottie said. "Just because Grace is trying to help solve the case doesn't mean she's gonna be able to do it by herself. Just focus on helping Delilah and let the rest take care of itself."

"You're right. We've got less than three hours before the convention ends and our suspects leave, and we're not any closer to finding Sybil's killer."

"Then let's stop gibber-jabbering and get a move on."

I hugged Lottie. She didn't have Grace's eloquence, but she had the mothering instinct down pat.

As Marco returned from his goodwill mission,

Lottie said, "I'm guessing the Urbans didn't show up for the memorial service. I saw them buzz past the aisle about an hour ago, pushing a casket on wheels."

"The casket races! Oh, no. I forgot about them." I glanced at my watch, then hopped up. "They started ten minutes ago, Marco. We need to get out there. That would be a great place to corner Ross about his alibi."

"We can't do it now. We have an urgent date with an envelope." Marco patted his jacket. "Grab your coffee and let's go."

I picked up my cup and gave Lottie a sheepish smile. "Do you mind? I know it's kind of boring for you here."

"Course not. I'm doing my part to help Delilah, too." She pulled a paperback out of her purse and patted it. "I've got my coffee and a romance novel. What else do I need?"

Marco had arranged with the security manager to use an empty hotel room on the second floor, right next to the elevators, one of the least desirable rooms because of the noise and lack of view. But it had a steam iron, a VCR/DVD machine, and a television, and that was all we cared about. Marco used a key card to get inside; then he made sure the door was double-locked while I filled the iron with water in the bathroom.

As I waited for the iron to heat, my cell phone began to vibrate. I glanced at the name on the screen, grimaced, then tucked it away.

"Your parents?" Marco asked, leaning against the doorjamb.

"Reilly."

"Reilly? Why didn't you answer it?"

"Because he's being a pest. This is the third time he's called in the last hour."

"Don't you think you should find out why he keeps calling?"

"I know why. He thinks he saw me on the fourth floor earlier. This iron sure is taking a long time to heat up. I wonder if it's broken."

"Back up a minute. *Did* Reilly see you up there?"

"He saw a woman who *didn't* look like me because she was wearing a wig." In the mirror above the sink I saw a flicker of skepticism in Marco's expression and I smiled to myself. He was just going to have to accept that I was fully capable of handling these little emergencies. I licked my fingertip, then touched it to the iron's sole plate. "Ouch. It's working."

"Wait a minute. You took one of Sybil's wigs out of the closet?"

"I needed a quick disguise. Clever, wasn't it?"

"That depends. Where's the wig now?"

"Wrapped in paper towels and buried in a trash can in the women's restroom near the bar. No worries, mate. Everything's under control. Abby Knight is on the job."

"I get nervous when you say that. Let's go back to why you needed the wig."

I sighed in exasperation. "Remember when you had

to leave Sybil's suite to go watch the videos and you asked if I could put the police tape back? Well, as it turned out, the couple in the next suite, Alicia and Walt Tyler—they sat at our table at the banquet, remember?—returned before I got the tape off their door."

"Damn, Abby, why didn't you tell me about this?"

"Because it wasn't a problem. I took care of it. When the Tylers left to call security from the hotel's house phone, I put on Sybil's wig, switched the police tape, and ducked down the stairs. Done and done. It just so happened that Reilly was coming out of the elevator with the security manager when I was going into the stairwell, but he really didn't get much more than a glimpse of my face, and most of it was hidden under that heavy wig."

"Then why does he think it was you?"

"Some fourth-floor guest reported seeing a shoeless redhead in the hallway talking to one of the maids. But don't worry. The snitch didn't see you, and I have an alibi. Okay, we have steam now. Bring on the envelope."

He held the flap end of the envelope over the huffing iron. "Are you sure no one can ID you?"

"Positive. I just don't want Reilly to start quizzing me on it because I don't like to lie, and I can only stretch the truth so far. That's why I'm avoiding his phone calls."

"So Reilly's still in the hotel?"

"He was an hour ago."

"I wonder if he came back for another look at the crime scene."

"Would that be bad or good?"

"If it means he's having doubts about the direction of the investigation, it's good. Hey!" He jerked his hand back and examined his wrist. "That steam is hot."

"Sorry." I slanted him a coy glance. "Want me to kiss it and make it all better?"

That sexy grin flickered at one corner of his mouth. "Later, baby. "

It took two more minutes for the gummed flap to loosen; then Marco took the envelope into the bedroom, sat on the bed, and reached inside. I stood at his shoulder, crossing my fingers in the hope that whatever was in there was Delilah's ticket to freedom.

"Let's see what we have here. This looks like a bankbook." Marco placed a small, thin blue book on the bed. "A homemade CD or DVD." He put a clear plastic case containing a generic disc beside the bankbook and reached inside again. "And one black plastic videocassette tape." He checked inside the envelope. "That's it."

I picked up the cassette and read the label on the front. "*Chester Cheater*. Running time sixty minutes. And get this. It stars Sugar Shackup and Chester 'Chest-hair' Domingo. Oh, man, that's bad. It has to be a porn movie of some kind. I wonder if it's a takeoff of Chester *Cheetah* from the Cheetos commercials."

"So it's a *corny* porn flick," Marco said as he examined the bankbook.

"Why would Sybil want to keep a porn video safe?"

"Maybe she's in it."

"You think? Maybe she's Sugar Shackup."

Marco mumbled something about that being preferable to Chest-hair Domingo, but his attention was on the bankbook, so I took the cassette and headed for the television. "I'll check this out and tell you about it afterward. Keep your eyes averted."

"Abby, take a look at this."

I walked back to see Sybil's bankbook, where Marco pointed out two deposits in the amount of ten thousand dollars each that had been entered on the first of every month. There were no other entries listed on the pages.

"Wow. Twenty thousand dollars a month. That's a lot of money for a product line that wasn't doing well. I wish I could make that much selling flowers."

"This can't be income from her business. She wouldn't deposit it in two separate amounts on the same date every month, even if her business was a success."

I waved the cassette in front of him. "Maybe she produced this kind of movie."

"Why would she keep just one of them?" Marco flipped back a few pages, studying the entries. "One of these deposits started last March, the month after her husband died."

"Could she have received payments from his life insurance policy?"

"That would have been paid out in a lump sum. Besides, she wouldn't have needed to keep it in a secret account."

I picked up the round case and opened it. The top side of the disk was blank, but on the back someone had written a name in the center in tiny black letters. "This has *Walker* written on it, Marco. Could this be about Colonel Billingsworth?"

"I don't know any other Walkers. Put it in the player, and let's find out."

Chapter Eighteen

I turned on the TV and the video player, inserted the disk, and hit PLAY. We sat on the edge of the bed watching as an emaciated man appeared on the screen. He was propped against pillows in a bed, obviously in a bedroom by the look of the ornate headboard behind him. He had an IV line in one arm and an oxygen mask over his nose and mouth, with a stand holding the oxygen tank beside the bed. Clearly, the man wasn't the Walker we knew.

From somewhere out of camera range, we heard Sybil's grating voice say, "Go ahead, Thad. The camera is rolling."

"That has to be Sybil's husband," I said as the sickly man removed his mask and began to speak.

"My name is Thaddeus Blount," he said in a weak, shaky voice, "and I am making this recording for my business partner and lifelong friend, Walker

Billingsworth, at the urging of my wife, in the hopes that Walker will join me in atoning for the shameful way in which we conducted our business."

"A confessional?" I asked as the ailing man stopped to breathe into his mask.

"Sounds like it," Marco said. "Did you catch that he was doing it at Sybil's urging?"

"Walker, old friend," Blount continued, "I couldn't live with our ugly secret any longer. It consumed my life, and I refused to go to my grave with it, too, so I've made my confession to my maker and to my wife, and I beg you to do likewise. Cleanse your soul before it's too late."

"Cleanse his soul?" Marco muttered. "What the hell did they do?"

"When you and I first started our business," Blount continued, "we were young men fresh from 'Nam, with no income, desperate for customers, so we made what we thought was a shrewd business decision. But what we did to the families of our fellow soldiers was—unconscionable and"—Blount's breathing became labored—"has been—a terrible weight—on my conscience—ever since."

When Blount's head fell back weakly and his chest shuddered beneath the thin material of his pajama top, Sybil instantly appeared on the edge of the screen, adjusting his breathing apparatus, patting his shoulder, whispering into his ear.

Marco sat forward, watching the screen intently. "Come on," he said tersely, as though he could will the man to speak. "Tell us what you did."

His agitation puzzled me until I remembered that his uncle had been one of the soldiers whose remains had been handled by Billingsworth and Blount.

After a few moments, Blount gathered the strength to continue, but his voice was fainter than before and he had to pause every few seconds for more air. "This hideous secret—has affected my entire life, including—my relationship with my wife. How could I bring myself to be—completely open and honest with her—when I've been lying to myself, denying that—what we did was wrong? Worst of all, though, was the guilt I felt—each time I thought of how we deceived—those grieving families—"

He stopped, gasping for another breath, his eyes bulging, his scrawny hand clawing for his mask, until he was able to clap it over his face and drag in more oxygen.

"You can do it, Thad," Sybil urged from offscreen.

Blount shook his head. "I'm too weak."

"Come on. You're doing this for Walker, remember?"

Blount nodded, then drew in several long mouthfuls of air, raised the mask away from his mouth, and struggled to lift his head from the pillow. "If you have a shred of dignity left, Walker, I beg you to do the right thing. Be brave, man. It's too late for me to make reparations, but you can do it."

He fell back against the bed and closed his eyes. "No more," he wheezed; then the video went black.

Marco punched the STOP button and removed the disc from the machine. I could tell from his choppy movements that his anger was simmering just below the surface.

"Wow," I said softly. "They must have done something terrible. I wonder what it was?"

"I don't know, but I sure as hell intend to corner Billingsworth about it." He put the disk into its plastic case, then picked up the black cassette and walked over to the television. "Let's see what surprises this has in store."

Marco tried to insert the cassette into the VCR side of the player, but it wouldn't fit into the slot. He examined the case again. "This is old. It must be in Beta format. I'll have to dig up an old Beta player somewhere."

"If it's old, maybe it's a porn movie starring Sybil in her younger years. Or maybe her husband is on it. Wait. I know! Her husband and the colonel are in it, and *that's* their ugly secret."

"It wouldn't have affected the families of the soldiers they cremated. I'll have to dig up a machine somewhere, so we can find out. The security manager might have one stowed away in the hotel's basement. I'm supposed to be back down there at five, but I'll go early so I can talk to him—" Marco stopped midsentence and reached for the bankbook again, a look of sudden comprehension on his face. "Of course."

"Of course what?"

"You know what this is about?" He slapped the book

against his knee, shaking his head in disbelief. "Damn. That Sybil was one gutsy woman."

"Wait. You lost me, Marco. Are you talking about the bankbook now?"

"The bankbook, the confessional, the porn movie . . . it's blackmail evidence." He reached for the plastic case containing the DVD. "This so-called confessional is where she got her husband to incriminate the colonel so she could blackmail him."

"Are you serious?"

"It all makes sense now. After Blount made his deathbed confession to her, Sybil must have leapt at the opportunity to use the information against Billingsworth. All she had to do was record it before her husband died."

"So that's why she kept urging him to go on."

Marco flipped through the pages of the bankbook. "It's all documented right here. One deposit started just after her husband passed away. That must have been Billingsworth's first payment. The other deposits started earlier, which means that by the time she began blackmailing Billingsworth, she was an old hand at it."

I sat on the bed staring at the evidence of Sybil's crime. Given what I'd heard about her, it wasn't hard to believe that she would resort to something as contemptible as blackmail. Still, how could she have betrayed the man whom her husband considered his dear friend?

"*Now* it makes sense why she couldn't go to the

police with this," Marco said, tapping the envelope. "Blackmail is a felony. Mandatory jail time. No way would she want these things to fall into police hands." He picked up the *Chester Cheater* videocassette. "If my guess is right, Sybil's other victim is on this. Someone made an X-rated movie and is living to regret it."

"I'm still shocked that Sybil would blackmail her husband's longtime friend. You'd think if she cared at all about her husband, she wouldn't have been able to do it."

"Let me spell it out for you, Abby," Marco said as he put everything back into the envelope. "It's about *M-O-N-E-Y.*"

"True. Crawford did tell us that she was almost paranoid about having enough money to retire on. Still, ten thousand dollars a month from each victim? That's a hundred and twenty thousand dollars per year just from the colonel. How could he afford it?"

"He did what he had to do to keep his secret safe."

"I'm amazed that the colonel could bring himself to say anything good about Sybil in his eulogy. You'd think he would have hated her."

"Are you kidding? Billingsworth must have been ecstatic when he found out she was dead. No more Sybil, no more payments, no more worries about that secret."

I smacked my forehead. "That's why he was so relieved when he came down to the storage room yesterday evening. Remember what he said after Reilly told him about Sybil? *'Thank God!'* I'll bet it just slipped out before he caught himself."

"Think about it, Sunshine. Billingsworth's entire life is based on his upstanding reputation—Purple Heart medal, Vietnam War record, a leader in the morticians' society, and even his phony military rank. Whatever he and Blount did, if it got out, he'd be ruined. It makes sense that he would have done everything in his power to keep it quiet. And you notice that Sybil's blackmail video only hinted at what that secret was. Without Sybil to provide the details, the video is useless." He paused a moment for me to absorb it. "Do you see where I'm going?"

"I see that you agree with Grace that the colonel should be a suspect."

"Don't you? He obviously had a motive."

I got up to put the iron away. "I'm not sold on the idea of him being a killer, Marco. He's a gentleman."

"And a liar. And think about Blount's confession. Blount felt compelled to clear his conscience, but Billingsworth didn't. Blount was begging him to set it to rights. That says something about Billingsworth's character, doesn't it?"

"I'll give you that, but really, Marco, can you imagine any reason why Sybil would undress for him? And then climb into a casket?"

"Billingsworth could have threatened her, or used force against her."

"If Sybil met the colonel in the storage room, she must not have been worried about her safety. And would he have put her clothes on the dummy? That's much too juvenile for him. That's something only the Urbans would do."

"Or something the killer might do to point a finger at the Urbans. Billingsworth did have the opportunity, Abby. Remember, Sybil died around six thirty, by best estimates. We didn't see Billingsworth until he went up to the podium. What time was that, around seven fifteen, seven twenty? So where was he from six o'clock to seven twenty? Does anyone know?"

"I guess we'll need to check it out," I said reluctantly.

"You bet we will. And I need to have a talk with him about what he did to those veterans." Marco tucked the flap into the envelope. "Now that I think about that phone call Sybil made to Crawford, her concern was for her belongings, not for her own safety. She must have believed someone was going to try to take them from her."

"But only her blackmail targets would have a reason to do that."

"You got it."

"It sure would help to know who that other person was, and if he, she, or they are here this weekend. Hey, maybe Chester Cheater is one of the Urbans."

"This is a Beta tape, Abby. The Beta format was phased out in the eighties. The Urbans probably weren't even two years old when this was made."

Damn. There went that theory. I wasn't ready to give up on the Urbans yet, however. Only they would have even thought about putting Sybil's clothes on that mannequin.

While Marco smoothed out the bedspread, I walked over to the window to think. There was something about gazing at the outdoors that cleared the cobwebs from my brain. All that blue sky and bright sunshine, plush green grass, flowery shrubs, and the reds, golds, and oranges of autumn leaves seemed to . . . Oops. This room had a view of the back parking lot.

"Ready to go?"

"Not yet. I'm working on a thought."

"In that case, I'd better take my shoes off and make myself comfortable."

"Sardonic remarks will only make my thought process take longer."

Marco pretended to snore.

"Okay, fine, you'll have to settle for an unfinished idea." I was about to turn away when I caught a sudden movement in the parking lot below. There among the rows of cars was a man in a long brown robe darting swiftly from one vehicle to the next, as though trying to stay hidden.

"What is it?" Marco asked, coming to stand beside me.

I pointed to the last row of parked cars. "I thought I saw Eli Cotton over there."

"That wack job is back?"

"I keep telling you, he's not a wack job, Marco. He's eccentric."

"Splitting hairs."

"Look. There he is by that silver Lexus. I wonder what he's doing."

"Probably trying to steal a car."

"Be serious. He seems to be watching the back of the hotel."

"He's probably looking for a way to get inside." Marco glanced at his watch. "It's two forty, Abby. We really need to get moving."

"Can I tell you my idea on our way?"

"I can't wait." He tucked the envelope inside his jacket, then we headed toward the door. Out of habit, Marco opened it just a crack and looked up and down the hallway before we stepped outside. "Let's take the stairs. It's faster."

"Okay, here's what I was thinking," I said as he pulled the door shut behind us. My cell phone vibrated again, but I ignored it. "We still don't know what triggered Sybil's call to Crawford, so what if one of her blackmail victims got into her suite to hunt for the envelope; then when Sybil returned to her room later that afternoon, she saw the mess, realized someone had been there, and that's why she panicked and placed that call?"

He paused at the stairway exit. "I still think the police caused the mess. Besides, look how hard it was for us to get inside her suite."

"Harder for some of us than for others."

"Don't start." Marco pushed the stairwell door open and we headed down the steps toward the lobby. "Think about it, Sunshine. If your theory is correct, that would mean at least one of Sybil's victims knew she had the blackmail evidence with her, and the only way that would be possible is if she had told him—or them—and why would she do that?"

"Well . . . how about to hand over her blackmail evidence for a final payoff?"

"It's possible," he said slowly. "I suppose Sybil could have arranged a business meeting rather than a tryst. But then wouldn't she have taken the tape with her?"

"Not if she was smart. And there's still the whole clothes-on-the-dummy joke. A blackmail victim wouldn't kill her, then advertise it."

"So much of this doesn't add up. Maybe once we see this Beta video we'll have some answers."

"Or we can get the guilty party to confess." I checked my watch. "We've got a little more than two hours until the exhibitors begin to pack up and leave. What should we focus on first?"

"Billingsworth." As Marco strode ahead to open the door, he muttered, "He has a lot of explaining to do."

"Wait, Marco. What about the casket races? They started at two o'clock. Shouldn't we try to catch Ross there before we go after the colonel? I'm afraid the Urbans will leave the convention after the races are over."

He paused with his hand on the door handle. "We'd better split up, then. I'll track down Billingsworth, and you see what you can find out from Ross."

"I wish I could think of some ingenious way to trick him into telling me what happened."

"You could always resort to flattery."

"Flattery didn't work on his brother. I'm thinking a scare tactic would be better. I should have hung on to Sybil's wig. I'll bet seeing me in that would shock him."

"Flirt with him. You're good at flirting."

"Really?" I batted my eyelashes at him. "What else am I good at?"

We heard footsteps coming down the steps, so Marco said, "We can discuss that later. Let's reconnoiter in half an hour at your booth."

He pulled open the door and we stepped into the lobby. "Half an hour," he reminded me, tapping his watch.

Suddenly we heard someone shout, "Marco!"

We both turned—I had to rise on tiptoe—and saw Reilly making his way toward us. Instantly, I ducked down and grabbed Marco's sleeve. "I can't let Reilly see me. What should I do?"

"Why don't you want him to see you?"

"Hello-o-o. Remember our fourth-floor break-in, and the witness who saw only one of us trying to get inside Sybil's suite? Oh, damn. Here he comes. Don't let him arrest me, okay?"

"Stay behind me." Marco took a few steps to the left, close to where a group of people stood in a line for the shuttle service to the airport. "Okay," he whispered, "see the bellboy with the luggage cart coming toward us? Keep low, circle around that line of people, and get behind the cart. You should be able to make an escape from that point."

"Got it." I didn't have to duck down far to stay out of sight, so all it took was another sidestep or two before I was behind a big cart stacked high with suitcases and garment bags, being rolled toward the sliding glass entrance doors. I kept even with the cart, crouching behind the bags ignoring the quizzical glances from the bellboy. Once I was outside, I breathed a sigh of relief—until I saw a police car parked at the curb, and then I had a moment of panic and scooted off down the sidewalk, around to the back of the hotel.

Please don't let him arrest me. Please don't let him arrest me.

Chapter Nineteen

According to the signboard I'd seen on Saturday, the casket races were supposed to take place in the rear parking lot. The only thing wrong with that was that the parking lot was full of automobiles. Surely someone had foreseen that possibility before they set the race's location, or had I been mistaken? I pulled out my cell phone and called Lottie.

"Hey, sweetie, where are you?"

"In the parking lot behind the hotel, trying to find the casket races."

"Hold on while I check the flyer. One of the Urbans came around with them earlier. By the way, did your mom reach you? She called me several times trying to track you down."

That would teach me to ignore my phone calls. "I haven't talked to Mom today."

"I reminded her that you were at a convention, but she still wants to hear from you. I didn't say a word about you and Marco investigating the murder."

"Good thinking. All she needs is another reason to worry."

"Are you in the east parking lot, behind the conference center? That's where the races are."

Oops. I was in the west lot. I shaded my eyes as I tried to figure out the quickest way to reach the other side. Because of the lay of the land, it appeared I had to make a choice: either backtrack around to the front of the hotel—where I might be spotted by the eagle-eyed Reilly—and continue up the sidewalk toward the conference center, then circle around behind it, or take a shortcut across the lot where I now stood and cut through a lovely wooded nature preserve to reach the far side.

That was a no-brainer. I began to wend my way through the rows of vans and cars to reach the woods. "So, other than my mom calling, what's going on there, Lottie?"

"Same ol', same ol', only less of it."

"Is Grace back from her coffee date yet?"

"She came back and took off again, saying she had to do some more investigating. She seemed excited."

Clearly, Grace was on to something. "Did she tell you anything about her conversation with the colonel?"

"Nope. She's being very tight-lipped about it. You know how Grace can be."

"Yeah. Mum's the word."

"You know, I've always liked that saying."

"It's the flower reference."

"That's it."

"Have you seen the colonel?"

"Not for a long while, why?"

"Marco had a—um—question for him." I didn't want to say anything more because I didn't want Lottie reporting back to Grace what we had found out. The wily Brit wasn't the only one who could be tight-lipped.

I stepped off the asphalt and into the woodland that spread over two acres and extended north to the sand dunes that bordered Lake Michigan. I stuck close to the southern edge, where the brush wasn't as high, crunching through a thick carpet of dry leaves made by the black walnut, sugar maple, white oak, cotton-wood, and beech trees that were native to the area. Green golf ball–sized walnut pods littered the ground, making a fast pace risky, which I learned when I stepped on one and skated a few feet before regaining my balance.

My phone beeped, signaling another caller. I checked the screen and saw the word MOM on it. "Lottie, my mom's calling. I should be back there within half an hour."

"Is it okay if I start packing up? No one's been down this way in a long time."

"Be my guest. Thanks." I switched to the waiting call. "Hi, Mom."

"Abigail, where have you been? I've been trying to reach you all afternoon. First you didn't show up for church today; then I saw the newspaper article about the murder at the Woodland Convention Center; then I heard from Lottie that you were there attending a conference at that very same place. Do you have any idea how upsetting it is to hear that my only daughter is at the scene of a murder?"

Would it have been less upsetting if she'd had two daughters? "Mom, there's positively no reason to be upset. I'm not in any danger. Hey, you should be relieved I'm not lying in a ditch at the side of the road."

"I don't find that amusing," she said in a hurt voice. "Do I make fun of your fear of clowns? You know I can't help worrying about you."

"I'm sorry. I've been really busy today. I did tell you I was going to be here this weekend."

"No, you didn't."

In the background I heard Dad say, "Yes, she did."

There was a pause, and then Mom said in a hushed, anxious voice, "I think I'm losing my mind, Abigail."

"You're not losing your mind. It's probably stress. Are you still worried about your gift for the baby shower?"

"I've been thinking about"—she sighed forlornly, as though she hated to finish the sentence—"buying a baby gift instead."

"Really? That's—too bad." I'd nearly said *wonderful* but caught myself in time. "Why?"

"Remember the spider-plant pot I made last January? You sold it in the shop for me."

Remember it? I'd tried my best to block it out. Her pot wasn't so named because it was designed to hold spider plants. It actually *looked* like a giant, hairy-legged spider squatting on a table. "What about it?"

"A friend called to tell me that it's being auctioned on eBay," she said with a sob. "As a gag gift. I have to go now. Here's your father."

A gag gift? Poor Mom. She had to be feeling like a failure. . . . Dear God, had I inherited that trait?

"Hi, honey," Dad said. "Sorry we interrupted your convention." Then he whispered, "See what I mean about your mom?"

"She's not morphing, Dad. She's having a self-esteem crisis." Not paying attention to where I was stepping, I nearly tripped on a rotted log. "I'll call you later. I'm in the middle of something right now." I closed the phone and slipped it in my pocket.

To get around the enormous trunk of a fallen tree, I had to go deeper into the woods, where the brush was dense and thorny branches plucked at my clothing. Wind gusts stirred the leaves beneath my boots. I didn't have my jacket with me, and under the canopy of trees, away from the warmth of the sun, the air was chilly, so I held my arms close to my body to keep warm.

Hearing a twig snap, I looked back, but all I saw were two squirrels chasing each other up a tree. A mosquito buzzed around my head. "Get away!" I said, batting it. I watched it circle above me, and when it swooped in for a landing, I clapped my hands together and squashed the little devil. "You were warned," I told the mangled bits in my palm, then crouched down to wipe the remains on dry leaves. Mosquitoes in October were just wrong.

I found a walking trail and followed it some distance until I realized it was going in the wrong direction, then stopped to get my bearings. Something crunched leaves behind me, and I turned with a jerk. The crunching instantly stopped. Was someone following me, or was it my imagination?

For a long moment I stood perfectly still, scanning the woods, but nothing moved. I started walking again, trying to make my footfalls as soft as possible, casting frequent glances over my shoulder, unable to shake the feeling that someone was behind me. *This isn't a horror movie, Abby. Little woodland creatures crunch leaves, too. Just keep moving.*

I went a few yards, then paused—and heard that nerve-wracking crunch of leaves again. So I did what every woman would do in that situation. I ran, plowing through rough scrub and not caring about thorns or mosquitoes or branches that grabbed my hair. Ahead I could see the outer edge of a parking lot, and I breathed a sigh of relief. Almost there.

Snap. Crunch.

Damn, how I hated that noise. I glanced over my shoulder and saw a man dart behind a thick tree trunk. Okay, *that* wasn't my imagination. Someone was definitely following me. Should I keep running or call his bluff? This time I chose the second option, since running through the woods hadn't deterred him. Plus, I was close enough to the parking lot that I knew I could escape if I had to.

"I know you're there," I called, trying to sound brave. "Show yourself."

When no one answered, I took out my cell phone and flipped it open. "Show yourself this minute," I called. "I have my cell phone open and I'm about to dial 911."

"Please don't call the police." A long, narrow face topped by wild gray curls peered out at me from behind an elm tree.

"Eli?"

He hesitated a moment, then stepped forward. "I'm sorry if I frightened you. I just wanted to be sure you weren't meeting your boyfriend."

"You should be sorry. That's a horrible thing to do to somebody. Why couldn't you have just called, 'Hey, I need to talk to you'?"

"I was going to, but I got nervous. I'm not supposed to be on hotel property." He picked his way toward me through the scrubby plants, slipping on a walnut, stopping to yank his burlap robe from the clutches of a thorny branch. "I really appreciated the legal advice you gave me yesterday. You're the only one who seems to understand my cause. Everyone else acts like I'm some kind of circus act."

Still not totally sure I could trust him, I closed my phone but didn't put it away. "I don't mean to offend you, Eli, but if you want to be taken seriously, you're going to have to ditch the burlap robe and put on a business suit like the other men here."

"Trust me, I've already gone that route," he said with a sigh. "No one paid attention then, either."

I glanced at my watch. "Look, I've got to be somewhere right now, so I don't have a lot of time. What is it you want from me?"

"I need to get inside the convention center."

"Eli, the cops took you away yesterday for sneaking inside. Why do you want to tempt fate? Besides, the conference is nearly over."

"Oh, it's not to promote my natural burials. You see, the police think I had something to do with Sybil Blount's murder, so I have to convince them I'm innocent."

"They suspect you because of the confrontation you had with her out front yesterday?"

"Well, that, and because I was hiding under a table when they found me. I told them it was their fault I was hiding, but they wouldn't believe me. I even tried to explain about my burial bags. You'd think, being cops, they'd be grateful to know there were inexpensive choices, but they didn't want to hear about it."

"How will getting inside the convention center help you convince the police of your innocence?"

Eli sighed again, clearly exasperated. "If I can find the man I saw in the exhibition hall last night, he can prove I had nothing to do with Sybil's death."

"How can he prove that?"

"He's the one who murdered Sybil."

Chapter Twenty

I stared at Eli in astonishment. "You know who murdered Sybil?"

"Yes," he cried, and then, as though startled by his own voice, he held a finger to his lips to hush himself, hunching his shoulders and pulling his head down into his robe like a turtle into his shell. "I told the police I knew who did it," he said in a whisper. "I told them I'd lead them straight to the murderer, but they just laughed at me. I even showed them proof."

My blood was really pumping now. "You have *proof?*"

Eli glanced over his shoulder, then reached into a pocket and withdrew his hand. Slowly, he uncurled his fist. "The murderer left these behind."

I stared down at the two bloodred rose petals on his open palm, and instantly the words of Angelique's rhyme sprang into my head: *"Find the petals and a killer, too."* My gaze went back to Eli's face. He was only a few feet away, watching me intently, his pupils fully dilated, giving him an eerie, almost crazed expression. Was Eli trying to trick me? Was he the murderer?

My cell phone began to vibrate. I glanced at the screen and saw that it was Reilly. For the first time that day, I was glad he'd called.

At once Eli's hand shot out to clasp mine, startling me. "Please don't answer that."

"It's just, um, a friend calling, but that's okay. I'll call him back later." I slipped the phone inside my pocket, wondering whether I dared try to make an emergency call from there. But Eli was watching me too closely. Without giving away my sudden trepidation, I decided to play along with him. "Can you describe the man you saw?"

"That's the problem. I didn't see his face because I was hiding under a table two booths away. I only saw his navy shoes and trousers."

"It's going to be difficult to find him, Eli. People were dressed up for the banquet last night. They won't be wearing those clothes today."

His haggard face sagged. "I hadn't thought of that."

"Where did you find the petals?"

"At the top of aisle two, by the funeral-clothing booth. The man dropped a bundle of clothing onto the carpet, and the petals fell out. He picked up the clothes but not the petals. I guess he didn't see them."

"Did you notice anything else about him? Was he alone? Did he say anything? Make any phone calls?"

"He was laughing. And then I heard music and he ran off."

The laughing would fit with one of the Urbans playing a prank. "What kind of music?"

Eli shrugged. "I don't know, but I'd recognize the tune if I heard it again."

"You told the police all this?"

"Yes!" Eli flapped his arms in frustration. "They wouldn't listen to me. They said I was making up the story to protect myself. Protect myself from what? I asked them. All I did was hand out brochures. Where's the harm in that?"

"Then why did you hide from them?"

"Because they told me when they took me away the first time that I'd be arrested if they had to come back again."

"Yet you still came back."

He waved his arms in the air. "Don't you see? This was my golden opportunity to spread the word. If I can get morticians to read my brochures, they'll understand that what I'm promoting is the right thing to do. I know how these people think, you know. I was the chief embalmer for a big mortuary for years."

That surprised me. It also made Eli more credible.

"Don't get me wrong," he said. "It was a good job. But then my conscience started talking. 'Eli,' it said, 'how can you condone the use of precious land to bury a bunch of boxes and cover them with big, ugly blocks of stone when that land could be turned into a nature preserve or a woodland? How can you work for people who sell extravagant coffins that most people can't afford anyway? What difference does it make what you're buried in? Who's going to see it when you're six feet under? Wouldn't the money be better spent going to the family or to a charity?' So I bought myself an industrial sewing machine and went into business."

I was finding it more and more difficult to believe that Eli had anything to do with Sybil's murder. As Grace had pointed out, his beef was with the funeral industry, not with Sybil. And if he had shut Sybil in the casket, why would he have stuck around? He could have fled the building before he was discovered.

"Eli, would you know the man's laugh if you heard it again?"

He nodded vigorously.

"Then maybe I can help you."

Eli's hollow cheeks folded like an accordion as he smiled. "Thank you. You don't know how much this means to me. See, I have a plan all figured out. There's an escalator at the back of the hotel that goes to the lower level. If I can get down there—"

"You won't need to get into the hotel." I pointed toward the parking lot where the races were being held. "Your man is right over there. All I need to do is get him to laugh for you."

My phone vibrated again. I had to give Reilly snaps for persistence. I pulled out the slim silver case and held it up. "I have to take this call or my friend will think something is wrong."

"Go ahead. Just please don't tell him I'm here."

"I won't." This time I meant it. I didn't want to frighten off the man who might be able to solve the murder. I checked the screen and was surprised to see that it was Marco calling. "Hi, what's up?"

240

"Where are you?" Marco asked.

"I'm about to step onto the parking lot behind the convention center. Where are you?"

"Heading toward the Midwest Funeral Directors' Association booth to see if I can find Billingsworth. He seems to be MIA. Have you talked to Reilly yet?"

"No, and that man just won't take the hint that I don't intend to talk to him."

"He's not calling about the fourth-floor thing, Abby. He wanted to alert you that Eli Cotton is on the loose."

I glanced at Eli, who was picking burrs from his robe. "Is that bad?"

"Cotton was being detained by the police for questioning in Sybil's murder, but he managed to slip out about an hour ago. Reilly thought he might try to find you."

So Eli wouldn't know we were talking about him, I said only, "Why would he do that?"

"Because Mr. Wack Job kept saying he had to find the little freckle-faced redhead who tried to keep him from being arrested. He had the crazy idea that you would help him, or as he put it, save him from certain death. So be careful. Stay close to the crowds and keep your eye out for him. The man is a loose cannon. He could be dangerous."

I glanced at Eli, who was smiling as he watched a butterfly flutter by. I turned away to say quietly, "Marco, he's not a wack job and he's certainly not dangerous. In fact, Eli knows who—"

I heard a sharp intake of breath and stopped

abruptly, turning wide-eyed toward Eli. "I'm sorry," I whispered. "It just slipped out."

He hunched down into his robe again, a frantic look in his eyes. "Why did you say that? I don't want to go back to jail. Now I have to leave."

"Eli knows who what?" Marco asked.

"Hold on," I said to Marco, then covered the phone with my hand and whispered, "Don't leave, Eli. I won't let them take you to jail."

"Abby, who are you talking to?" Marco asked.

"I'm talking to"—at Eli's pleading glance I finished—"myself. I've really got to get to the races now, before the Urbans leave. I'll let you know what happens afterward."

"Abby, hold up a minute. Is everything okay there?"

"Better than okay. Some evidence just came to light that is going to point to the killer."

"What kind of evidence?"

Eli was frantically shaking his head.

"Marco, I'll explain later."

"Sunshine, you're worrying me. I know someone else is there. Is it Eli? He found you, didn't he? Okay, keep him talking and try not to upset him. I'll be there in a few minutes."

"Marco, I can handle it. You go see the colonel—"

Too late. The line was dead.

Why wouldn't Marco trust me? Annoyed, I snapped the phone shut.

"Your friend is on his way, isn't he?" Eli asked, chewing on his lower lip.

"I'm sorry, Eli. Yes, he's coming."

Eli's deep-set eyes widened fearfully as he looked around, as if expecting the cops to jump out from behind the trees to arrest him. Snatching my hand, he put the petals in them and curled my fingers around them. "Keep these for me." Then he turned and ran into the woods.

"Wait, Eli. How will I find you?"

He was too far away to hear me. I uncurled my fingers and stared down at the velvety red petals. *Hmm.* I'd been hoping to find a way to get Ross to talk to me. Maybe these would help.

Slipping the rose petals into my pocket, I headed for the clearing, stepping from the shade into bright sunshine. Ahead was the black asphalt parking lot of the convention center, which started at the loading docks behind the building and ended at a long stretch of sand dune due north. The dune sloped gradually to a flat sandy beach and ended at the lake.

The parking spaces near the building were filled with the exhibitors' vans and trucks, but the entire rear portion of the lot was empty. There was a crowd of men at the back hooting, thrusting manly fists into the air, and chest-butting each other, not dissimilar to what cavemen must have done eons ago.

As I drew nearer, I saw Ross standing behind a casket painted to look like an Indy 500 race car, with four wheels attached to the bottom, red and black racing stripes down each side, and the UMS logo on the front and rear. Seated inside, his hands on a steering lever, was Jess the Mess, wearing racing goggles and driving gloves. Five other colorful casket–race cars were lined up beside theirs, each with a driver inside and a team partner behind.

A man holding a whistle near his lips called, "Everyone ready?"

Ross crouched behind his casket-car, hands braced on the rear. "Bring it on, dude."

At the whistle, the men behind the caskets pushed their entries over the top of the sand dune, then stood back and let gravity do the rest. Far below, two men stood at the finish line, waiting to call the winners.

As the crowd cheered, I stepped up beside Ross to see the action. If I hadn't been on a mission, I would have enjoyed watching the crazy caskets speed down the dune, spewing sand, forging ruts that immediately filled up again, and hitting depressions that tossed the drivers from their seats. "Won any races yet?" I asked.

"No, but I'm about to win this one. Come on, Jess!" he hollered. He glanced my way briefly but didn't seem particularly surprised to see me. "Did you come to cheer us on, Red? We could use a cheerleading section."

At that moment a loud clamor went up as the first casket crossed the line. It wasn't Jess's, though. "Damn, I thought we had it that time," Ross said. He knuckle-pressed a guy standing nearby. "Nice job, man."

"Yeah, better luck next time," the other guy said. He

noticed me and winked. "There's your lucky charm, Ross. Put her in the driver's seat."

"No, thanks," I said. "I prefer real cars. Listen, Ross, I need to talk to you."

He gave a sharp sigh. "If you're here about Sybil, I'm done talking. She's a dead issue."

"A dead issue. Good one," his buddy said, and they knuckle-pressed again, snickering.

Ignoring the tasteless remark, I said, "You might change your mind when you hear what I have to say."

"Sorry. Not interested."

"Really? Because I know it was either you or Jess who killed Sybil."

Ross quickly ushered me a few feet away. "Jeez, will you keep it down?"

"You want me to keep it down? Then make this easy for both of us. Tell me which one of you was actually at the bar last night."

"Okay, I get it now. You're on another fishing expedition." He said quietly, "Watch out, Red. One of these days you'll reel in something you weren't expecting."

"Is that a threat?"

"Define it any way you want," he said with a smug grin.

Common sense said to stay cool—after all, Ross was a murder suspect, and that meant he could be dangerous—but his cocky attitude really pushed my buttons. "What are you going to do? Lock me in another phone booth—or maybe a casket this time?"

"A little help here, bro," Jess called as the drivers

grunted their way up the sand dune, pushing their casket-cars in front of them.

"Get lost," Ross said to me, starting toward his brother.

"I'm not going anywhere until you tell me which one of you was at that bar last night."

He spun around and came back, throwing his arms up in exasperation. "Do you honestly think I'm going to confess *anything* to you? Did you forget I was *cleared?* Now, go play with your flowers before I get my lawyer to slap a restraining order on you."

Well, that approach hadn't worked. I turned around to scan the parking lot for Marco. Not that I needed his help, but what was taking him so long? "Fine, Ross. I'll go—straight to the detectives. I'm sure they'll be fascinated to hear what I dug up."

"You are so full of it."

"Wanna bet? I have a witness who saw you dressing the dummy." I mentally crossed my fingers, hoping my ploy would work.

"Who?" he said.

"You think I'm going to name him and risk finding him stuffed in a coffin, too?"

Ross chortled. Boy, how I wished Eli had stuck around to hear that laugh. "If you're so sure I killed Sybil, why didn't you go to the detectives in the first place?"

He had me there.

"You wouldn't be trying to blackmail me, would you, Red?"

"You're an idiot. Why would you assume . . . Wait. Was *Sybil* blackmailing you?"

He straightened with a frown. "Go away. I'm tired of you."

Jess came back dragging his casket-car, grumbling, "Thanks for the help."

"Hey, man, it's not my fault." He stabbed a finger in my direction. "Blame her."

Jess dropped the car onto the sand and took off his goggles. "Are you back at it, Red? What is it this time? Are you trying to convince Ross to say something against me?"

"Actually, he was about to tell me why Sybil was blackmailing the two of you."

"No kidding. Was Sybil blackmailing us, Ross?"

"It's news to me, bro. Hey, here's an idea, Red. How about I give you the name of our lawyer, and you can ask him?"

"Oh, that's right. Your daddy hired a mouthpiece for you, didn't he?"

Ross held out his arms. "Hey, he insisted, and it's his dime."

"Everyone ready?" the man with the whistle called.

Jess pulled his brother aside to whisper something, but Ross shook his head.

"Suit yourself," Jess said, and climbed into the car. "Just remember what I told you."

"On your marks," the whistle blower called as the drivers readied themselves. "Get set."

Jess adjusted his goggles and Ross braced his hands

on the back of the casket-car, ready to spring forward. The man blew the whistle, and the race began.

Frustrated, I checked my watch. It was three fifteen, leaving me with only one hour and forty-five minutes to go. Out of desperation I approached Ross again. "You know that witness I mentioned? Well, guess what? He found something you dropped near the dummy."

Ross patted his pants pocket. "Wallet's here. Key card's here. Wait. I know. My cell phone." He checked his other pocket. "Nope. Got that, too. I guess you've got the wrong guy."

Wanting to wipe that arrogant smirk off his face, I almost showed him the petals but at the last second decided they'd be safer in my pocket. "You know the red rose Sybil wore in her hair? Well, some of the rose petals ended up in the clothes that you ran off with. They fell onto the floor when you were dressing the dummy. The witness picked them up after you left."

I saw a sudden flash of panic in his eyes and I thought I had him at last, but then that shrewd look reappeared. "Is that supposed to scare me into confessing? Look, I'll be the first to admit I'm not a genius, but even I know that a couple of rose petals your mystery witness *claims* I dropped can't prove a thing. A smart lawyer would tear that argument to shreds. Nice try, Red, but it would take more than that to connect me with Sybil's death."

Crap. Ross was more savvy than I thought.

His cell phone began to play the appropriately

selected "SexyBack." He pulled out a thin phone and flipped it open. "Isn't this a coincidence? Here's my lawyer now. And here come your reinforcements, ready to clap handcuffs on me and lead me away. Like that's going to happen anytime soon. Sorry, Red. You lose."

I swung around to see Marco, Reilly, and four county cops in full uniform striding across the parking lot. With a defeated sigh, I started toward them. I'd made a gigantic mess of things. What was I going to tell Marco?

Chapter Twenty-one

I was still two yards away when both men started in on me, talking over each other.

Reilly: "Where's Eli Cotton?"

Marco: "Did he threaten you in any way? Are you okay?"

Reilly to his men: "Fan out. Comb the woods, and search inside the hotel and convention center."

Marco: "Why didn't you keep him talking?"

Reilly: "Why the hell haven't you been answering your phone? I've been trying to reach you for almost two hours."

Marco: "What new evidence were you talking about?"

I clapped my hands over my ears and walked right between them, heading toward the convention center. One really peeved person was all I could handle—and that was me. But I couldn't decide what peeved me the most. Was it that I hadn't stopped to analyze Eli's "proof" before trying to get Ross to talk? Because if I had, I would have known that his proof was really hearsay, and not evidence at all. Or was it that the Urbans seemed to be a step ahead of me at every turn?

Maybe Marco was right. Maybe I shouldn't be handling this without him overseeing me. He and Reilly were on either side of me at that very moment, still firing questions at me.

At the door, I finally gave in. "Okay, you want to know what happened? Eli Cotton told me he witnessed the killer drop rose petals in the exhibition hall, and I tried to use that information to force a confession from Ross. But he realized before I did that I didn't have solid evidence, so he clammed up. It's my fault because I took Eli's information without analyzing it."

I held up a hand as both men began to speak. "Eli ran away because I told him you were coming, and he knew he wasn't supposed to be on this property. He took off to keep from going back to jail, but please believe that he isn't dangerous. He's just an oddball who's passionate about natural burials."

Marco and Reilly started to talk again, but I stopped them. "Can we get some coffee first and continue the discussion afterward? I really need a double espresso with—"

I tried to open the door, but Marco put his hand on it. "Abby, would you stop talking for one minute and listen to me? Ross Urban couldn't have killed Sybil."

I blinked at him in surprise. "What?"

"Ross couldn't have done it," Marco said. "He's not on the security video that covers this exit. He wasn't the one who stashed the smock and the rose in the trash."

"Then there must be a problem with that camera, because my gut is still telling me that Ross was involved in Sybil's murder, and my gut doesn't lie."

"There was nothing wrong with the camera or the videotape," Reilly said. "The real murderer conned you, Abby. You were suckered in by his story."

"The real murderer? Who are you talking about?"

"Eli Cotton," Reilly said.

"You are so wrong. Eli's harmless, and besides, he doesn't even have a motive. But he did see the killer—"

"Let me guess," Reilly said. "He saw the killer drop the rose petals by the mannequin, but he can only identify the man by his shoes, his slacks, his laugh, and a tune he can't remember."

The petals in my pocket felt suddenly warm against my thigh. "Why don't you believe him?"

"Because Eli Cotton *was* on the security video," Marco said.

"You watched it?" I asked. "When?"

"I didn't watch it. The detectives did." Marco's gaze shifted briefly toward Reilly, but neither of them said anything more on the subject. Obviously Reilly had given him that info.

"Well, of course Eli is on the video," I argued. "We know he sneaked inside. I'm sure there were other people on that video, too."

"But none with a motive," Reilly said. "Discounting Delilah's, of course. Cotton had the means, the motive, and the opportunity."

"Motive? Are you talking about that little confrontation he had with Sybil out in front of the convention center yesterday?"

"Sunshine, Eli used to work for Billingsworth and Blount. He was their chief embalmer until Sybil had him fired."

Damn. Eli hadn't told me that. He'd made it sound like he left because his conscience bothered him. Why had he lied?

"The camera caught Eli entering around six o'clock and leaving around six-thirty," Marco said, "then later being escorted out around ten, when we saw him."

I rubbed my temples, starting to feel a headache coming on. "Okay, back up a minute. The camera caught him entering once, but leaving twice? That doesn't make sense. How did he get in the second time?"

"It doesn't matter how he got in, only that he *was* in," Reilly said. "It's called opportunity. The current theory is that when Cotton snuck inside the convention center last night through the rear exit, he saw Sybil waiting for her date in the storage room. They argued about him being banned from the convention, he shoved her in the casket, wiped off his prints with

252

the smock, stuck her rose inside the smock, and dumped them in the trash."

"Then he came back inside the convention center through the front entrance and hid under a table?" I asked. "Why would he do that? And why would he keep the rose petals?"

"Because he's a wack job," Marco said.

I rubbed my aching head. "Could you please not ever use that term again?"

"Cotton probably kept the petals as a souvenir," Reilly said. "Sickos do that, you know. Keep something that belonged to their victim. He probably got a thrill out of showing them to you."

The rose petals in my pocket began to sear into my skin. I didn't want to believe what they were telling me because my gut was telling me otherwise. But how could I convince them they were wrong? "So you think Eli was able to convince Sybil to strip off her clothes and hop into a casket?"

"She might have already stripped in anticipation of her tryst," Marco offered. "Or he might have forced her."

"When he was taken out of the building that evening, did he have a weapon on him?" I asked. "Gun, knife, burlap cutter, garlic press?"

"It wouldn't have to have been by force of weapon," Reilly countered with a scowl, meaning that Eli hadn't been packing any kind of anything.

"What about Sybil's date, then? If she was meeting someone, he must have shown up at some point, right? Why hasn't he been found?"

"My guess is that he didn't want anyone to know about his date with Sybil," Reilly said. "If he went to the storage room and it was dark, or he didn't see her, then he probably left. And now he doesn't want to come forward because he'll be found out."

I still wasn't buying it, but I couldn't think of any more arguments. "So you're saying neither of the Urbans had anything to do with Sybil's death?"

"That's how it appears at this point," Reilly said. "At any rate, the DA is convinced Cotton is the killer and will be convening a grand jury tomorrow to indict him."

"Does this mean Delilah has been cleared?"

"Yep." Reilly hooked his thumbs in his big leather belt, as if he were solely responsible for Delilah's deliverance. "She's as free as a dove. Get it? Delilah Dove?"

Got it. Threw it away.

Marco put his arm around my shoulders. "And after I meet with Billingsworth to get some answers, we can pack up your booth and get the hell out of here. I'm thinking of having a dinner celebration at the bar. A nice bottle of merlot, your favorite thick-sliced grilled ham and Swiss cheese sandwich with extra-dark french fries on the side."

"And a dill pickle," I added without feeling.

"We'll invite Sean, too. And afterward," he said in my ear, "we can slip back to your apartment for a little dessert. How does that sound?"

Any other time it would have sounded like an invitation to paradise, and that low husky murmur in my ear would have spiked my heart rate into the ionosphere. But at that particular moment I was bummed, so I merely circled my finger in the air. "Yippee."

"Come on, Abby," Reilly said. "Aren't you relieved?"

"Of course I'm relieved. I'm very happy for Delilah, too, but I firmly believe you've got the wrong man. It simply doesn't make sense that Eli would kill Sybil, dump all the evidence except for two rose petals, then return to the building to hide within shouting distance of the scene of the crime."

"Then what do *you* think happened?" Reilly asked, folding his arms across his chest with an attitude that said, *Give it your best shot.*

"Ross met Sybil in the storage room, tricked her into stripping, closed the casket, ran off with her clothes, and dropped the rose petals when he dressed the dummy. Eli was hiding under a table nearby, saw the petals fall, then scooped them up after Ross left."

"For what reason?"

"For proof."

"Proof of what?" Reilly asked. "It doesn't prove anything."

"Exactly. It doesn't prove Eli killed Sybil, either."

"How do you explain his coming and going?" Reilly retorted.

I said crossly, "I can't."

"What about the smock and the rose in the trash can?" he countered.

"I can't explain that, either," I muttered, "but I still don't agree with you."

Marco held up his hands to stop our arguing. "I think we *can* agree that Delilah is off the hook, and leave the rest up to the investigators. Okay?"

I glanced from Marco to Reilly, both stubbornly refusing to believe that Eli could be innocent, and realized that arguing with them was futile. It would take solid proof to change their minds, and all I had left was a videocassette of unknown content. I knew better than to mention it in front of Reilly, and I wasn't sure I even wanted to remind Marco about it later. As far as he was concerned, Delilah was safe, and we were done.

But I wouldn't believe Eli was guilty and I wasn't about to let the poor man be railroaded. I knew that the real killer was lurking nearby, and unless someone could prove otherwise, I was determined to find him.

"I need coffee," I told them. "You're both still welcome to join me."

Marco opened the door for me, and I marched up the hallway past the storage room, halting briefly when I saw the crime-scene investigators hard at work. "Why are they still here?" I asked Reilly.

"It takes a long time to process a crime scene. Everything has to be examined." His radio squawked, so he pulled it from his belt clip and stepped away from us to answer it. He returned moments later to say, "I've got to go. Eli slipped under the net, so they're bringing out the dogs."

"Dogs? Are you kidding me?" I was so furious I spun around and stamped off toward the food court at the back of the exhibition hall.

Poor Eli. All he had wanted to do was promote his burlap-bag business. Now, because of some very thin, totally circumstantial evidence, he had a police force and search dogs on his trail, and Things One and Two were racing caskets down a sand dune. Life was so unfair.

I was the only one at the Starbucks counter, so I placed my order for a tall hazelnut-flavored coffee, loaded it with cream, and took a seat at a table. Marco joined me moments later with his standard black java. For a while I just sat and sipped the sweet beverage, thinking over my encounters with Eli and the Urbans, letting all the information settle in.

"Find the petals and a killer, too," Angelique had recited. Well, Eli had the petals. Did that mean he was the killer after all? Were my instincts wrong? Was it possible I'd been the victim of a clever con job?

No to all of the above, and I'd bet my beloved old Corvette on that.

Marco put his hand over mine. "Don't be too hard on yourself. You just got off track."

"The detectives are the ones off track, Marco. They're so caught up in all that circumstantial evidence, they can't think logically. They're not looking at the whole picture."

"It doesn't matter, Sunshine. The reason we got involved was to make sure Delilah was cleared, and that's happened now, so you have to let it go. It's not our problem anymore."

Right. Like it was that easy.

He pinned me with those yummy chocolate eyes. "Let's hear an affirmative answer."

"I'm totally and completely satisfied that Delilah is off the hook."

Marco studied me for a moment, then moved on, apparently deciding that was the best he would get. "I'm going to track down Billingsworth; then I have to run to New Chapel to take care of some bar business, but I'll be back here at five o'clock to help you haul everything out to the van. Between now and then, hang tight inside the building. Eli Cotton is out there somewhere, and since he came looking for you once, he might try again. He's going to be pretty desperate now. There's no telling what he'll try next."

As Marco prepared to leave, I remembered that he still had the cassette. "Did you contact Crawford about Sybil's envelope?"

"Why?" he asked guardedly.

I took a sip of coffee, trying to figure out how to get it from him without raising his suspicions. "Since I'll be bored out of my mind, I might as well call him and set something up. He might want to come right over. So, where is it?"

Marco's eyebrows drew together. "Are you positive that's all you want it for?"

"*Pffft.* Of course I'm positive. I'm always positive.

Positive outlook, positive approach to life, positive ions—"

"It's in a shopping bag under the table at your booth. I told Lottie to watch it for me."

If only I had known that thirty seconds ago. "Great. I'll take care of it."

"Aren't you going to ask for Crawford's business card so you can call him?"

"That was my very next question."

Giving me a skeptical glance, Marco stood up and pulled Crawford's card from his pocket, holding it just out of my reach. "Abby, if you're planning anything, I want to know about it right now."

Planning. Hmm. There had to be a way around that. "Marco, the only thing I'm planning to do is pack up the booth."

Still giving me a skeptical glance, he handed me the card, then leaned down to press a kiss on my cheek. "See you later."

I smiled at him. And then I started plotting.

Chapter Twenty-two

As soon as Marco was gone, I swallowed the rest of my coffee, then headed for my booth, where I was surprised to see that Max had returned and was helping Lottie pack up. At the Music of the Soul booth across the aisle, Angelique was seated at her harp with her eyes closed, playing a melody that sounded slightly familiar, but not enough to identify it. That was possibly due to the annoying way in which she played it—a rapid cascade of notes followed by a long pause followed by another cascade, then another pause . . . almost like a person tumbling down a flight of stairs, hitting the landing, then tumbling down again, from the forty-third floor of a skyscraper. That last flight of steps couldn't come any too soon.

When Max caught sight of me, he strode toward me and put his arms around my shoulders. "Thank you, Abby. Thank you so much."

"You're welcome," I muttered against his shirt front.

He stepped back, smiling broadly. "Lottie told us how hard you and Marco have been working to help Delilah. Whatever you did, it worked, and I can't even begin to express our gratitude. You were our guardian angels."

"We were very glad to be of help," I told him. No sense spoiling the mood by divulging that it hadn't been our snooping that had done the trick. I liked the idea of being angelic.

"Anyone want coffee?" Max asked. "My treat."

Lottie waved her hand like a woman going under for the last time, but I turned down the offer. I'd had enough caffeine for a while. I went into the booth and crouched down behind the table to peek inside the shopping bag Marco had left. Yep, the envelope was still there, and the DVD, bankbook, and black cassette were inside. Leaving the package in the shopping bag for the time being, I stood up. "Max, you don't happen to have an old Beta tape player tucked away at home, do you?"

"Sorry. We got rid of that a decade ago. The camera shop in town might have one, but they won't be open until tomorrow morning."

"That won't work. I need it now."

"What about asking the people at the *Make It Easy* set?" Lottie asked as she took a seat at the table and removed one of her pink leather flats, bending down to rub the bunion on her foot. "Didn't Chet Sunday do a show this morning on transferring old photos and tapes?"

Duh. How had I forgotten that?

Lottie bent down to tug the offending shoe back over her foot. "What do you need it for?"

Time for a diversionary tactic, since Sybil's tape was another thing I didn't want Grace to know about. Pretending not to hear her, I walked into the aisle and looked in both directions. "Isn't Grace back yet?"

"I haven't heard from her since she said she was going to do some more research. And of course the stubborn woman refuses to carry a cell phone, so there's no way to track her down."

At that, the harp music stopped abruptly and Angelique came swirling toward us, stopping a few feet away to strike a ballet pose, arms forming an oval above her head, balancing on one foot with the other tucked under her like an albino flamingo. *"Dolce et con affetto,"* she said in her paper-thin voice.

Lottie sat up and said crossly, "Would you mind translating for us mortals?"

Angelique came down on both feet, her arms flapping at her sides, as if someone had just let out all her air. She threw Lottie a chilly glance. "Grace has gone with her friend Walker."

"Where?" Lottie asked.

"Grace didn't volunteer that information, nor did I ask," was her flippant reply, as she glided back to her booth and resumed her seat before her golden instrument.

Lottie pushed back her sleeves and stood up, as though she were fully prepared to thrash the hapless harpist. "Is Jolly Roger implying there's something going on between Grace and the colonel?"

My diversionary tactic had worked too well. "I don't think that's what she meant. Angelique likes Grace. She wouldn't spread malicious gossip about her."

"Then why can't she just say what she means?" Casting a glower in Angelique's direction, Lottie sat down again, grumbling, "*Dolce et con affetto,* my sweet a—"

"I can translate." Handing Lottie a cardboard cup, Max said, "It's been a long time since I played an instrument, but if I remember, *dolce* means *sweetly* and *con affetto* means *with affection.*"

"See?" I said to Lottie. "Nothing malicious in that." I held my hand alongside my face so Lottie wouldn't see me mouth, "Thanks, Max."

"Now, if you ladies will excuse me, " Max said,

"I'm going out to the loading docks to see if I can reserve a time slot for you. It'll be easier to load your van from there instead of carrying everything across the parking lot. I'll be back soon."

"Thanks again," I called.

Lottie waited for Max to leave, then said to me, "Sweetly, with affection? So what is Angelique saying? That Grace and the colonel are sweet on each other?"

"I'm sure what Angelique means is that the colonel is sweet on Grace. Remember Grace's plan was to flirt with him to get information? Well, obviously it worked." When had I suddenly become an expert on Angelique's intentions?

"That'd better be what she meant," Lottie said with a huff.

An announcement over the PA system interrupted our conversation: "There will be a closing cocktail hour at five o'clock in the hotel lounge. Appetizers and aperitifs will be served. And don't forget to pick up your souvenir bag before you leave."

A cocktail hour? That would give me a little breathing room, since it was almost four o'clock.

"What the heck kind of souvenirs do a group of morticians hand out?" Lottie asked.

Across the aisle, the harp went silent as Angelique suddenly covered her face and burst into noisy tears. I could see her shoulders trembling.

"That is one strange woman," Lottie said, shaking her head. "I don't know whether to wring her scrawny neck or gather her up in my arms and rock her like a baby. Maybe I should go over and see if I can help."

"Why don't you let me do that? I need to talk to her anyway."

I walked across the aisle and stood at the end of her harp. "Angelique," I said softly, "are you all right?"

Sniffling, she quickly wiped away her tears with the backs of her hands. "I'm fine. What do you want?"

"I'd like to talk to you for a minute."

"Then sit on a stool, please. My neck will hurt if I have to keep looking up."

I'd have to be standing on stilts for that to happen. But I was all about humoring her, so I pulled up a short, black padded stool and perched on it. "Remember the poem about the rose petals you recited to me yesterday evening?"

She began to strum the harp strings. "I've set it to music. Would you like to hear it?"

Um . . . no. But figuring it might be the only way to win her cooperation, I nodded enthusiastically.

She seemed pleased and began to play, singing along in a high, reedy voice, "Roses are red and violets are blue-ew-ewew. Find the petals and a killer, too-ew-ew-ew." She quieted the strings, then put her hands in her lap and looked at me, clearly waiting for some words of praise.

It was one of those awkward moments that called for a quick decision. Did I boldly plunge forward with the truth and possibly ruin any chance I had of getting her cooperation? *Angelique, on a scale of one to ten, the poem would rank a one, tops, because frankly it stunk. And neither the verse nor the melody are original because I've heard variations of both before.*"

Or did I go with my other option—the little white lie? Cowardly, yes, but guaranteed to leave us both happier than the truth would.

Answer: "That was amazingly *dolce,* Angelique!"

She gave me a tired sigh, as though I could have done better, then began to absently strum the strings with her right hand. "Why did you ask about the poem?"

"Because I wondered how you knew the killer would have the rose petals."

"It told me so."

"*It* being . . . ?"

"The petal I found outside the storage room. Its spirit spoke to me."

A talking rose petal. I had no comeback for that. Bloomers's blossoms had never so much as whispered to me. Maybe my floral knife had intimidated them. Or, as Grace might say, maybe I just hadn't listened. "Where did you get the tune? Did the petal sing, too?"

"If it had *sung,* I would have told you so," she fairly hissed. "The melody came from"—she waved a thin hand in the air—"far, far away."

"How far?"

"I wasn't actually thinking about what I was hearing, because that was when I found the petal"—Angelique paused as her lower lip began to quiver—"and then I found Sybil, and that's when I realized that whoever had met her in that room had taken the rest of the flower with him." At that she covered her face and began to sob. "If only I could have saved her."

I wasn't sure whether I should attempt a hug or just let her cry, so I glanced across the aisle at Lottie for help and she gave me a questioning glance, as if to ask, *"What did you do to her?"*

I shrugged, then made a motion with my arms to show hugging, then I pointed toward Angelique. Lottie shook her head. Whew. A few consoling words and I was off the hook. "Don't blame yourself for Sybil's death, Angelique. Help me find her killer instead."

She peered up at me with swollen, red-rimmed eyes. "How?"

"What do you remember when you came through the exhibition hall yesterday evening?"

She pulled a tissue out of her pocket and blew her nose. "I've already gone over everything with Grace."

"She has a bad memory. You'd better give it to me again." *Forgive me, Grace.*

"Okay," she said reluctantly, then closed her eyes to concentrate. "I remember that the big overhead lights had been dimmed . . . and the whole room felt very desolate. I didn't see anyone around, not even when I turned the corner into the back hallway. That was when I saw the rose petal and picked it up."

"When did you hear the melody?"

She stared at the floor, her brow wrinkling in thought. "Right before I turned the corner."

"But you didn't see anyone in the hallway?"

"No. I felt an icy chill though, like dead souls swirling all around me."

Or maybe she'd felt a rush of air when the killer opened the back door. "Play the tune for me again, please."

She obliged, but all those cascading notes were too distracting.

"Would you like to see the petal?" she asked.

Without waiting for my answer, Angelique rose in a fluid motion and glided over to a three-tiered stand at the back of her booth, where she had a stack of CDs in plastic cases. She pulled a case from the bottom and brought it back to show me. Through the clear plastic I saw a single rose petal, identical to the ones now in my own pocket.

"Listen," she whispered, holding it against my ear.

I listened for several seconds but heard nothing, not even the ocean. "Sorry, it's not talking to me."

Giving me an annoyed glance, Angelique put the case back, then went to sit at her harp, her delicate fingers strumming the strings as tears continued to course down her white cheeks. My phone began to vibrate, so I excused myself and slipped away to answer it.

"Abby, dear," Grace said in a quiet voice, "would you be good enough to join me in Walker's suite? We're in room four sixty-two on the fourth floor. I'll leave the door unlocked."

There was an expectant tone in her voice that made

my pulse beat faster. "Is everything all right, Grace?"

"Everything is fine. But will you hurry, please? Walker is ready to confess."

Chapter Twenty-three

The colonel did it?" I blurted, but Grace had already hung up. I stood there with the phone pressed to my ear, too stunned to move. Grace had solved the case—damn it.

"Don't that beat all," Lottie said with a laugh after I'd told her. Then she saw my face and donned a serious expression. "Take Marco with you. It might be dangerous up there."

Dangerous? The thought hadn't even occurred to me. Grace was alone with a murderer, and I was thinking solely of my wounded pride. That snapped me out of my funk. "Marco went back to New Chapel," I called, starting up the aisle. "I'll phone him on my way."

I did a speed walk up the aisle, turned the corner, and cut past aisle one, where I could see Chet Sunday onstage with a reporter taping an interview in front of an audience. Serpent Sue was there, too, front and center, in an aqua cashmere sweater.

As I dashed up the main hallway, I noticed that the coffin–phone booth had been taken away. Good riddance, I thought with a shudder, pulling out my cell phone. I hit speed dial number two and headed up the connecting ramp and into the hotel lobby, waiting for

Marco to pick up. When the call went to his voice mail, I left a brief message, then stepped onto the elevator. I got off at the fourth floor, read the brass sign so I'd know in which direction to go, then raced up the long hallway on the left, watching the door numbers until I found the colonel's suite. I pressed my ear against the door but didn't hear anything, so I knocked quickly and said, "It's me, Grace."

"Come in, dear. It's open."

I stepped into a suite that was identical to Sybil's. Inside, I found Grace seated on a beige sofa beside the colonel. Both of them were calmly sipping tea, as though confessing to murder was an everyday occurrence. It was totally surreal.

"Abby," Grace said, rising, "have a seat. I've already poured your cuppa."

I sat in a chair adjacent to the sofa and accepted the cup. Grace sat down beside the colonel, who kept his cup to his lips and his gaze lowered. His normally florid face appeared ashen, except for two spots of color high on his cheekbones.

"Walker and I had a long chat this afternoon," Grace began, "and after much soul-searching he's decided to clear his conscience. He's simply too honorable a man to keep such a troubling matter to himself any longer. This became all the more evident when I explained how vital this information was to your investigation."

So now we were back to *my* investigation instead of *our* investigation. Grace must have decided she'd had enough of playing detective.

"First I need your word, Abby, that this will go no farther than to Marco. I want Walker treated as if he were one of Marco's PI clients."

The colonel was about to confess to murder and I was supposed to keep it to myself? "But, Grace, this is—"

She held up her hand. "It will be up to Walker what happens next." Patting the colonel's hand in a maternal way, she said, "There's nothing to do now but get on with it, love."

He gave her a fond smile. "Thank you, Grace. You've made this much easier for me."

"You're a good man, Walker," Grace said. "Never doubt that. We've all made mistakes that we regret."

I wouldn't have classified shutting someone in a coffin as merely a mistake, yet I couldn't help but admire how Grace had established a deep bond of trust with the colonel in just a few hours. He darted a glance my way as he took out a handkerchief to mop his sweating face, and I noticed then that his eyes were bloodshot and red rimmed, as though he'd been either swigging down the booze or fighting back tears.

In a very dignified manner, he set his cup and saucer on the coffee table and rose, walking to the window to stare outside, his back erect and his hands clasped behind him in a military posture. After a moment he sighed heavily, and keeping his back toward us, began to speak.

"Thaddeus Blount and I opened our funeral home in an old Victorian house that we'd borrowed every dime to buy, but once we'd set up business, we had very little money to spend on advertising. As a way to draw customers, we came up with the idea of offering free cremations for veterans in the hope that we would get return business from the soldiers' families. We went to the VA hospital to spread word of our offer, and it worked after a fashion. But we didn't make much money, so to keep from going bankrupt we"—he paused to take a breath and let it out, as though building strength to finish—"sold cadavers to medical schools."

"Question," I said, as that tiny part of my brain that retained traces of legal knowledge kicked in. "These cadavers, were they your—um—clients?"

With his head bowed, the colonel nodded.

"Did the clients' families give you permission to sell their bodies?"

He hesitated, then slowly shook his head.

Wow. No wonder he wanted that kept quiet. The lawsuits alone would destroy him. "Did you bury empty caskets?"

"No," he said forcefully, "we never sold bodies tagged for burial, only those to be cremated."

"So what did you put in the urns?"

"Chicken-bone ash."

I glanced at Grace in astonishment, but she only put her fingertip to her lips to warn me to keep quiet. So *that* was the secret Billingsworth and Blount had shared. Not only had they sold cadavers, but then they'd duped the families with chicken-bone ash. If that wasn't fraud, I didn't know the law. Come to think of it—well, never mind. An image of Marco's aunt carefully dusting around that urn on her coffee table came to mind. Marco would be furious when he found out.

The colonel continued, "We weren't proud of what we did, believe me, and as soon as we could, we stopped, and never spoke of it again. I'd managed to put it out of my mind entirely until Sybil came to me after Thad died. She told me my old friend had left me a taped message, which I found very touching—until she played it for me. You can imagine my shock when Sybil demanded money to keep it quiet."

He stopped to wipe his brow again. "I tried to convince her that the scandal would damage the good name of Blount along with mine, but she didn't care, and I knew Sybil well enough to take her threat seriously. What else could I have done? I would have disgraced my wife, who has stood by me all these years, and my sons' reputations would also be tainted. You can imagine my turmoil. So I started meeting her demands, even though paying a sum that large was depleting my life savings. Thad and I had made a good living on the funeral home, but I wasn't wealthy by any means. If I had continued to pay her, my funds would have been gone within fifteen months, and I simply couldn't let her do that to me."

He dropped his head into his hands and muttered, "I just couldn't let her do it."

I was about to ask him a question when Grace mouthed, "Wait."

Finally, the colonel raised his head, distress etched in the fleshy folds of his face.

Here comes the confession, I thought, wishing I had a tape recorder. Too bad Reilly wasn't here to witness this.

"So I did the only thing I could," he said in a voice heavy with regret. "I cashed in my 401(k) retirement fund so I could pay her off once and for all."

Wait. What? That wasn't a murder confession. I gave Grace a look that said, *What gives?* She signaled for me to be patient.

"Somewhere in Sybil's house there's a DVD with my name on it," the colonel said sadly. "I only hope it never sees the light of day."

"Thank you, Walker," Grace said. "Now I believe Abby has some questions. Abby?"

"Okay, let me make sure I understand this," I said to him, putting my cup on the table. "You didn't kill Sybil?"

"Kill her?" The colonel barked, puffing up his chest like an outraged pigeon.

"I thought Grace said on the phone—well, never mind. I must have misunderstood."

"Please be assured, young lady, that I had nothing to do with Sybil's death."

"Perhaps you should tell Abby about your conversation with Sybil yesterday, Walker," Grace gently coaxed.

The colonel took a deep breath. "Last week Sybil called me to arrange a meeting for this weekend. It was set for yesterday afternoon at three o'clock in her suite, and I knew instantly that she was going to up her demands. So I told her that I was running out of funds and that I'd have to either quit paying and take my chances or pay her a lump sum in exchange for the DVD and be done with it. She wasn't happy, but I held my ground, so she finally agreed to it. I think she sensed my desperation and knew I'd reached my limit.

"Yesterday afternoon, as she made her rounds of the exhibitors, she stopped to tell me that she had to change our meeting time. I didn't think anything of it then, but looking back, she seemed very edgy. I didn't see her again until her body was found."

"Do you know why she changed the time?" I asked.

"No, and I didn't ask. I could barely tolerate the sight of that woman."

"Do you have any guesses about who might have killed her?"

"Several people come to mind—the Urban boys, Eli Cotton, and Sybil's other blackmail victims, if they're attending the convention."

"Do you know who her other victims were?"

"Unfortunately, no. The only reason I'm certain there are more victims is because of a comment Sybil made. It hearkens back to when she first gave me her blackmail demand. I was in a complete state of shock, as you can well imagine. This woman had been my best friend's wife. We'd dined together, vacationed together, and then she turned on me just like that. So I said to her, 'How can you stoop to such a despicable act, Sybil? Thad would be deeply ashamed of you.' And her reply was, 'It gets easier with practice.'"

"Wow," I said. "It sounds like she was a pro. You mentioned the Urbans as potential suspects. Is it possible she was blackmailing them?"

"Anything is possible. I wouldn't have thought her capable of blackmailing me, but that proved to be a mistake. Who knows who else she targeted."

"Do you know if she was having affairs while her husband was alive?"

"No, I don't. It wasn't until Thad died that rumors of her dalliances reached my ears, but as I said, anything is possible."

"Did the rumors link her with younger men as a rule?"

"Sadly, yes." The colonel sighed. "I wonder how much my old friend knew about the real Sybil. I never felt they were a good match. She'd lost her first husband under questionable circumstances, and it hadn't taken her long after being hired to latch on to Thaddeus. I can only imagine her glee when Thad made his deathbed confession. What an opportunist she turned out to be. Although I may be damned for saying so, I'm immensely relieved she's gone."

While Grace murmured consoling words, I sipped my tea and thought over what the colonel had said. He didn't know that I'd seen the DVD or knew of the existence of Sybil's bankbook or the other video, but his story certainly fit with what I'd learned so far. I was satisfied he hadn't killed Sybil, but if I ruled out the colonel, Angelique, Chet, and Eli, by process of elimination that left one of the Urbans. The final bit of proof had to be on that *Chester Cheater* video. It was my last hope.

I stood up, eager to find a machine to watch the tape. "I need to get going, but thank you, colonel, for your honesty and bravery in sharing your story with me. I appreciate how difficult that was for you."

Grace walked me to the door and stepped into the hall. "Does this help the investigation, dear?" She already knew the answer, but she had to hear me say it.

"Yes, it does. Thank you, Grace."

"Do you see now why I was flirting with Walker?"

"Yep."

"Shall we discuss why you didn't want me investigating?"

Nope. I pointed to my watch. "I'd really like to, but time is flying, Grace."

"Then I would think you'd want to be quick about it, dear." She gave me a firm smile.

Go on. Let her see how selfish you are. I drew a breath and on the exhale said, "I was afraid you'd solve the case before I did."

"Yes, I thought that might be it." Grace put an arm around me. "But you see, I was on the wrong path, wasn't I? Don't worry, love. With your tenacity and courage, you'll solve it. You're a natural. Now, off you go. Time is flying."

A natural! "Thanks, Grace. You might have been on the wrong path, but you did help a lot." I gave her a hug and headed toward the elevators, beaming. Grace's opinion meant a lot to me. My phone vibrated. I flipped it open. "Hey, Houdini. How's it going? Are you missing me yet?"

"I can barely function," Marco drawled. "Listen, I just got your message. Did Billingsworth confess?"

"Yes, but not to murder, only to paying Sybil's blackmail demands. I'll give you the whole story when I see you, but in a nutshell he didn't kill her. Now I need to find a Beta player."

"No, you don't. We're done investigating."

"What about your buddy in hotel security?"

"He doesn't have one."

I pressed the DOWN button. "Chet Sunday might. Remember the show he did this morning? I'm going to get the *Chester Cheater* cassette and head over to his set now. I hope his crew hasn't dismantled it yet."

"Forget about the Beta player, Abby. Go back to Billingsworth. Did he tell you what the big secret was?"

I really didn't want to be the one to tell Marco that his aunt had been dusting around chicken-bone fragments for the past thirty-five years, so I made a crackling sound, then said, "You're breaking up, ——arco. You ——ust be out of ——ange. Call me ——ater."

I snapped the phone shut, stuck it in my pocket, and stepped onto the elevator. Too bad there wasn't a law class on artful dodging. I would have aced it.

When I got back to our booth it was four fifteen, the only time slot left at the loading dock. Lottie and Max had packed up all the brochures, cards, and photo albums from the table, and Max had carried a load to the van. Lottie had stayed behind to take down the wall decor.

"What happened with the colonel?" she asked as I dropped to my knees and lifted the table skirt to retrieve my purse and the shopping bag.

"He's not the killer. I'll tell you about it later, because right now I have to get back to Chet Sunday's booth."

I opened the bag, and my heart stopped. There was nothing inside.

Chapter Twenty-four

A re you looking for that yellow package?" Lottie asked.

I sat up and banged my head on the edge of the table. "Ouch. Yes. Have you seen it?"

She opened her huge purse and pulled out the big manila envelope. "Sorry, sweetie. I didn't mean to give you a fright. I was afraid you'd forget it and someone else would come across it after we'd packed up and gone."

I breathed a sigh of relief as I opened one end and pulled out the cassette. Lottie peered over my shoulder, reading the label on the spine. "*Chester Cheater*? Is that a video game?"

"I don't think so." I turned the case to show her the front.

"A porn flick?"

"That's my guess, but I won't know until I find a Beta tape player. We think Sybil was blackmailing at least two people, the colonel being one of them. I'm hoping this tape will show the identity of the second one, because it may also identify a suspect."

"I thought you were sure it was one of the Urbans."

"I still think they were involved, but Beta tapes were phased out in the eighties, so it doesn't seem possible that Ross or Jess is on this tape."

Lottie tapped her chin. "Could it be that their daddy is in the movie and he's the one Sybil was black-mailing?"

"That's a possibility. But somehow I can't see a high-powered businessman like Conrad Urban putting up with some Mickey Mouse blackmail demands. I doubt even Sybil would have the nerve to attempt that. She was smart enough to know he'd retaliate somehow. . . ."

An idea popped into my head. I glanced at Lottie and saw she was thinking the same thing.

"Maybe Conrad killed her," we said in unison.

"Maybe," Lottie mused, "Conrad Urban concocted the whole scheme to lure her to the storage room and let his boys carry it out."

"Means, motive, and opportunity. You might be on to something, Lottie, except wouldn't that be a risky thing for a dad to do to his sons?"

"I don't see Conrad winning any father-of-the-year awards, do you?"

"I see your point. Still, having Ross dress the mannequin afterward doesn't sound like something a smart, high-powered businessman would do."

"Maybe Ross just couldn't stop himself from playing one last prank on her," Lottie said. "You know the old saying—boys will be boys."

I had to consider it. As Marco had pointed out, so much just didn't add up.

"*Chester Cheater* must be a send-up of the cartoon cat Chester Cheetah from those Cheetos commercials," Lottie said. "Or was that before your time?"

"I remember the character from a video game. He was orange and white and wore dark glasses and a black beret."

"That's him. He called himself Mr. Cool. He was supposed to be a beatnik." Lottie sighed wistfully. "You probably don't know what a beatnik is."

Mr. Cool? Why did that ring a bell?

"One of my boys—I think it was Karl—dressed up as Chester Cheetah for Halloween one year." She chuckled at the memory. "He could imitate that lazy, hep-cat voice perfectly. *'I'm too cool to fool.'*"

Wait. I'd heard that phrase, and very recently. But when? Where? Who? I pressed my fingers to my temples, trying to stimulate my memory cells. *Mr. Cool, Mr. Cool. Come on, brain. The clock is ticking.*

I was getting something, a sliver of a conversation I'd had yesterday . . . with the Urbans! *"We're too cool to fool.*" Yes! That was it. Jess had used that phrase Saturday morning, after I'd confronted him and Ross about their phone-booth prank and the sign on Sybil's skirt.

"Why do you want to embarrass her?" I'd asked them, after hearing about the joke they'd played on Sybil. *"What has she done to you?"*

"Nothing," Jess the Mess had said, *"and that's the way we want to keep it. We're too cool to fool. Hey, Ross. Let's get her again."*

"Dude, what should we do?" Ross had asked.

"You're asking me? Come on, Mr. Cool, you're the one with the ideas."

I tucked the cassette inside my purse and slung the strap over my shoulder. "There has to be a connection between this tape and the Urbans, Lottie. I heard Jess refer to Ross as Mr. Cool, and he even used that *too cool to fool* catch phrase, and that's just too coincidental. Maybe Sugar Shackup is their mother, or maybe Conrad produced the flick. All I know is that if I don't find a Beta player soon, I'm going to explode from curiosity, and that won't be a pretty sight. Freckles all over the ceiling—"

"Get going," Lottie said with a chuckle, giving me a gentle push.

I hurried up the aisle toward Chet Sunday's booth, hoping the set with his electronic equipment was still there. But when I rounded the corner at the top of aisle two, I could see from that distance that the *Make It Easy* set had been stripped down to the backdrop and the camera equipment. Chet had stuck around, though, standing center stage beside a businessman in a black suit who was speaking through a microphone to a sizable crowd.

I spotted Serpent Sue and edged in beside her, trying to find out what was going on. She glanced down at me and bared her fangs in recognition. No lipstick on them today. "You couldn't stay away, either, huh?" she asked, turning her wistful yet somehow pathetic gaze back to Chet.

"Are you kidding? A free chocolate buffet couldn't have kept me from attending." I nodded toward the stage. "What's going on?"

"Didn't you hear the announcement earlier? The president of Habitation Station is presenting Chet with an award."

"For what?"

She waved away my question as a triviality. "Saving the planet or something."

Saving the planet. Wow. Quite a feat for a television personality. "I must have been outside when the announcement was made. Are you sure the award isn't for humanitarian of the year?"

"No, it had something to do with the planet. Maybe Planet Hollywood?"

"When did the speech start?"

"Five minutes ago." Sue heaved a lustful sigh. "Look at Chet up there. Isn't he just too yummy? I can't get enough of him, although I sure would like to try. Hey, maybe we can form a Chet Sunday fan club.

I'll bet he'd really go for that. What do you think? Should we ask him?"

"Actually, I'm working on a murder investigation."

"Really? Are you a cop?"

"No, I'm just helping a friend."

"So why do you need to see Chet?"

"To see if I can borrow his tape player."

She waggled her finger at me. "This investigation is about Sybil Blount's death, isn't it? I had a feeling she didn't pull that lid shut on herself."

Okay, time to move on.

With Chet otherwise occupied, I went around behind the set to see whether the electronic equipment was still there. Instead, I found a member of his TV crew loading a crate onto a dolly.

"Looking for someone, baby?" He was chewing— or should I say smacking—a stick of spearmint gum, which I could smell from four feet away. He had a stocky build, a big beer belly, a shaved head that showed off the overhang of his low Neanderthal fore-head, and an ugly lizard tattoo up one side of his neck. He was dressed in a brown jumpsuit with the words MAKE IT EASY on the front. I would have added to that phrase: TO PUKE.

"Bet you're waiting for Chet, am I right? Yeah, he's a popular guy, our Chet, so's you might wanna take a number . . . or you could take your chances with Lizard Lover Luke." He used a fat thumb to point to himself, wiggling an inch-thick eyebrow. "That's me, if ya didn't know. Lizard Lover Luke at Yahoo-dot-com."

"Thanks, um, Lizard, but I just wanted to check out Chet's equipment."

"You and every other chick in this building," he said with a snicker.

"His *electronic* equipment," I said with a scowl. "I came across an old movie and I'm looking for a Beta cassette player so I can preview it. I thought I remembered that Chet had one for the show today."

"He's got one, but you'll have to ask Chet about using it. He brings all his own electronic stuff with him, and it's already been loaded into his big RV. It's sitting out at the loading dock right now."

"Terrific," I muttered.

"Listen, if you ask Chet real nice, he might give you a private screening. He's got quite a set up in that RV—leather sofas, big-screen high-def TV, full bar, mood lighting—the works. He travels everywhere in it. Had to cost him some big bucks, I'll tell ya that."

"A private screening? I thought Chet was all about being a decent guy."

"Sure, he's a decent guy. No need to get yourself in a stew, baby. I ain't insinuating anything's gonna happen that you don't want to happen. But I ain't saying he doesn't have some fun along the way, either. Look, it can't hurt to ask him, can it?"

"Sure. Thanks for the help." Private screening. Yeah, right. The only way I'd watch *Chester Cheater* was alone. But even if Chet agreed to let me use his tape player, I'd still have to wait until the end of his award ceremony, and time seemed to be moving at warp speed. But what choice did I have? Thank goodness for that cocktail party. One hour could make all the difference.

When I rejoined the audience, Chet was giving an acceptance speech. I glanced at my watch, dismayed to see that it was almost four thirty.

"I would like to tank you again, Mr. Pelliman, for bestowing this award on me. I accept it with great honor and vow to continue my efforts to make this great country of ours a cleaner place for us to live."

Cameras flashed and the audience clapped as the Habitation Station president shook Chet's hand. I immediately moved toward the stage to catch Chet before he left, but his fans were faster, quickly forming a line in front of me. Serpent Sue was third, so I sidled up beside her and began to chat as if we were longtime friends, hoping to casually insert myself behind her without causing a rebellion in the ranks.

"I hope Chet appears here next year, don't you?" I said in a bubbly voice, as if that had been our ongoing topic of conversation.

Serpent Sue turned to look in both directions, as though she didn't know where those words had come from.

"*Psst.* Down here."

"Oh, there you are." She patted the top of my head. "You're so short I didn't see you."

Height remarks made me incredibly fractious, but

since I needed to latch on to her I tucked away my comment about her Amazonian stature and gave her a smile.

"I don't know if Chet will ever come back to our convention," Sue said sadly, her bright pink lips wilting like an aging tulip. "With Sybil gone and all. I mean, say what you will about her, she was the driving force that got him to come."

Hearing grumbling from the troops behind me, I knew it was time to make my move or be ousted. There was no worse foe than a queue of women who'd been cut in front of one time too many. I drew Sue down and said quietly, "If *you* ask Chet, he might come."

Her fangs came out in full force. "You think?"

"And if we *both* ask, there's no way he'll refuse."

"That's a super idea!" she effervesced, and tried to link her arm through mine, but gave up when she discovered she'd have to bend sideways. So she put her arm around my shoulders instead and we stepped forward as one. I glanced around at the angry army behind me and shrugged, as if to say, *Out of my control. Sorry.*

They didn't believe me, and I didn't have time to care.

"Hi, Chet," Sue said eagerly, squeezing her arms against her boobs to make them look bigger. "Remember me? Sue Antioch? From Chicago?" She smiled, revealing those feral eyeteeth, and instantly there was a glimmer of recognition in his gaze.

"I remember you, Sue. And you," he said, pointing at me, "are Nikki's friend . . . Ruby."

"Abby."

"Whatever. Do you ladies have someting for me to sign?"

"Did you hear that? *Someting,*" Sue said to me, running her hand down Chet's arm, making sure he had a great view of her cleavage. "I just adore your Russian accent, Chet."

"I'm from Croatia, but tank you," he said politely.

I tried to give Sue a smug smile, but she was thrusting her pen and a piece of hotel stationery at him and paying no attention to me.

"Oh, Chet, you absolutely have to come back to our convention next year!" she gushed, nudging me in the ear with her elbow.

"We'll be totally devastated if you don't," I added, trying to match her enthusiasm.

"Well," Chet said slowly, eyeing the V in her sweater, "I'll have to tink about it."

Sue knew exactly how to start that process. She lifted one shoulder to her chin, arched one eyebrow provocatively, and pouted her lips à la Marilyn Monroe. "What can we do to bring you back, handsome?"

She nudged me with her foot this time, but the only famous persona I could possibly incarnate was Pippi Longstocking, and somehow she paled beside Marilyn. So I kept my reply to a hearty, "Ditto."

Looking ill at ease in front of his fans, Chet said,

"Why don't you step up onto the stage and wait until I finish here, and then we can discuss it?"

"Sure," Sue said, and motioned for me to follow as she wiggled her way up the steps, obviously still channeling Miss Monroe.

I followed, but I didn't wiggle. I was running out of time and, as we stood there watching Chet sign autographs and chitchat with his fans, out of patience, too. "Listen," I said to Sue, "when Chet comes up here, would you mind if I asked my favor first? I'm in a real time crunch. Then you can have him all to yourself."

"Okay."

That was easy. Waiting was not. I paced, stewed, checked my watch, and paced some more. Finally, the last fan left, clutching the convention brochure with her hero's handwriting on it, and Chet sauntered up the stairs and made straight for Sue.

I held up my hand to get his attention. "Excuse me, Chet, could I ask you a favor?"

But his focus was on Sue—and her low-cut sweater. "Now, what is this about you wanting me to return next year?" he asked her.

"You will come back, won't you?" she asked in a breathless voice, squeezing her boobs for him again. "I'd—we'd—be so grateful."

He smiled. "You didn't ask what I charge."

"And you didn't ask what I'd be willing to pay." She whispered something in his ear that made him blush.

If I didn't need that tape player, I'd be so out of

there. But I had to stand there like a mope until Sue got her way.

Chet turned so he was angled toward her, where he apparently thought I couldn't see what he was doing; then he picked up Sue's hand and flipped it palm up so he could rub his thumb in the center. "Maybe I can tink of someting," he murmured.

Ew. I really didn't like this side of Chet. His wholesome handyman image was quickly dissolving into a puddle of lecherousness. But I couldn't let a little dirty water stand in my way.

As they gazed lustfully into each other's eyes, I said, "While you two are busy *tinking,* would you mind if I popped into your RV, Chet, to use your Beta cassette tape player?"

Without even taking his gaze away from Sue, he said, "What for?"

Duh. "So I can watch a tape. I'll only need about ten minutes and you won't have to lift a finger. I can get Lizard Lover Luke to let me in. Please? It's very important."

"Sorry. I don't let people use my personal equipment."

"I totally understand, but I promise I'll be careful. I wouldn't ask if I wasn't desperate, but it's hard to find those Beta machines."

"Do you have to watch this tape *now?*" he said, giving me a frown, probably because I'd spoiled the mood.

"Yes. Right now. I'll be quick, though."

Sue held a finger to her pouting lips. "Sh-h-h! Don't

tell anyone, but she's investigating Sybil's death." Then her eyes opened wide and she said excitedly, "Oh, wow. I just had a terrific idea." She leaned close to him to whisper, "Why don't we all go to your RV? You know, for a little threesome?"

Chet turned a speculative gaze on her, and at her suggestive wink, he eliminated the last shred of hope I had for any wholesomeness when he murmured, "A treesome? Maybe so."

Maybe not. I didn't want anywhere near that forest. Trying to look disappointed, I leaned between them and said quietly, "You know, that's a tough invitation to turn down, but I don't have a single minute to spare, so how about letting me inside for ten minutes to watch my tape, and then you two can have the RV to yourselves?"

Sue gave Chet a doe-eyed, pleading look, cooing, "How about it, lover?"

Chet pondered it for a moment, then smiled slyly. "I tink that just might work."

Chapter Twenty-five

When we arrived at the loading dock, Lizard Lover Luke was pushing his empty dolly up a wooden ramp toward us. "Hey, boss," he said, "that was my last load. I got your slide-outs all tucked away, so all you have to do is disconnect the power when you're ready to roll. I'm going to take off now unless you need me for something else."

"You're done for the day, Luke," Chet said. "I'll meet up with you in Minneapolis tomorrow afternoon."

"Sure thing." As Luke passed me, he said quietly, "I see you get to check out his equipment after all, heh-heh."

Crawl under your leaf, lizard boy.

"This way," Chet said, and led us down the ramp to where the RV was parked, although calling the vehicle an RV was about as appropriate as calling a full-size Hummer a go-cart.

Chet Sunday's customized motor coach had a full diesel truck cab and extended an impressive fifty-two feet in length, with three hydraulic slide-out rooms that extended the living space to an astounding 378 square feet. I knew all this because I'd watched the show in which he'd given viewers a tour of the interior. Being somewhat of a car buff, I was fascinated by the whole concept. I also knew Chet drove the coach himself, preferring it over air travel, not that I blamed him. The inside was as luxurious as a suite in any five-star hotel, which, sadly, I'd seen only on the Travel Channel. It sure beat being squeezed into an airplane seat the size of a tissue box.

The outside of the coach was painted gold with MAKE IT EASY in thick black letters, and a smiling Chet leaning jauntily against a ladder, holding a paintbrush, as though he'd just painted the words himself. The ladder, toward the front of the coach on one side, cleverly disguised a door; on the other side it framed one of the windows. Next to Chet on both sides was a big ad for Habitation Station.

Chet used his key to unlock the ladder-disguised door, an oak-paneled beauty on the inside, with a small tinted-glass window near the top. All the windows were tinted black, no doubt for security reasons. The door was located near the truck cab, which naturally had its own door for the driver. Two steps up and we were inside the coach, staring around in amazement.

Chet spread out his arms. "My little home away from home."

Little? Hardly. We were standing in the living room, which contained a white leather sofa and recliner on one side and a fifty-inch LCD big-screen TV built into an oak cabinet on the other. The windows above the sofa and chair were covered in white pleated shades, separated from each other by brass sconces, with recessed lights in the ceiling. The floors were oak with a black walnut border, with plush, cream-colored carpeting under the seating and dining areas.

"It's a little crowded now," he said. "The slide-outs have been pushed in."

"What's a slide-out?" Sue asked.

"Where the floor slides out to expand the room," he explained. "This coach has three slide-outs, one for the living area, one for dining area, and one for the bedroom."

"Oh, a bump-out," she said, finally getting it.

"Bump-outs are for campers," Chet said. "This is a custom motor coach, top of the line."

Well, weren't we impressed?

I turned to my left, where beyond the sofa I could see a kitchen/dining area, complete with oak cabinets, marble countertops, and built-in refrigerator, microwave, oven, and cooktop. The round oak dining room table sat four, with white leather chairs that matched the other furniture.

"Oh, please give us a tour," Sue begged, hanging on to his arm.

Chet glanced at his watch. "We'll have to make it quick."

"I hope that's the only thing we make quick," she said with a giggle.

Barf bag, anyone?

"The cab is up front, through that last doorway," Chet said, pointing toward an opening in an oak-paneled wall. "I like to keep it closed off from the living area. It makes me feel more at home when I'm back here."

"I see what you mean," Sue said, stretching her long body out on the sofa.

"This is my media room," Chet said, stepping through the first doorway.

The small space between the living room and the cab contained a short white sofa opposite a wall of built-in electronic equipment, with a desk below. Toward the front and one step down was the cab, with white leather swivel chairs and state-of-the-art driving equipment. Thick, custom-made folding panels had been pulled across the front windshield and locked into place for privacy, blocking all daylight.

"As you can see," Chet said, pointing out the various electronic components, "I have a computer, a flat-screen monitor, live tracking satellite, surround-sound stereo, DVD/VCR player, eight-track recorder, turntable, and right at the top, a Betamax tape player."

Woo-hoo! No need to show me the rest of the coach. I'd found everything I needed. Restless Sue, however, had moved on.

"Wow," she called from the rear of the coach. "I've never seen a round bed before."

"Wait till she sees the sauna," Chet said to me with a chuckle.

A sauna in a motor coach? No way. The videotape would have to wait a few more minutes.

I followed Chet toward the back of the coach, through the living room and kitchen, and into a short, oak-paneled hallway, where he stopped to open a door onto a small space lined with red cedar benches and marble on the walls. "Here is the sauna."

Sue came running up to peer inside. "A sauna! Oh, Chet, we *have* to try it out."

"The bathroom is across the hall," he said as Sue slipped past him and wiggled her way to the bedroom, where I caught a glimpse of an expanse of bed and mirrored walls.

Keeping one eye on Sue, who was sprawled on the bed and appeared to be getting ready to take off her sweater, Chet said to me, "I'll set up the tape player; then we will leave you alone."

"Thanks. I really appreciate it."

He led the way to the media room and turned on the TV and the tape player, then picked up a remote control and pointed out the PLAY button, as if I'd never operated one before.

"Now let's see if you can work it," he said.

To humor him, I took the cassette out of my purse and inserted it into the slot, then pressed the PLAY button. The monitor flickered; then suddenly we were looking at a sweaty, naked couple moaning and writhing in happy delirium on red satin sheets. *Yikes*. I quickly hit the STOP button and risked a glance at Chet, who seemed as astonished as I was. Darn. I should have made sure the movie was rewound.

Embarrassed, I scratched the tip of my nose, a nervous habit I'd picked up in law school. Come to think of it, I'd had a pretty sore nose that entire year. "Um, I didn't know what was on that tape."

"Perhaps you'd rather I made you a DVD copy so you can watch it at home? Alone? Then you won't have to waste your time here." His eyes shifted toward the bedroom, and I knew he was in a hurry to get back to Sue.

"How long would that take?"

"Ten—fifteen minutes at the most. I have to set up my equipment first."

"Chet," Sue sang out. "Are you coming?"

"Listen, you've got company, so if you don't mind, I'll just catch a few minutes of the tape, then slip out. That way I won't be a bother."

"It's not a bother. Just leave everyting to me."

"Really, no, but thanks anyway. You go do—whatever—and I'll let myself out when I've finished."

He studied me. "You're stubborn, aren't you?"

"I like to think of myself as determined."

"Okay, then. Make yourself comfortable. We'll be a while." He stepped through the doorway and closed it behind him.

I waited until I heard Sue giggle; then I put my purse on the floor beside the sofa, pressed REWIND on the remote, and sank onto the soft leather. When the machine stopped, I hit PLAY and MUTE, then leaned back to watch. The movie title appeared, followed by the names of the actors. The movie opened with a shot of what was obviously a college dormitory. A girl was lying on her stomach on her narrow bed, reading a book. Her blond hair was wound into a tight, prim bun on top of her head, and she had on owlish wire-rimmed glasses and a thick, old-fashioned terry-cloth robe. I could see where *that* plotline was headed.

I moved closer to the monitor, where I could also see that the girl definitely wasn't a young Sybil. Cross off that idea.

Hearing a tap on her door, the actress, whom I assumed was Sugar Shackup, called, "Come in," and her door opened to reveal a studly male student with a square jaw, heavy mustache, black-framed glasses, and curly brown hair. He wore plaid pants, a gold chain, and a shirt that was open to halfway down his chest, revealing muscular pecs and curly chest hair.

Wait. Chest hair . . . Chester? It had to be Chester

Domingo. I moved even closer to see his face. Could that be Conrad Urban? I couldn't see any resemblance to Ross or Jess, but the thick mustache and glasses hid a lot.

All at once the monitor went dark, along with everything else in the room, leaving me in pitch blackness. I couldn't even see my hand in front of my face. Had the tape player overloaded the circuit?

Within seconds, to my great relief, the door opened and Chet appeared with a flashlight in his hand (and clothes on his body). "The electricity is down. I'll have to go outside to check the power supply. Stay where you are, and I'll be just a minute."

"Do you have another flashlight?" I rubbed my arms to banish the goosebumps. There was no way I was going to sit in a dark, confined space.

He produced a blue plastic disposable lighter from a cabinet. "There's a candle in the storage compartment behind the passenger seat. You can use it until I get the juice back on."

I followed his flashlight beam and stepped down into the cab, where I found a short, vanilla-scented pillar on a brass candleholder in the compartment. Chet waited until I'd lit the candle; then he started to close the door, shutting off the media room from the rest of the trailer.

"Keep it open, please," I said nervously. "Just until the lights come on."

He obliged. I put the lighter and the lit candle on the desk, then sat down to wait. I could hear Chet talking to Sue as he moved through the coach; then I heard the door open and close, and then silence. Still on edge, I stood up and went to look at the various electronic components, trying to distract myself. Thank goodness I had some light.

A few minutes later the door opened again, then quietly closed. Then I heard nothing more. Strange. Why would Chet come back inside before the electricity was on? Or maybe it was Sue leaving, deciding to follow him outside to see what the problem was.

After a long moment of wondering, I called, "Sue?" Silence.

A sound from a distant room, like a soft rustle of cloth, raised more goosebumps on my arms. Was someone inside or not? "Chet? Sue? Are you there?"

More silence. Maybe I'd imagined the rustle. Then a hard thump, like a shoe against wood, told me it hadn't been my imagination after all. Someone was in the coach and didn't want me to know it. What I did know was that I needed to get out of there, so I picked up the candle and moved quietly toward the doorway.

Just as I reached it, the hair on the nape of my neck prickled. I stopped, listened, and heard breathing that wasn't my own. Someone was on the other side of the doorway. My heart hammered wildly as I took a step back, trying to think what to do.

Suddenly, there was a blur of motion and the candle snuffed out, leaving me once again in the dark. Only this time I had company.

Chapter Twenty-six

"Who's there?" I demanded, trying to sound fierce as I eased backward toward the desk. I felt for the lighter with trembling hands and flicked it, trying to get it to spark. It caught at last, producing a weak blue flame. I held it to the candle, but before the wick caught flame, a mop of springy gray curls and a long, gaunt, hollow-cheeked face appeared in the doorway.

"Eli! You scared me half to—"

"Sh-h!" He stepped into the room and pulled the oak door shut behind him, cutting us off from the rest of the coach. "Put out that light. I can't take any chances."

Any chances? What was he talking about? "I'm claustrophobic, Eli. The light helps."

"Put it out," he whispered harshly, moving toward me. "The police might see it."

"That's okay. They won't hurt you. I'll talk to them."

He jerked the candle out of my hand and tossed it onto the small sofa. "Just do as I say."

By the dim, flickering blue light, I could see that his pupils were dilated and his mouth showed foamy spittle in the corners. For the first time he looked truly deranged, and I was scared. "Okay, Eli. It's going out."

I flipped the lighter shut, cutting off the thin flame. Fearfully, I widened my stance and raised my fists in front of my face, ready to either defend myself or run like hell. How could I have been so off the mark with Eli? I should have listened to Marco and Reilly, but no, I had to trust my instincts. They never lied. Boy, when I was wrong about a person, I was *really* wrong.

Even worse was knowing that the cops probably wouldn't think to search Chet's darkened motor coach. Even if they approached it, all they'd have to do was talk to Chet, who'd tell them Eli wasn't there. What was I going to do?

I could hear Eli moving around the small space, but I couldn't tell what he was doing. "How did you know I was here?" I whispered.

"I saw you go in—" Eli stopped moving. "What was that?"

"What was what?" *Please be Chet please be Chet please be Chet.*

"Sh-h-h!"

I didn't hear anything except for the blood pounding in my ears. Damn it, why hadn't Chet turned on the juice? Being in total darkness was more frightening than anything else because I had no way to prepare. "Eli, you'd better get out while you can. Chet will be back any minute—he only went to fix the electricity—and you don't want to tangle with him."

"I know where he went," Eli snapped. "I cut the cord to get him out of the way."

Out of the *way?* For what, to kill me?

To think I fell for Eli's story about wanting to get inside to hand out brochures! He'd been after Sybil right from that first confrontation in front of the convention center. No, more like from the moment she'd had him fired from Billingsworth and Blount. Then when he suspected that I was investigating the murder, he'd started stalking me. And all the while I had railed against the injustice of picking on a man whose only goal was to promote his burlap bags.

I took a slow, steady breath to calm my rising fear, knowing I'd never escape if I panicked. I needed a plan. *Think, Abby! Where's the nearest door?* I tried to picture the cab. There was a door on the driver's side, but I'd have to maneuver the step between the swivel chairs, crawl over the driver's seat, and fumble for the handle, all in the dark. The door was sure to be locked. What if I couldn't find the button to unlock it before Eli found *me?*

Suddenly, big hands clamped down on my upper arms from behind, causing me to let out a startled gasp and instinctively try to twist away so I could aim a good kick. But he was stronger than I thought, and hustled me across the small space until my knees hit the sofa. "Sit," he commanded.

I sat, trying to keep my breathing even so I didn't faint. Time seemed to be passing in nanoseconds as my mind raced in fear. Wasn't it supposed to happen just the opposite way? Wasn't time supposed to slow down when a person faced death? *New plan, Abby. Come on!*

If only I had my cell phone! But it was in my purse, on the floor next to the sofa, just beyond my reach. If

I could scoot over a few inches, then ease my hand down the side of the sofa, slip it into the purse, and get the phone open far enough to hit the SEND button, it would call the last number dialed—Marco's number.

But how would he know where I was? Foolishly, I hadn't told Lottie or Grace where I was headed. The only people to see me enter the motor coach were Eli, Sue, and Lizard Lover Luke, and he'd probably already left for home. I didn't have a clue as to where Sue had gone. Maybe Eli had gotten her out of the way, too.

I moved closer to the edge of the sofa but froze when I heard Eli kneel down in front of me. I couldn't see him, but I could smell his garlicky breath. "Listen to me carefully. It's almost five o'clock. I need to get back inside the convention center before everyone leaves."

I had to keep him talking so I could slip my hand into my purse. It was an open-topped tote bag, and my cell phone would probably be at the bottom, which meant I'd have to dig through everything on top. "What are you going to do in the convention center?"

"I told you when I saw you in the woods," he said impatiently.

"Look, I'm a little rattled right now, so would you mind refreshing my memory?" *Lip gloss, pack of tissues, box of mints, comb, checkbook, receipt, receipt, receipt . . .*

"I have to find the man with the shoes."

Not that again. "The man who killed Sybil, right?" *Where was my phone?*

"Right, and you have to get me inside before he leaves, without the cops seeing me. So here's what you'll have to do. At the west end of the—"

"Time out. Are you telling me that you're keeping me in this dark, stuffy space to explain how I'm going to get you inside the convention center?"

"What did you think?" he asked, clearly exasperated.

That Marco was right about you being a wack job. "You cut the electricity to get Chet out of the motor coach so you could duck inside to talk to me?"

"Have I been talking gibberish?"

"All you want from me is my *help?*"

He leaned into my face, washing me with his sour breath. "I. Need. You. To. Get. Me. Inside. Do you get it now?"

"Got it."

"Listen carefully. There are two cops stationed at the corner of the west end of the building, and another pair on the east end. There's also a team with dogs out in the woods. There's probably more cops inside each entrance. When Chet returns with his floozy, wait until they're in the bedroom, then slip out the side door. You can't go through the cab because it's locked. Go through the loading-dock door and find me a disguise that covers my head."

"Where am I supposed to find a disguise?"

"You'll come up with something. Then bring it back here and rap twice on the cab window so I'll know it's you. Understand?"

Oh, yeah. I understood—that I had a way out. What I didn't understand was why he was making it so easy for me to escape. If he wanted to harm me, his plan made no sense. Was he stupid *and* dangerous or just crazy?

Does it matter? Actually, it did, because strangely enough, my gut feeling about Eli had returned, stronger than ever. Ah, I'd found the phone at last. I pried it open with my thumb and felt for the SEND button.

All at once the lights and television burst on, making me blink as my eyes adjusted, and sending Eli to his feet in surprise as the videotape resumed where it had left off. Eli was wearing jeans and a denim shirt, and without the brown robe he looked as normal as any other wild-haired, hollow-cheeked madman.

I pressed SEND, then laid the open phone on top of the jumble inside my purse and carefully slid my hand out so he wouldn't suspect what I'd done. I needn't have worried. Eli was standing in the middle of the room staring at the monitor as the actor on the video said to the actress, "I hear you're looking for a tutor," then laughed lasciviously.

I reached for the remote to turn it off, but Eli cried, "Don't stop it." He stepped up to the monitor and tapped his finger against it. "What's the actor's name?"

Why did he care? Hoping Marco had answered his phone and could hear me, I said, "Eli, listen, if you want your plan to get inside the convention center to work, you'd better—"

"Tell me the actor's name," he demanded, flapping his arms against his sides.

"I believe he's Chester Domingo."

Eli pounded the screen with his hand. "This has to be the guy, only a younger version. It's the same laugh I heard when I was hiding under the table. He's in the convention center right now." Eli spun to face me, his pupils huge and black. "Get me in there—*now!*"

At that moment a door opened deeper inside the trailer and footsteps came toward us. It had to be Chet returning at last.

With a look of alarm, Eli held a finger to his lips, then quickly darted into the cab area.

Chapter Twenty-seven

I pressed STOP on the remote, grabbed my purse, and started for the door. I'd get Marco and come back for the videotape.

"Some buffoon cut my electrical cord," Chet said as he stepped inside the room. "I'm afraid you won't be able to use the video player until I have it fixed. We're running on limited battery power, and it would cause too much of a drain. But don't worry. I've contacted an electrician, so have a seat. He said he'd be right out. It shouldn't take long."

Here was my chance to tell him that Eli was in the room, but an alarm was sounding in my head. Why would Chet have to call an electrician? Mr. Make It Easy didn't need help in that department—he'd given a demonstration of cord splicing on one of his shows only a few weeks ago. I'd watched it with Nikki. What was going on here?

Chet's cell phone began to play the *Make It Easy* song. He took it out of his shirt pocket, looked at the screen, then shut it off. But the song continued to play in my head. *"Make it e-e-e-asy on yourself . . . ,"* except I was hearing Angelique's words: *"Roses are red and violets are blue-ew-ew . . ."*

It was the same tune. Her words, his theme song. That was a strong coincidence. "Where's Sue?" I asked nervously.

"She had to go. Would you like a drink?" Chet asked, opening a cabinet. "I have a full bar."

"No, thanks." My mind raced back to the conversation I'd had with Angelique when she described her hunt for Sybil.

"When did you hear the melody?" I'd asked her.

"Right before I turned the corner."

"But you didn't see anyone in the hallway?"

"No. I felt an icy chill, though, like dead souls swirling all around me."

Angelique must have heard Chet's cell phone. But if she hadn't seen him when she turned the corner, then he must have just walked out the back door, which was why she'd felt the chill. Still, why would Chet be leaving the building through the back exit while the banquet was going on? Was it another coincidence?

While Chet poured himself a glass of scotch, I studied him, mentally adding curly hair, a heavy moustache, and thick glasses, then removing his short beard. Oh, my God. He was Chester Domingo— Sybil's other blackmail victim. That was one coincidence too many.

Now I understood why he'd been stunned by the porn video playing on his monitor, and why he'd tried to keep me from watching the tape. His lie about the electrician was no doubt another attempt to get the video back. Or maybe he was stalling to find out whether I had uncovered his secret. Or maybe he *knew* that I had uncovered it and was deciding what to do about it, in which case I needed to get out of there.

"I don't really need to watch that video right now," I told him, tightening my grip on my purse. "But I'll take you up on your offer to make a copy for me." I turned to leave, but he blocked my way.

"Surely you're not leaving so soon?"

"Actually, I have to be someplace." I tried to squeeze around him, but he wouldn't budge. "Excuse me," I said firmly, as a frisson of fear crept up my spine.

He dropped all pretense of politeness, his mouth curving into an ugly sneer. "Where did you get that videotape?"

"Someone gave it to me. Look, it's no big deal. Keep it. I don't need it."

"*Who* gave it to you?"

I wasn't about to tell him how I got it, so what lie would he believe? "Ross and Jess Urban. They made copies and handed them out as a joke."

"They own a Beta recorder?"

"They're rich. They have resources. And you know they love to play pranks on people."

"Come on, Nikki's roommate, you can come up with a better story than that."

"You've totally lost me now, Chet. Look, my boyfriend is supposed to meet me at my booth at five o'clock. He's probably there right now, and if I don't get back soon . . ."

Chet grabbed my arms and pulled me close, lifting me on tiptoe. "You got the tape from Sybil, didn't you?"

"Why would she give it to *me?*"

His grip tightened, bringing tears to my eyes. "Do you want me to keep squeezing?"

"Okay," I gasped, and immediately his fingers relaxed. At least if I could keep him engaged in conversation, Marco would have a chance to find me.

"Sybil called her lawyer yesterday and asked him to come get the video because she was worried you'd try to take it from her. He told her he couldn't get there until this morning, so she gave it to me for safe-keeping."

Chet's grip tightened. "If Sybil had given her lawyer my name, he would have gone to the police as soon as he learned she was dead, and they would have questioned me." He gave me a vicious shake. "You're only making it tougher on yourself with your lies."

A lump of fear in my throat made my voice sound thick. "Fine. Here's the honest truth. Sybil really did contact her lawyer about some belongings she wanted him to keep for her. My boyfriend and I suspected it might be blackmail evidence, so we broke into her room and took it so we could find out who her victims were."

"For what reason?"

"The police were questioning our friend. We didn't want her charged with murder."

He shoved me backward, onto the sofa. "So you know Sybil was blackmailing me."

"You weren't her only victim." I pulled my purse strap back onto my shoulder, praying that my phone was still connected and someone was listening, if not Marco, at least Eli—if he hadn't managed to get out of the cab somehow. "And so what if you were in that movie, Chet? Many actors started out that way. Does anyone care?"

"My sponsor cares!" he shouted. "Do you tink I would get the Humanitarian Award if it got out that I had made a pornographic movie? Do you tink they'd keep me on as their spokesman? I'd be ruined." He began to pace around the small room, waving his arms in the air. "My career would be over. Finished. I'd be washed up. At my age, what would I do?"

"So you set up a meeting with Sybil in the storage room to try to buy back the tape?"

Chet said nothing for a long moment; then he stopped pacing and stood with his head bowed. I eyed the doorway, wondering whether I should make a run for it.

"Sybil was already there," he said at last, his voice low and strained. "She'd been with one of her young conquests. I was on my way to the banquet and heard her calling for help. I opened the door, and there she was, sitting in that coffin, spitting mad. 'Chet,' she said, 'give me your jacket. That bastard Ross ran off with my clothes.'"

My instincts had been right on two counts: Eli wasn't the killer, and Ross *had* been involved, just not in the way I'd expected.

"You see," Chet said, crouching in front of me as if he were about to explain a football play, "if Sybil had cooperated with me, she'd be alive right now. I told her I'd give her my jacket as long as she let me buy the videotape. I even upped the offer I'd made earlier, but she said she preferred a steady income. I pleaded with her to change her mind, but she only laughed."

Demonstrating with his open hand, he said through clenched teeth, "So I pushed her face down into that casket and slammed the lid. I could hear her yelling, 'Let me out or I swear to God I'll destroy you.' And I almost did, but then I thought, Sybil can't ruin me if she's dead. So I put the toolbox on top, wiped off my fingerprints, and walked out the door."

Boy, had he deluded himself, because the tape would still be out there. I was tempted to ask more, but Chet glanced at his watch, then pushed to his feet. "This way, please." He gestured toward the doorway.

I rose warily, keeping my purse firmly clamped under my arm. "Where are we going?"

He merely gestured again, so I took a breath and hurried past him. I couldn't believe he was letting me go that easily, but I wasn't about to stick around to question him.

Just as I reached the side door, he grabbed my arm. "Not that way."

Shivers of apprehension shook my insides as he led me toward the hallway. "What are you doing, Chet?"

He didn't reply, and that frightened me even more. I tried to jerk my arm free, only to have him tighten his grip. Nearly sick with fear, I grabbed a door frame and hung on. "Look, Chet, I swear I won't tell anyone about your movie. I don't want to see your career ruined."

"You tink I'm stupid? My reputation is at stake here, and I will not allow anyting or anyone—not Sybil, and definitely not you—to destroy it."

"Just get rid of the video. Then it's just your word against mine, and who's going to believe a small-town florist over a superstar like you?"

"I can't take that chance."

"Eli, help!" I shouted, sinking to my knees as Chet pried my sweating hands off the frame.

"No one can hear you," he chided. "The coach is soundproof." He grabbed me around the middle and threw me over his shoulder, knocking the wind out of my lungs and sending my purse flying off my shoulder.

Please, Eli, for God's sake, do something! Surely he

realized the danger I was in. Or had he managed to open a window and escape?

With blood rushing to my head, I renewed my efforts to get free, yelling like a banshee, pinching Chet's back, and attempting to drive my knees into his chest, but he merely slid me farther over his shoulder, gripping me around the upper thighs, making it impossible to move my legs. He stopped in front of the sauna, opened the door, and tossed me onto the floor inside, then left, shutting the door behind him.

I staggered to my feet, bruised from the fall, but grateful Chet hadn't done anything worse. I grabbed the recessed handle and turned it, but the door didn't budge. He'd obviously locked it from the outside. I turned to glance around. There were no windows in the tiny room and only one dim, recessed light over-head, so I pounded on the thick marble outer wall even though I doubted the sound would carry through it.

A moment later, the door opened and Chet came in carrying a roll of gray duct tape that I knew was meant for me. Petrified, I climbed onto the cedar bench and held my arms in a defensive position. "Stay away."

He laughed just as he had on the video and pulled off a long length of the heavy tape. "Turn around and put your hands behind your back."

"Don't be an idiot, Chet. You can't get away with two crimes."

He didn't seem worried. I pressed my back against the wall for leverage, and when he came at me, I kicked out with my foot. But Chet knew the counter-move, and suddenly I was on my stomach, my chin against the wooden planks and my arms pulled behind me.

Quickly, he bound my wrists, then flipped me onto my side on the narrow bench and tore off more tape. When he leaned down to put it over my mouth, I jerked my head away, my heart pounding so hard it shook my rib cage. "Are you so cold-blooded that you could m—?"

He grabbed a fistful of my hair to hold my head steady as he pressed the sticky tape over my mouth. Overwhelmed by feelings of suffocation, I began to hyperventilate, panting through my nose. I whimpered in dread as he ripped off yet another length of tape, this one to stop my breathing. I had only minutes to live. *Marco, where are you?*

All at once the motor coach lurched backward, sending Chet sprawling onto his rear. "What the hell is going on?" he bellowed.

I felt the engine vibrating the bench. We were moving!

There was another lurch, forward this time; then, jerking at first, the coach began to pick up speed. But who was driving? It couldn't be Marco or the cops. It had to be Eli.

Where was he taking us?

Chapter Twenty-eight

Chet opened the sauna door, then locked it behind him and charged up the hallway. I heard his boots pounding the oak boards as he ran toward the cab. Quickly I sat up and swung my legs to the floor, so glad that he hadn't bound my ankles. I managed to get to my feet just as the coach swerved to the right, sending me tumbling back onto the bench.

I rose again and stepped up to the door, pressing my ear against it, trying to hear what was happening outside.

"Open up!" I heard Chet shout. "Whoever you are, open this door at once!"

Eli must have locked himself in the cab.

"Do you know how much this coach cost? Half a million dollars. I swear to God, if you do *anyting* to it, I'll wring your neck. Pull over right now, before you kill us."

I couldn't hear what Eli shouted back, but whatever it was, it made Chet even angrier. He hammered the door with his hands. "If you don't stop right now, I'll break down the door."

At once I heard what sounded like a body slamming against a hard object and guessed Chet was trying to bust into the cab. I couldn't imagine what Eli was thinking, but if it were me, I'd be feeling the stress.

Then I heard a welcome sound—sirens, many of them. The coach swerved and I fell sideways. The sirens were all around us now. It had to be the police. Why wasn't Eli stopping?

Suddenly, there was a loud *bang*, and I could only guess that Chet had gotten into the cab. I heard him shouting; then there was a screech of brakes; then a terrible impact that threw me forward. I hit the wall hard. And then there was nothing.

"Abby? Can you hear me? Where are you?"

I opened my eyes but couldn't see anything in the pitch blackness. Where was I? Why did Marco's voice sound so far away? I tried to answer and realized something was stuck to my mouth. I went to pull it off only to find that my hands were bound.

"Abby? Can you hear me?"

Marco, I'm in here. I tried to remember where here was, but my head hurt and my brain felt fuzzy, as if it were cloaked in a heavy blanket. The air was stuffy and hot and singed my nose when I breathed. Slowly I sat up and was able to push to my feet, but as soon as I tried to step forward, I hit a wall. I stepped backward and hit another wall. Had the Urbans locked me in the phone booth again?

"Abby! Shout out your location."

That was Reilly. I kicked the wall with my shoe in reply, but it made little noise. Sirens blared, as though the phone booth were surrounded by police cars, which triggered a memory of a crash and a tumble through space. And then I remembered. I was in Chet's sauna.

I had to find the door. The marble was thinner there, providing a better chance of being heard. I dragged one elbow along the wall, turned the corner, and kept going until it hit the handle; then I started kicking again. I pressed my ear against the door and heard footsteps in the distance, so I kicked until my foot tingled and my toes were numb.

The door opened and thick gray smoke poured into the tiny space. A face appeared in the midst of it, and although he held a cloth over his nose and mouth, I knew him at once by those gorgeous brown eyes. Marco! What a welcome sight he was.

Quickly, Marco lifted a corner of the tape that covered my mouth; then in one swift pull, he removed it, the stinging pain causing tears to spill down my cheeks. At once he clamped a damp towel over my face, then picked me up and carried me out of the smoldering wreck.

I looked over his shoulder and saw that the entire front of the coach had been smashed in, the driver's side was separated from the passenger side by the huge trunk of an oak tree, and black smoke was pouring from under a piece of crumpled metal that must have been the hood. Had Eli and Chet survived?

I was taken into the back of a rescue van and deposited on a padded bench, where my hands were cut free at last. My hunky hero knelt before me, gazing at me with those eyes I loved so dearly. "Sunshine, you came this close"—he held his fingers a millimeter apart—"to being toast."

As if I needed a reminder. I threw my arms around his ribs and hugged him tightly, soaking up the heat from his body as I trembled from shock and my teeth clattered against one another so hard I feared they'd chip.

"Can she have a blanket?" Marco asked, wrapping his arms around my shivering form. And then a comforting warmth fell over me.

It was only when I felt the shudders subside that I was able to stop my teeth from chattering so I could talk. "Is Eli okay?"

"He was injured in the crash—some contusions and broken bones—but he'll live."

"What about Chet?" I asked as a medic crouched in front of me and pressed the end of his stethoscope against my chest.

"A few bumps. Nothing that needs hospitalization."

"Hey," Reilly called, climbing into the back of the vehicle. "How are you doing in here?"

"Reilly!" I almost knocked the EMT over in my haste to stand up. "Don't let Chet get away. He killed Sybil."

"Calm down, kid," Reilly said. "Chet's not going anywhere. We know what he did. Marco heard enough that we were able to piece everything together."

"Then my call went through?"

"It went through," Marco said, wrapping the blanket around me once again. "I just didn't know where it was coming from."

"Thank God. I was so afraid you wouldn't be able to hear what was going on."

"I heard you talking to Eli," Marco said, "and I figured you'd called me for that reason. But then when Chet started talking, I knew you were in serious trouble. I contacted Reilly, but he already had men searching the grounds, and we didn't know where else to look. It wasn't until I heard Chet shouting at Eli to pull over that I realized you were in a vehicle."

"A few minutes after that," Reilly said, continuing the story, "I got a report that Chet's motor coach was careening away from the hotel with an electrical cord dangling behind it, and that's when we put it all together. When Eli was pulled from the cab, he told us he'd decided the only way to clear his name was to bring the killer to us."

"He was going to drive that thing all the way back to the New Chapel police station?"

"No, to the state police outpost," Reilly said. "It's only a few miles up the interstate."

"Eli saved me," I told them. "Chet was about to suffocate me when Eli drove off with the coach. See? My instincts weren't wrong after all. And Ross *was* the one who met Sybil in the storage room and took her clothes as a prank. Chet came by afterward and heard her calling for help. She asked him for his coat; then they started arguing over the blackmail video, and when she refused to give it to him, he snapped."

"Whoa," Reilly said. "What blackmail video?"

Marco said, "We'll discuss that later. Right now, let's let the medic finish so we can get out of here."

"Did you ever find the colonel?" I asked, while the EMT checked my pulse rate.

"No, but I have his phone number. He and I are going to talk, believe me."

"You're not going to arrest Eli, are you?" I asked Reilly.

"For what?"

"For carjacking Chet's motor coach."

"I didn't see him do that. Besides, who's going to complain? Chet? I think he has bigger problems now, don't you?"

"Thanks, Reilly. That's a relief. Poor Eli. He was so sure he knew how to identify the killer, but he didn't realize he'd seen Ross's shoes, but heard Chet's laugh. I'm glad he's been proved innocent. I just hope Ross gets what he deserves. If it wasn't for him, Sybil wouldn't have been locked in the storage room."

"Forget about it," Reilly said. "You know the law. What he did was stupid and juvenile but not criminal. Don't worry. Those two jokers will be in trouble again before you know it, and then they'll get what's coming to them."

"Unless their dad intervenes again," I said with a frustrated huff. "Is it okay if we leave now? I want to get back to the convention center. Lottie and Grace and Max must be frantic, wondering what happened to me, and I don't have my cell phone to call them. My purse is still in the coach."

Reilly glanced at the medic, who was checking my

skull for signs of injury. "Does your head hurt?" the EMT asked.

"Yeah, but it's no big deal. I'll take some aspirin when I get home."

"You sure you don't want to have the ER doc check you out?" Reilly asked. "You might have a concussion."

"I can watch for that," Marco assured him, giving me that sexy little smile.

"If you feel okay," Reilly said to me, "then there's no reason to stick around. I can get a statement from you tomorrow. I'll try to get your purse for you, too."

"Thanks, Sarge. You really are super."

Reilly merely gave me a nod, but I could tell he appreciated the compliment.

"Here, use my phone," Marco said, reaching into his pocket. "I know Lottie and Grace are worried, because I was talking to them when your call came through."

I took the slender silver case and punched in Lottie's number. She answered in a panic, thinking it was Marco on the line. "Did you find Abby? Is she all right?"

"It's me, Lottie."

"Abby? Lordy, girl! We've been in a stew, worrying about you."

"I'm fine. Marco and Reilly are here with me. You can let Grace and Max know that we caught the killer."

"No fooling?"

"You're not going to believe this, Lottie. It was Chet Sunday."

"Well, blow me over with a bag of feathers." She

covered the phone to tell Grace, then said, "I'll call Max and Delilah right now and give them the news. Max left before all the drama started."

Then Grace got on. "Abby, I'm so relieved you're all right. You gave us quite a fright, you know. And your mother has rung Lottie at least five times looking for you, so we told her you were busy. I thought it best not to upset her."

"Good thinking. No need for my parents to know what happened. I'll call them in a while. Thanks for covering for me. And Grace? You know that talk we had earlier? I really appreciated it. You got me back on track."

"You were never off track, love. You just needed a bit more light to see the path."

I ended the call and handed the phone to Marco; then we got into Reilly's squad car for the short ride back to the convention center. Grace and Lottie were waiting at the back entrance and took turns hugging me and turning me around to check for damage. Later, after strong cups of coffee from a kind clerk at Starbucks, who was just about to close up shop and took pity on us, Marco and the two women packed up the booth in the nearly deserted exhibition hall while I rested on a chair and related my tale of Eli, Chet, and the harrowing motor coach ride.

"Good gracious," Grace said at the end, shaking her head in wonder. "I'm almost at a loss for words. I guess you'll have to settle for that old saw, all's well that ends well."

"Hear, hear," Lottie said.

"You know what we need?" Marco said as the four of us toted boxes out to the van. "A hearty dinner and a couple bottles of wine."

"Sounds good to me," I said.

"Delightful," Grace added.

Lottie shoved her box into the back of the van and turned for another. "I could go for a tall, frosty beer myself."

"You got it," Marco said. "Dinner and drinks on the house. You want to ride with me, Sunshine?"

As if he had to ask.

"We'll meet you at Bloomers to unload," he told Lottie and Grace, "and then we can head for my bar."

Or so we had hoped. But on the way, Marco's cell phone rang, and I had a strong hunch it was going to be bad news again. Which one would it be this time, his bartender or a family member?

"For you," Marco said, handing me the phone.

Raising my eyebrows in surprise, I said, "Hello?"

It was Nikki. "Abs, omigod, you've got to get home right now. I've been trying to reach you for an hour. Thank God Marco's number was in our caller ID. Why did you turn your phone off?"

"Nikki, slow down. What's wrong?"

"Someone left a big box outside the door with your name on it. I was going to bring it in, but it's pretty heavy, so I thought I'd check it out first. I made a tiny cut in one corner and peeked inside and—oh, Abby, there are two big, ugly fish lying at the bottom."

"Fish?"

"Yes! They're in a net."

Oh, no. The Urbans were at it again! *Watch out, Red. One of these days you'll reel in something you weren't expecting.*

"What's happening?" Marco asked.

I held my hand over the phone. "The Urbans left two fish at the apartment." I uncovered the phone and said, "Nikki, you've got to get that box outside right now."

"They left *fish* at your apartment?" Marco repeated, starting to get angry.

I nodded. "Nikki, it's a prank. Take the box to the stairs and push it down, or get it into the elevator. Those fish will probably start to stink soon, and if that fish juice leaks through the bottom of the box, we'll never get rid of the smell."

"Abby, there's no smell. I'm not even sure they're real fish."

"Trust me, Nikki. You don't want to wait around to find out."

Marco whispered, "Tell her we'll come help her. Give us ten minutes."

"Marco said we can be there in about ten minutes."

I held the phone between our heads so Marco could hear her reply. "Don't bother. I've already pushed it to the top of the stairs. I'll give it a good shove, then drag it over to the Dumpster. Then I'm heading for a party, so don't wait up for me. Oh, I almost forgot. Call your mother. She left about seven messages."

I ended the call and examined Marco's slim phone.

"Maybe I'll get one like yours. I like not having to flip it open, especially when I'm trying to send you a message in the dark."

"Let's hope that doesn't happen again. So, what's the significance of the fish?"

"Ross made a remark about me fishing for answers when I tried to question him this afternoon. I'll tell you more about that later, because if I don't call my mom soon, she'll freak."

I dialed my parents' home phone number, and my dad picked up. "Hey, honey, good to hear from you. Where have you been? Your mother has been trying to reach you."

"I was a little, well, tied up. Is she there now?"

"She just left for the grocery store."

"Do you know why she left all those messages for me?"

"Sure do. You know that gift she was sculpting for Marco's sister's baby shower? The one that was giving her so much trouble?"

"Was that when she was throwing clay? Wasn't she making a lamp?"

"You're not even close. She finished it this afternoon and was so excited that she took it to your place to show it to you, but no one was home."

Oh, no! "Did she leave it there?" I asked in dread. "In a big box?"

"Yes, did Nikki find it?"

"Tell me it wasn't two giant fish, Dad."

"It's a bassinet."

"A baby bassinet?" *Then what had Nikki seen?*

"A different sort of bassinet. You remember your mother's footstool? Or her palm tree?"

How could I forget a stool made up of four feet, or a coat rack made of lifelike human hands, palms up, reaching out on long human arms?

"Think about it, Abby. A bass-in-net."

"Oh, Dad, no." I covered the phone and whispered the details to Marco, who merely shook his head in amazement.

"It's not too bad, really, honey," my dad said. "Two big yellow bass make up the cradle. They face each other, with their tails curling up on each end and the center scooped out to hold blankets. The cradle sits in the bottom of a strong net that hangs from a tall, curved stand. I guess you could say it's modern funk."

"Gee, it sounds—terrific, Dad. I can't wait to see it. Tell Mom I'll call her later."

I hung up and immediately dialed my apartment phone but got no answer. That meant Nikki was on her way to the Dumpster with my mom's gift.

"I'm doomed," I told Marco.

"Do you want to see if we can get there in time to save it?"

"It's too late. Nikki will already have pushed the box down the stairs, dragged it across the parking lot, then tipped it over the side of the big garbage bin. It'll be in a thousand pieces." Although . . . that wasn't necessarily a *bad* thing, considering that if it somehow escaped harm, that hideous 'bass-in-net' was what Marco's family would forever remember my mother for.

What I'd have to do was come up with a really good explanation for what happened to her gift so Mom's feelings wouldn't be hurt. Then maybe I could talk her into going in with me on a real bassinet for the baby, since the shower was only a week away.

"I have an idea," I said. "Let's go back to my apartment after dinner."

"Now you're talking." We stopped at a red light and he leaned toward me for a kiss that whetted my appetite for more. "Do you have anything particular in mind?" he murmured, nibbling my jaw.

"You bet I do." I turned my head to kiss him. "We're going to pour ourselves glasses of that Cabernet in my fridge, light a few candles in my bedroom, get real cozy, and"—I kissed him again—"come up with a whopper of a fish story."

"A fish story?" Marco pulled his head back to see whether I was serious; then the light changed and his attention went back to the road. "So we're on a fishing theme, huh?"

"Yep."

"Then tackle this one." He gave me a lustful glance that heated areas inside me to the sizzle stage, making me tingle all over. "If you bring the bait, I'll bring the pole."

Oh, baby. What an evening this was going to be. "You know I'm hooked."

With a wicked grin, he put his arm around me, and I snuggled against his shoulder.

Cod, how I loved that man.

Center Point Publishing

600 Brooks Road ● PO Box 1
Thorndike ME 04986-0001 USA

(207) 568-3717

US & Canada:
1 800 929-9108
www.centerpointlargeprint.com